WATER THE COLOR OF SLATE

A Novel by
Mary Ann Noe

Black Rose Writing | Texas

The author grants the final approval for this literary material.

First printing

ISBN: 978-1-68513-298-9
PUBLISHED BY BLACK ROSE WRITING
www.blackrosewriting.com

Printed in the United States of America
Suggested Retail Price (SRP) $21.95

Water the Color of Slate is printed in Bookman Old Style

*As a planet-friendly publisher, Black Rose Writing does its best to eliminate unnecessary waste to reduce paper usage and energy costs, while never compromising the reading experience. As a result, the final word count vs. page count may not meet common expectations.

Author photo by Barb Geiger

To those who can see beyond

WATER
THE
COLOR
OF
SLATE

Chapter 1
Louise Wright

I arrived at the big house on the west side of the village without being seen. Once on the back porch, I took a deep breath to steady myself before I tapped on the window glass.

The curtain barely moved as a hand shifted it. A moment later, Rose swept the door open, creating a shaft of light, drawing me like a flame draws a moth. "Louise Wright! What on earth are you doing here at this time of night? I thought you were coming tomorrow."

"Rose..." My voice dwindled. "I couldn't wait."

"Come in, come in." Rose took my elbow and pulled me into the kitchen.

The girls were upstairs already, behind closed doors, alone, silent. I needed it to be that late.

"I need your help," I whispered, barely able to speak for the flood of tears threatening to burst.

"Come, come, come," she whispered back. She motioned me to follow to the next room, her personal parlor, closed off from the front of the house. Small, tastefully furnished with coral velvet chairs sent from out East and carved tables nearby. No damask drapes here, only sheer lawn curtains, barred and bordered with lace.

She must have been about to sit down for a moment, a tea set sat on a table near the fireplace, steam languishing up from the pot's spout.

She took my hand and led me to a chair close to the hearth. I shivered.

"It's a cool night. Let me stoke up the fire a bit," she said.

I shook my head. I didn't trust myself to speak.

She pulled her chair to face mine and perched on the edge. She bent forward and grasped both my hands in hers. "Now. Tell me what's wrong. You're as white as a sheet, Louise. This isn't like you."

I looked down, letting my dark hair drop to shield my face. "I...I don't know what to do." A deep sigh rose unbidden. I raised my eyes to hers. This had to be done. "You're the only one I know who can help me."

Chapter 2
Lou

Lou MacManus frowned at the girl standing in front of her. The girl jammed her hands deep into her pockets. Fists, crammed in. Ungrateful... Lou forced her thoughts to a halt.

Kapi was planted with hands cocked on her hips. She wasn't quite as tall as Lou, but that didn't cow her one bit. "I hate you!"

Well, you ain't nothing to write home about either. She sure wasn't, what with her torn jeans and baggy plaid shirt, to say nothing of her sullen face. But Lou forced herself to not say anything.

"I don't see why I have to stay with you. Granny—" Kapi spat out the word.

"I'm nobody's granny."

"So whaddam I suppose to call you? Bitch?"

Lou's hand cracked against Kapi's cheek before she thought. The girl recoiled and smoldered. She grabbed her long brunette braid and held it across her mouth.

Lou pursed her lips. "You, girl, can call me Lou. Everyone else does, so you might as well." She turned away and headed for the kitchen before Kapi could reply. Lou wasn't going to let any teenager walk out on her.

Kapi's voice splintered through the kitchen door. "What the hell do you know, old lady?"

Lou turned back and swung the door open. She winced as her knees complained at the sudden movement. She raised one finger. "No need to talk to me like that. Now get outta my sight."

Kapi spun, her braid swinging behind, and strode out the front door, slamming it for good measure. As if Lou didn't already know how the girl felt about her. Kapi's mother never did take to Lou either, and apparently it was genetic.

Lou let the door from the kitchen to the living room swing shut. She plodded to the sink and braced her hands on the edge. The backyard out the window usually felt like home, the real part of her home. She knew, though she couldn't see them from the window, that tiny pearls of rain edged the miniscule leaves on the apple tree in the back corner. Even though it was early, small spears of daffodil leaves poked up through the debris in the flowerbeds. In another month, the whole border along the lot line would be awash with yellows and oranges.

She smiled and thought of Wordsworth. Some of her tension seeped away down the sink drain. Soon the roses would green up. The ones by the garage's south wall had stripes of green along their canes already. Cutting grass was still a distant concept, and for that she was grateful. One of these years she'd have to hire somebody to take care of her yard. But not yet. Even with her arthritic knees, she wasn't that feeble. It was a small yard, after all. Just enough to fit with her small bungalow.

After the first warm day—Be realistic, Lou. After the first warm week—she'd ask Heddy to help her lower the porch swing so she could sit outside and admire her gardening handiwork or read. Maybe she could get back to the enjoyment of reading poetry. She'd run dry over the winter when she heard she might end up having to take in Kapi.

She shook the cobwebs out of her mind and turned to the stove. She grabbed the teakettle, grateful the water was still hot. A whole pot would be too much. If she brewed a whole pot, she'd gulp it down, then spend most of the morning sitting on the john. One cup, that would do it.

Blueberry tea calmed her. The whole ritual of swirling hot water in the cup to warm it, then setting the silky bag of leaves in before pouring on the steaming water. Lou hovered over the cup, watching the color creep out from the bag. You could paint a watercolor with the blues drifting in the water if you didn't hurry things. When the water went from indigo to almost purple, she pulled out the bag. Drinking it became almost secondary.

Her neck tightened up again. What was she going to do with the girl? She was a handful. And it was probably only going to get worse. Lou had her own life to live. She didn't need to be saddled with a mouthy fourteen-year-old.

Lou turned to reach for the cookie tin and caught sight of herself in the nearby mirror. Her free hand went automatically to her hair. Always that wide swath of white that wouldn't cooperate among the dark. The dark hair that refused to fade to gray. The white streak looked like a ski track swooping from just above her forehead to down over one ear. The rest of her hair was tame and flat, nothing special. She leaned in to the mirror. The encroaching white streak would have to stay.

She stroked her neck. Few wrinkles. Her face had the usual, but her dark eyes still shone without the sags and bags that drooped on most women her age. She faked a smile and her skin creped up around her eyes and mouth. Who're you trying to fool, old woman? she thought. Those high cheekbones aren't coming out to play anymore. She ran a hand up along the side of her face, pulling the skin taut again. Her hands had turned into her mother's. Breakfast sausage fingers and knobby knuckles. At least the rest of her was spindlier. She curled her fingers into fists. Can't even tighten 'em up anymore. She wiggled her fingers, making them into spastic spiders, then swatted one at the mirror. Pah! Go drink your tea before it gets cold.

Lou pulled out a shortbread cookie from the tin and dunked it in the tea. She propped herself against the counter and gazed out the kitchen window again. She sighed and sipped.

The girl would just have to get used to Lou's routines. Routines, nothing about this was routine. She'd have to get used to Lou's schedule, such as it was. She wanted time to sit and read. Alone.

But since she retired, who cared if she stayed in bed until ten? Eating breakfast was sacrosanct, but the rest of the day usually unraveled at its own pace. Lou just went along for the ride. Who cared if, instead of a sit-down lunch, she stuffed her pockets with bags of granola to eat as she walked? Who cared if she ate at all?

Maybe that would be a blessing in disguise. Heddy was always harping on her to eat more regularly, bringing in casseroles in little ramekins, or fresh veggies from the garden. Lou called it Meals Without Wheels.

Now she wasn't about to kowtow to any teenager telling her when and what to eat. Neighbors were one thing. Kids were another.

Years ago, nothing had surprised her more than when she found out she was pregnant with their own kid.

Sam's response was predictable. "Early enough to get rid of it?"

She couldn't imagine getting rid of "it." That's why she'd waited so long to tell him. Sam MacManus, her "loving" husband. "Too late the doc says."

He grunted. "Guess you'll be doing most of the work." Then he left for his job. That was the day her "loving" husband just plain left. The gravel truck rolled over, and he was trapped. Killed instantly, the doctors told her, though she wasn't sure that wasn't just kindness on their part.

So there she was. Alone and pregnant. Neither one of them really wanted a child, but when she found out she was pregnant, she was going to see it through. Come hell or high water, she was going to see it through. Just like she'd seen her marriage through.

Lou sighed and slurped her tea. She pushed her butt against the swinging door and headed into the living room. More of an all-purpose room, really. Early on she'd commandeered the dining table. None of the chairs matched. A couple were from Heddy's parents' cottage up north. Another was her grandmother's. The others? Lou couldn't remember. The rustic tabletop was really a long slab of maple from a tree in her grandfather's yard that he'd milled down and smoothed. Well, as smooth as could be expected. Level enough to hold cups without tipping, but a gentle dip here and there attested to the tree's refusal to be totally civilized. Around the edges, Grandpa left the bark, though gaps here and there showed heavy use. The top was attached to wooden trestles he fashioned. Lou loved it. She never ceased to marvel at the man's talents.

Right now, the table was piled high. Everything had its place. Bills to be paid. Bills already paid and waiting to be filed. Receipts of things to return. Post-it notes of reminders—books to pick up at the library, the half-finished notes of spring plants to buy and coax into being, lists of people to call or write. And then scatterings of things she'd forgotten about. What was that stack of pink papers anyway? She couldn't recall.

What on God's green earth was she going to do with all this stuff? Before Kapi, it all lived in the spare bedroom, Lou's pseudo-office. But that room was reclaimed so Kapi had somewhere to sleep. Some of Lou's papers and more were relocated to this table, the rest apportioned to almost every other horizontal surface in the house. Some of it was important and needed attention. Maybe she should start by throwing away the stuff on the table that didn't need attention. Or had once, but now it was too late.

Lou shook her head and returned to the kitchen. Organizing all that stuff could be done later. Maybe much later, she hoped.

The front door banged open and Kapi stomped across the living room and into the kitchen. She planted her hands on her hips and glared. Raindrops glistened on her hair and eyelashes.

I'm supposed to say something first? Fat chance. Lou set down her teacup and mimicked Kapi's stance.

"So, it's raining outside," Kapi said, as if challenging Lou to a duel. "You're not going to make me—"

"I'm not going to make you do anything," Lou snapped. "But there's rules around here. I expect you to follow them." She turned away and took her cup to the sink. Rinsing it would keep her from saying something stupid.

"So? Are there rules about eating? Like, lunch?"

Without turning around, Lou asked, "Why? You hungry?" If she scrubbed the bottom of the cup any more, it was apt to dissolve.

"Starved." Chopped off, but clear.

"Fine. I've got soup."

"Fine." Kapi was on the move.

Before Lou could swing from the sink, Kapi returned to the living room. Lou set the cup down and followed. What's she up to now? "Don't you know food's in the kitchen?" She couldn't keep the sarcasm out of her voice.

"Gotta make room here." Kapi set her hands on the piles of papers on Grandpa's maple table. She pushed them all to one side, then, with a snarky look at Lou, slid everything right off the table onto the floor. "Oops," she said, her dark eyes snapping.

Lou backed up against the little computer desk just beyond the big table. "Don't you dare touch this stuff. My poetry books and stuff." She reached behind to slap her hands on the stacks of papers and books there. "Computer is off limits too."

That gleam, that crooked smile. The lack of movement to pick anything up. This was going to be one helluva relationship.

Chapter 3
Louise Wright

When I was ten, my father bought me a pony and taught me to ride. A lovely golden pony with creamy tail and mane. I rode before, naturally, but never with my own mount. And never astride. I giggled. "Papa, Mama will be..." I couldn't come up with the right word.

"Scandalized?" Papa offered. "Yes, Louise, without a doubt." A short guffaw popped out. Then he frowned, but that too was gone before it established itself. "We must consider her feelings. We agreed you must have a mount for yourself, that much is true. She just never agreed to the style of riding."

"But Papa," I said, tugging at my skirts to try and cover my legs more. It didn't help much.

"No, 'but Papa,'" he said, waggling a finger at me.

We approached our house, set cheek by jowl with the neighbors. It had but a tiny front garden that my mother filled with flowers.

"Holla! Mother, come out and see what we've purchased!" Papa called.

My mother appeared at the front window, sewing, undoubtedly, in the front parlor so she could observe anyone going up and down the street. It was a relatively busy street, though not equal to the thoroughfares of downtown Green Bay, so she had plenty to keep her interest. A moment later, the front door opened, and she stepped out onto the shallow stoop.

"Louise Wright, what on earth are you doing?" She crossed her arms, never a good sign.

"Tread lightly, girl," my father whispered to me.

I waved and grinned. "Look, Mama! My very own pony! Thankyouthankyouthankyou!" I thought if I kept talking, she would loosen her pursed lips. But I ran down fairly quickly at her look.

My mother. Her beautiful dark hair set off her wonderful skin, full of deep light like the inside of a mother-of-pearl clam. That made her eyes look even brighter. Green, they were, but not deep like any emerald, but more like celery-colored, light and sparkling. I loved her eyes. Usually, they were flanked by laugh lines, because she smiled and laughed so much.

But now. Well, now, they seemed darker. She shook her head, but it was directed at Papa, not me. "Astride. What were you thinking, Stephen?"

"I was thinking how much I'm going to need a helper soon. Someone who can keep up with me." He started to dismount.

"Oh, no, don't you come down yet," Mama said. Her eyes cleared, and the laugh lines came back, though her mouth was still tight. "You take Louise down to the mercantile right now and buy her a riding coat..."

I didn't even hear the rest of their exchange. A riding coat! A long coat, split down the back of its skirt so riders could keep their legs warm and dry. No trying to bunch up a coat or skirt around a saddle and still keep legs covered. A girl could keep her modesty. Not only that, I could swirl that coat around when I walked. What a picture! I couldn't wait!

"...and boots," Papa was saying. "She needs proper riding boots. And perhaps a riding skirt." He sent his most engaging eyebrow-raise at Mama.

Mama sighed. But I could see she was won over. Her mouth was smiling. "All right, Stephen. But do it right now, before people start talking." She turned to go back in the house, but at the last minute, she spun back. "Louise, you are my mystery girl, always surprising me." She blew me a kiss. I laughed and returned the favor.

"Boots." Papa leaned in his saddle, to impart a secret perhaps. "Men's boots, Louise. None of those fancy lady's boots for you. We want good sturdy boots."

"Like yours, Papa?" I asked.

He lifted one foot in the stirrup as we turned our mounts and set off for the mercantile. His boots were dark with oil and use, polished every evening when he came in from his work. A decent heel allowed him to set his foot firm in the stirrup. "Like these?" He nodded. "Yes, I think so, Louise. Perhaps a softer leather, but certainly tall enough to keep your legs from chafing. None of those low fancy things that they sell to the society ladies."

I giggled. "Those society ladies don't ride like this anyway."

He joined my laughter. "They certainly do not. They gad about in carriages and traps mostly." He cleared his throat. "Your mother said you should ride sidesaddle to protect...ahem...your tender parts. Gave me quite the fight." He looked sideways at me. "Until I reminded her that she rode astride before we married and I made her a virtuous woman."

"Oh," I said. I didn't really understand. But then, the two of them were always sharing looks and smiles, over what I didn't know. But it led me to the shocking realization that they must have had a life before I came along. Some things I wasn't privy to share. I sighed. "Is that why she drives her trap now, instead of riding a horse?"

"Oh, she'll ride once in a while. But she's more concerned with decorum now."

Decorum. A word I'd not encountered before. But it must have to do with protecting her tender parts.

***

The first few summers, Papa took me around town to make sure I knew my way around on horseback. I think he also made sure everyone in town knew me. They'd keep an eye on me, surely. When winter came, the pony and saddle were relegated to the barn. My chores didn't lessen, however. Mucking out the stall and laying down fresh hay was an ongoing task. I didn't mind so much. The pony was gentle and friendly, nuzzling my pockets in a search for an apple or carrot. Though Mama forbade me riding on the frozen slippery streets—and Papa backed her up—I found enough to do in currying and caring for the pony.

When spring arrived, I oiled my boots and saddle in preparation. Mama's usual admonition rang out, along with the return of the robins' mating calls, when I readied myself to ride out with Papa. "Stay with your father, Louise, but ride home before lunchtime." She waved me down the drive from the front door.

I made as if to be too far away to be heard, but I always waved back. I didn't want to be caught in a lie. If I didn't make any promises or acknowledgments, I couldn't be held accountable.

I rode with Papa to the harbor, but only to the turn in the road that took him onto the docks. He was in on my secret, and turned a blind eye to my early escape.

Most days, I rode about town a bit, before setting out west of town. I followed the farm tracks between the fields, but avoided the farmsteads themselves. I didn't need anyone reporting back about a girl galivanting around alone. Sometimes I stopped and dismounted, letting the pony graze before heading back to town. I never went far.

Before I was given free rein, as it were, I had to prove myself worthy of trust, as well as a competent rider before Papa would allow me a taste of freedom. That took a couple of years. By that time, I outgrew the pony. Even Mama agreed I needed a full-grown horse. She offered her mare, the lovely little horse she hitched to her trap to set out on the town.

"Your Bridie?" Papa said, surprise in his voice. "That is not fair, Mother. You would never have a chance. Louise would have that mare out and about every day, and you would be stuck in the house, or walking." He shook his head. "She needs her own mount."

Mama conceded. "Of course, you're right, Stephen." She gave him a sideways glance. "And you've already picked out a mount, haven't you?"

He harrumphed and had the good grace to blush above his beard. "She's a real beauty, she is."

"Yes, Louise is." Mama shook her head. "And I'm sure the horse is too." She drew me into a warm embrace. "All right, you two. You win. Go finalize the deal."

Papa clapped his hands together. "She'll be delivered by dinnertime."

How my mother put up with him, I'll never know. But I knew she could wrap him around her finger too. I could always feel the love radiating from them when they were together.

So, I received my own beloved mare. Papa made sure to work with me every single day that summer, and I became an accomplished horsewoman. I still rode astride, to the consternation of the society dames, and probably to the jealousy of their daughters. I know that Papa's fellow workers merely shrugged, and accepted me as I was.

I continued to ride out and about. But only until lunchtime. Then Papa and I would rendezvous and return home together.

Chapter 4
Lou

The papers stayed on the floor for three days. As they walked past, a piece would occasionally flutter up and settle in a new spot. Finally, Lou got up in the middle of a sleepless night and crept downstairs. With only a flashlight to help, she sorted out the bills to be paid and various other papers, and scooped the rest into a recycle bag. Luckily, Kapi left Lou's desk alone, so her books and such were safe. For now.

The grass was wet on her bare feet when she schlepped it out to the bin, but she wasn't going to give Kapi the satisfaction of watching her clean it up. Kapi should be the one picking up, but Lou didn't want to open that bag of tricks.

She slid back into bed and tucked her toes under the heavy bedspread folded at the foot. Her feet were still damp between the toes and she slid them around looking for the warmest corner. She burrowed deeper into the blankets and fumed until she heated up enough to stick one foot out from under.

This is stupid, she thought. I shouldn't be the one awake at two in the morning while that little twit sleeps the sleep of the... "just" didn't fit. "Damned" had yet to be proved. She replaced it with "wicked." And promptly fell asleep.

***

Lou awoke to the rattle of pans and the smell of coffee. Through the fug of sleep she heard Sam in the kitchen. By the time she dragged herself awake, she remembered Sam was dead, and the morning coffee was the only decent thing he did for her in their three years together. Was that the only thing keeping her with him? She tucked her foot back under the blankets and checked the time. Sam was gone, and good riddance to him. At least he left her with a son, Mac, that lovely "it" Sam wanted her to get rid of.

Eight o'clock. She grunted, unwilling to get up and face Killer Kapi in the kitchen. In spite of herself, she smiled at the juvenile alliteration. It sounded like something from that old game of Clue. Kapi in the kitchen with the knife. Which brought her back to the current poem she was supposed to be writing bouncing around in her head. It retreated in indignation at the distraction of Kapi's arrival. Didn't appear to be forthcoming now either. Lou didn't blame it for sulking in some back corner of her brain.

This would get her nowhere. She sighed, tossed back the covers and rolled herself upright. She could come up with no good reason for staying in bed. Morning was precious to her, but today she didn't want to haul her 75-year old body anywhere near the kitchen. Even if the sun was out. Even if Heddy was coming over later with a promised loaf of fresh-baked bread. Even if... Lou quit trying to think of other enticements.

Might as well get it over with. If she was foraying into enemy territory, even if it was her own kitchen, she was not going unarmed. That meant cleaning up and getting dressed. Which she never did before she had a cup of something hot. One coffee in the morning, usually. Tea for later. However, that would draw the slings and arrows of Kapi's disgruntled humphs or downright derisive laughter. Lou hadn't purchased a new nightgown in years. In fact, she didn't wear nightgowns, though Sam thought she did. She had a bottom drawer full of the darn things.

Pajamas. That was her thing. Men's pajamas. She didn't need Kapi's comments on her oldest, rattiest, most comfortable pair, so she retreated to the bathroom and took up her routines out of sequence.

By the time she got to the kitchen, the coffee pot was empty and Kapi was rinsing out a mug. Her hair was back in a thick braid, but stray ends leaked out all over, making her look like she'd stuck her finger in an electrical outlet.

"You leave any?" Lou asked to Kapi's back and got nothing but a shrug.

"I made coffee for me," Kapi said.

Lou frowned. She's hopeless. "Don't wash the pot. I'll make me some."

"I'm not washing anything," Kapi said. "I'm outta here." She grabbed her jacket from the back of a chair and swung it across her shoulders.

Lou got to the back door before Kapi. "Where do you think you're going?"

"Out. What's it to you?"

"I said you have to follow the house rules."

"No, you said you expect me to follow the rules. That's not the same."

Lou wanted to lay out a tarp before the acid in Kapi's tone burned through the kitchen floor. "What is expected—and demanded—is that you follow the house rules. Just like everyone else who lives here." Echoes of her warnings to her son. "Your father followed the rules and so will you."

"Your son is dead, remember?"

It was a low blow. Lou scowled at Kapi, but couldn't bring herself to say anything.

"Can I go now?" Kapi moved to sidestep Lou.

Lou found her voice. "House rule. Tell me where you're going."

"Why?" She reached for her backpack, black like almost everything else she wore.

Typical toddler answer. Lou pushed down her anger. "In case something happens to you. Or me. I need to know how to get ahold of you." *Not that I'd want to. You fall, you're on your own, honey.* But she couldn't disrespect Mac that way. She had to handle this somehow. "Please." There. Now was that so hard? She dared not answer that one.

"All right, all right. I'm going to the library, okay?" Kapi said. She slung her backpack over one shoulder.

"It's not open until ten." Lou tried to keep from growling.

"It'll be open by the time I get there."

Lou risked a glance at the clock on the stove. 9:43. "Fine. Be home for lunch."

As Kapi ducked into the hood on her sweatshirt, Lou thought she saw a shadow of a nod. Lou stepped away from the back door. "Sun's out. Good day for a walk."

By the time Lou got more thoughts together, Kapi was out the door and down the driveway.

"That went well." Lou shook her head. "Hopeless." But she meant the situation just as much as the girl. The girl. Mac's stepdaughter. She didn't look like Mac, of course, but her connections to him were there, and that made Lou's heart hurt. How could she be so different from her "beamish boy." Having Kapi around was one more reminder that her son was dead.

"Hey, Lou!" Heddy's voice always preceded her by a mile.

Lou stuck her head out the back door and motioned her neighbor over.

Heddy pressed her way through the hedge that separated their houses. They tried carving an opening one year, but in spite of plenty of traffic, the hedge got the upper hand. Whips of branches seemed to grow overnight, determined to close ranks. But Heddy's bulk was enough to keep it passable, more or less. The grass succumbed, however, and a narrow track stayed mangled and a bit dusty. After rain, muddy.

Heddy stepped up on the porch and walked out of her floral gardening boots. Her faded green pants billowed as she came in the door. "No need to get dirt on your kitchen floor." She said the same thing every time. She made a beeline for the coffee pot, same as always. "What's with the empty coffee pot?"

Lou pushed a sigh out of her nose. "Kapi. She made just enough for herself. Little..." She stopped herself.

"Ha! Finally found someone to match wits with, eh?" Heddy grabbed the pot and filled it with water. "Set 'er up. I need a strong waker-upper this morning."

"None here then. This is de-caf."

Heddy sighed and shook her head.

Lou ground the beans and got everything going before she sank down at the small table by the window that remained inviolate. No papers ever found their way there. "I don't know what I'm going to do with that girl." She folded her hands on top of her head.

"She's had a hard time, Lou. It can't be easy for her coming here either." Heddy pulled out the nearest chair, hitched up her pants and sat down.

It always amused Lou how, when Heddy sat, she created a series of steps with her body: belly roll, stomach roll, breast roll, chin roll. The reward was her smile at the top of the stairs.

"She's only got you left, right?" Heddy said, leaning forward and setting her formidable arms on the table. She ruffled her hands through her orange hair.

Lou laughed when Heddy decided to go wild with the hair dye, but she'd gotten used to it. She couldn't imagine—or even remember—the other Heddy with dishwater blond hair. Teasing her about trying to cover up gray hair, none of which she had anyway, got Lou only a laugh and a flap of the hand. Not much bothered Heddy. Good thing. Heddy could give as good as she got.

Lou levered herself upright. "I know all that. I'm the only one left. I know, I know. Even though she's not mine, I'm the only one." She rummaged around for clean mugs, just to keep her hands busy. "Doesn't make it any easier." She drummed her fingers on the counter, willing the coffee to finish.

To deflect more of that conversation, she said, "By the way, where's that bread you said you were bringing over?" She swapped out the coffee pot for a mug and caught the last of the brew.

"It's cooling. I'll drop it off later." Heddy swiveled and draped one arm over the back of her chair. "Say, since when did you switch back to coffee? I thought you swore off the stuff after Sam and went back to tea for good."

"One coffee in the morning's okay. Besides, this is unleaded. Won't get me all wired up," Lou said. "I'm wired enough already."

Heddy reached for the mug Lou offered her. "No picker-upper here then," she muttered. She blew on the coffee and took a noisy sip.

Lou caught it. "Seems like you don't need much of a picker-upper anyway. You must've been up pretty early to get bread baked already." Lou hoped the conversation would steer clear of Kapi and that whole situation. Though that wasn't likely to happen.

Heddy was not about to be deterred. "So. Tell me more about that grandkid. That must take some getting used to. You got her forever?"

Yup. Here it comes. Lou took her time stacking a few shortbread cookies on a plate. "Looks like." Some things were hard to talk about, even with a best friend. She came back to the table and set the plate between them. "Becca brought that girl into the marriage. Mac adopted her. But Mac died when she was little, she doesn't remember a lot. And now the car accident killed her mother. I'm the only one left. The courts gave her to me." She went to the sink and dumped out her coffee. "I need tea."

"I wondered if you'd come to your senses. I'm the only visible coffee drinker in the kitchen this morning," Heddy said. She wriggled her ample toes and paddled her stocking feet on the floor. Steam put a shine on her face as she cradled her mug.

They sat in silence for a few minutes, the way people do when there's no need of talk.

"So, what are you going to do?" Heddy asked. "I mean, she's here, but do you think this'll work out? I know Mac's wife never took to you. Do you think Kapi will?"

Lou snorted. "Who knows? We sure haven't gotten off on the right foot. Maybe she'll follow the rules, but just. She knows there's nowhere else to go, but..."

"But what?"

"Well, she's acting like she wants me to kick her out."

"Probably because then it all becomes your fault, not hers." Heddy shoved half a cookie in her mouth.

"What are you now, a psychologist?" She reached for a cookie before they were all gone. "But what good would throwing her back on the courts do? I can't exactly give her back." Lou hid behind her teacup. "She's…Mac's. Even if she's adopted, she still belonged to Mac."

Heddy reached out a hand and laid it on Lou's arm. "You have more than enough on your plate, Lou. If there's anything I can do…"

Lou's smile lifted only one corner of her mouth. "I know. Honestly, I can't think of anything. Other than listening to me grouse about her. I've got to figure out something to keep her busy. To keep us both busy, I guess."

Heddy hitched up one shoulder, as if shifting a bra strap into place. "Weren't you going off somewhere this summer, like you usually do? Soak up some new atmosphere? Find some great scenery? Or something?" Heddy asked. "Why not get her out of town? Get you both out of town, matter of fact."

"Yeah, right." Lou scratched her nose. "Like she really wants to go traipsing all over Hades and half of Georgia with an old woman. Who'd wanna do that?"

Heddy laughed. "Well, me, for one." She held up a hand. "Don't even think about it. I have a job to attend to, remember?" She blew on her coffee and sighed. "Someday. Someday I'll take off with you." She shook a finger at Lou. "You can make this work. I know you can. Besides, you wanted to get away for a while anyway, didn't you? Kapi'll just have to come along for the ride."

"Some ride! Like the worst corkscrew roller coaster, the way she carries on." Lou shook her head. "Not a fun idea, trapped in a car with a snarly girl."

Heddy shrugged. "You never know. Worse things have happened." She took another cookie.

They had. Worse things already happened. Mac died a long and lingering death from some kind of chemical exfoliant sprayed where there were supposedly no troops. So much for military intelligence. Kapi's mother killed in a car accident. Kapi pawned off on a "grandmother" she didn't know. And Lou stuck in the middle of it all. The worst.

Chapter 5
Lou

Days of rain pulled a blue funk down on the house. Lou tried writing a letter, but it was like pulling a cork out of a wine bottle with a paring knife. Everything came out crumbled. Finally she gave up. For a day or two, anyway. The letter could wait.

She diverted herself by heading out to the woodpile along the side of the house. Struggling into the house with a sling full of firewood, Lou let the door slam behind her. She set the wood on the hearth, and creaked down to her knees. Even though the sun finally started to break through, the days of intermittent rain lowered a damp and flimsy blanket over the living room. A good fire in the middle of the afternoon would go a long way to warming up the place. It was worth a try.

The living room ran across the front of the house, and deep. The room would be flooded with light if not for the covered porch protecting the whole width of the house. As it was, the sun still provided decent light through a front wall of windows.

When she bought the house, Lou kept the plush maroon love seat left behind, even though maroon wasn't her favorite color. But she liked the shape and comfort of the piece, as well as the look of her antique brass reading lamp that swooped like a swan's neck over one end. However, she ripped down the heavy maroon drapes as quickly as she could. Who would put maroon drapes with yellow walls? To say nothing of the weight of the damn things, cutting out all the light. She switched to blue gingham tie-backs and matching valances. She never closed them, figuring if anybody wanted to look in, they were welcome.

The rough stone fireplace took up most of one wall, though the staircase stole a chunk as it wound up and around the back of the fireplace. The fireplace boulders came from the lakeshore when the house was first built, and Lou couldn't bear to change that.

She had an old television, but it was relegated to a position on the back wall, next to the swinging door leading into the kitchen. The only way to watch it was to rearrange the chairs. The message was clear. The fireplace and its attendant plump chairs, scarred tables and lamps took precedence. Even her desk stood against the wall opposite the fireplace. Luckily, anyone ensconced in the chairs admiring the fire didn't have to face the overflow of notebooks, papers, books and other paraphernalia on and around the desk and the nearby big maple table. Of course, the maple tabletop was empty now. Not the desk, luckily. Kapi missed that mess when she swept the big table clear. Good thing. That would induce apoplexy. Lou loved all of her house, but the living room was a favorite spot to park. She reached in to build the fire.

Kapi was out on the back porch. Lou heard the creak of the swing's chains. *Good place for her*, Lou thought. They'd gone through the days pussy-footing around each other to keep from firing salvos across the divide.

The front door rattled and Lou swung around on her haunches. Through the panes in the door, she could see Heddy, arms wrapped around a cardboard box. Lou didn't bother to get up off the floor. The door swung open and Heddy swayed in. The box clinked with every step.

"Since when do you use the front door?" Lou asked.

"I wasn't about to disturb your guest out back." Heddy bumped the door shut and pried her shoes off. "No need to get dirt on your floor. Here, I brought back the canning jars." She looked toward the kitchen, then appeared to think better of it and deposited the box on a small settle bench by the door.

"Empty, I suppose," Lou said.

Heddy laughed. "You did give me the stuff to eat." She took off her jacket and threw it on the loveseat. "The tomatoes made great chili, by the way. Do you need some help?"

"Nope. Been lighting fires forever. Figure I haven't forgotten how yet." She slid the mesh screen back and flicked on the long-nosed lighter. She poked it in and held steady while the cardboard toilet paper roll stuffed with dryer lint caught fire. She closed the screen and levered herself up into the nearest armchair. Heddy already took over the other one. Both chairs sported mismatched pillows, and were worn deep and wide.

"You are a wonder, Lou," Heddy said. She wriggled her ample rump into a comfortable position.

"Why? 'Cause I can light a fire?" Lou put her slippered feet up on the old chest that served as a catch-all table between the two chairs. Lou cleaned up the pile of her notebooks and magazines earlier. She didn't need another "Oops" there.

Heddy ruffled her short orange hair. "Not everyone can make a good fire. To say nothing of taking in a lost child."

She sent Lou a quick look before dropping her head back and closing her eyes.

Lou ignored the lost child comment. "Trick is keeping some of the ashes in the firebox. Too many people clean everything out and then expect the fire to take like that." She snapped her fingers. "Cleanliness is overrated." She settled back and closed her eyes too.

They sat listening to the snap and hiss of the wood.

Finally, Heddy said, "This house big enough for the both of you?"

Lou didn't open her eyes. "Plenty." It was a lie and they both knew it. The house had two cozy bedrooms upstairs; a bathroom up and a half down; a mudroom with washer and dryer off the kitchen; ample porch space. The house was fine. But the people in it weren't.

Heddy snorted. "Right. I see you haven't cleaned up everything." She waved her hand toward the desk against the wall, overflowing with papers, pens, notebooks, as always. Book stacks grew like mushrooms on the floor. "I don't see how you can find anything around here."

"I've had to condense some." Lou shifted in her seat and frowned. "Do you know she's taken over my spot?"

"The fireplace nook?" Heddi gave a sympathetic growl.

"Can you believe it? Without a single Captain-may-I." She sighed and settled back in her chair.

Halfway up the staircase behind the fireplace, a nook backed up against the chimney. Somewhere along the line, someone turned it into a tiny sitting area. It was Lou's haven, especially on a cold winter night where she could settle in for a few minutes before continuing on up to bed. A rose plush area rug that lapped up against the walls. A stuffed chair that wrapped itself around her, Lou's current book balanced on its arm. And that wonderful brick chimney wall that radiated warmth and welcome behind the chair. Heaven.

To Lou's consternation, Kapi commandeered the nook.

"Well, at least it keeps Kapi out of your hair," Heddy said.

"It's my spot," Lou said. "I love that last bit of warmth from the chimney." Warmth before getting into a cold bed, even when Sam was alive.

"The hearth is the heart of the home," Heddy said.

"What?" Lou came back to earth. "Yeah, the heart." She wondered if Kapi knew that homes could have a heart. Her mother sure hadn't radiated much warmth. And Mac, poor Mac. Struggling with cancer for so long. He couldn't have given off too much heat either, his mind so taken up with...

"Dying," Heddy said.

Lou jolted upright. "What did you say?"

"The lawns are finally drying. It's been so darn wet. Why? What did you think I said? You jumped like a stuck frog."

Lou flapped her hand at her. "Nothing. You want a cup of tea?"

"Naw. Just relax. I can't stay too long, but I wanted to bring your jars back before they got lost in my kitchen." She elbowed the pillow behind her, punching it into place.

Lou snorted. Heddy's kitchen was bigger and a lot newer that hers, but it was full to the gills with craft projects and cookbooks. "Are you sure you didn't lose a husband or a boyfriend in there?"

Heddy rolled her head to look at Lou. "I forgive you, you old coot."

Heddy had a boyfriend living with her for a while. For several years, in fact. But that all fell apart long ago.

Lou pursed her lips. "My mouth has a mind of its own."

"You think I haven't noticed?" Heddy smiled. "He was a louse anyway. Some people just don't get it." Her voice took on a whine. "'You're getting older, Heddy. When you gonna settle down?' They don't realize I *have* settled down. That's why I live alone." She burrowed deeper in her chair. "You have the most comfortable furniture."

"That the reason you come over here?" Lou said. "To sit in my chair?"

"Nope. I come over because there's no room to sit in my house." She shrugged. "Well, at least in the kitchen."

"Thanks for helping me get the swing down. I'm always glad to get that done. It means spring is truly here," Lou said.

"No problem. My youth gives me strength," Heddy said.

"Decades younger than me ain't nothin' when wisdom comes with age, honey." They both laughed.

"And speaking of youth, how is that young lady out there doing?" Heddy asked. "How long has she been here? Two weeks? Did she have to finish her school year here, or...?"

"She probably would've gotten suspended. She's a troublemaker."

"Really? Her records show her as a criminal type?"

"Naw. She was a good student, according to what they all said." It was grudgingly given. "Anyway, they said she didn't have to enroll for the last couple weeks of here. Figured it might do more damage on top of everything else."

"Would've helped get her out of the house," Heddy said. "It's gotta be tough on both of you, bumping against each other all day long."

Lou shifted her shoulders. She scooched forward to poke at the fire.

The back door banged open and shut. A moment later, Kapi tramped through the swinging door from the kitchen. She stopped cold, like a dog coming up on a chicken without warning.

Heddy didn't miss a beat. "Hi, Kapi." She shot out her sweetest smile, the one that bowled almost everyone else over. It seemed to have no effect. But at least Kapi didn't bolt.

Kapi dipped her head, the only acknowledgement that she'd heard.

"So," Heddy jumped in, "you're done with school for the summer? Do you like to read?"

Lou bit her tongue to keep from putting her own two-cents in.

"Yeah, I like to read."

"Great! Me too," Heddy said and opened her mouth to rattle off a list of her favorite titles, but Kapi got there first.

"I'm going up to read." She flashed a book, but too quick to show the title. She padded across the living room and disappeared up the stairs.

Lou rolled her eyes as Heddy put a finger to her lips. "I know," she whispered. She moved to the edge of her chair. "Okay, Lou, gotta run. I've got garden plants to buy. Say, wanna come along? It's such a gorgeous day..."

"You know what? I think I will. I want to see if they've got their hanging baskets out yet. I need a couple for the front porch."

Heddy tilted her head toward the stairs. "Wanna ask...?"

"Absolutely not!" Lou cleared her throat. "We need some time for ourselves."

Heddy raised her eyebrows in a brief moment of silence before she launched herself up from the chair. "Okay then. Let's go."

Lou closed the glass doors on the fireplace, confining a fire that moved from hollering to growling and now was only grumbling. She walked to the bottom of the stairs. "Kapi! Back in a couple hours. I'm going to the garden center with Heddy." She turned back to Heddy. "House rule." she whispered. "Tell where you're going and who you'll be with."

"Yeah, fine," came crackling down as Lou went to the door and grabbed her jacket.

"C'mon," Heddy said, slipping her arm through Lou's. "You need a breath of fresh air."

Chapter 6
Louise Wright

My father went from Papa to Father when he started to take me along on his business excursions to meet the boats coming into Green Bay's harbor. The town swelled to well over two-thousand people by that time. On my fourteenth birthday, he told me he was taking me to the docks and warehouses. He said, "It's time you learned the business, Louise. Your mother and I discussed it, and we think you're ready to take on more responsibilities. You already help me with the bookkeeping, but you should know the business from the bottom up." He harrumphed. "So, I think 'Papa' is a bit too..."

"Juvenile? Informal?" I plugged into the pause. "Perhaps 'Father' would be better. More..." I wiggled my fingers. "More businesslike, yes?"

Father smiled and nodded. "Papa is fine at home, but Father would make sure *you* were taken seriously too. I'd like that."

I agreed. From then on, most mornings we set off together.

Father dealt in all sorts of merchandise: food stuffs, lumber, raw logs floated down from the woodlots, furniture up from Chicago, everything he could buy and sell. And he was good at it. Store owners all over the city came to him to acquire the goods citizens demanded. Times with him were exciting, and demanded close attention. He wasn't one to wait on slowpokes.

That was the same year my mother met me at the breakfast table, dressed to go out driving. She slapped her fine leather gloves against her palm and exhorted me to hurry. "Come along, Louise. Grab your riding gloves and hat. It's time." She pivoted and skipped out the back door into the yard.

"What? Wait! Where are we going?" I took the last piece of bacon and shoved it in my mouth. "What is it time for?" But she was out of earshot. I swept my hat and gloves off the table by the back door, clattered down the back steps to catch up.

Mother's trap sat in the drive, but Ruby, my mare, was harnessed. I could hear Bridie protesting in the barn. These were not the usual doings, I'm sure she was thinking. I clambered up next to Mother, who sat, reins already gathered in her hand. She scooched over a bit to make room for me, and lifted her carriage whip from its holder next to her.

I frowned. It wasn't her whip, with its lovely carved handle. This one was plain, although the wood had a lovely grain. "That's not yours," I said to her, wagging my finger toward it.

She smiled. "No, darling, it's yours. It's time you learned to drive a carriage."

This was going to be a grand morning! I enveloped her in a hug. "Oh, thank you, Mother! I'm so excited! Here, I can take the reins." I leaned over, but she pulled them out of my reach.

"Oh, no, you don't." But she was laughing. "You're a fine horseback rider, but you've not handled a horse in harness. If you're going to help your father, he may want you to drive a team, and you might as well start small, with my trap." She shook her head. "Heaven only knows what else he has in mind for you. I can only hope to prepare you for anything."

I settled back and folded my hands in my lap. "I shall give you my highest attention, Mother." I hoped my excitement wouldn't bubble to the surface and ruin the moment. "Why do you think he wants me to learn everything about the business? Doesn't seem very...ladylike, does it?"

Mother snorted. Not a very ladylike response. "Plenty of women help run businesses. Often, they're behind the scenes, but don't you think they're not wielding power where they can." She tapped me on the nose. But your father said he doesn't have a son to inherit, so he's bound and determined to teach *you* everything."

It was my turn to snort, and we shared a laugh.

"Here. Ruby knows your voice, and your hand on the reins." Mother handed me her—my—carriage whip. "This may be called a whip, but you know very well from riding with me that no one should actually whip a horse. A touch for guidance is all that's needed. A reminder." She tweaked my ear. "Like this. You're reminding her that you are the driver, even if she can't feel your legs pressing and guiding her, as she can when you ride astride. That's what the whip is for. A simple touch of guidance from behind." She brushed a loose strand of hair behind my ear.

It burst upon me. Just the kind of guidance she gave to me. A gentle touch from behind. I knew she would always be back there. She handed me the reins.

"You're in charge, my dear. Go slowly until Ruby gets the hang of it," she said.

And we were off.

***

We stored the carriage in the barn for the winter, along with the well-oiled harnesses. Spring couldn't come quickly enough for me, although Father and I continued to visit the docks until the bay froze over. Then it was indoor work, or occasionally taking the team of draft horses out to the lumber camps and mills.

Mother took me in hand more often than not, leaving my father to carry on the business without me. She was determined to make a well-rounded lady of me. I already made the rounds of soirees and lectures, thanks to Mother's insistence over the years. Now she tutored me in the domestic arts: cooking, cleaning, sewing, all those tasks necessary to make a household run smoothly. We had a housekeeper cook, but Mother and she formed a bond based more on affection and respect than on condescension or fear.

As spring delayed and delayed, I despaired of ever seeing dry roads so I could get the trap out and harness Ruby. My hands itched to handle the reins. And yet, the weather didn't cooperate.

"Stop fidgeting, Louise. Pay attention, or your stitches will all have to be picked out and redone." Mother's voice brought me back from watching the rain sheet down the parlor window.

The weakness in her voice filtered down into my soul. I certainly was not paying attention. How did I miss that? I cast my mind back over the winter months. Her voice was stronger in the fall, I was sure of it. I shifted in the chair to better face her head on. "Are you...Do you have a cold, Mother?" She sent me a smile, but her eyes were faded, her cheeks flushed. I felt it in my bones. It was more than a cold.

"No, child." She bent to her stitching again, hiding her face from me.

If I didn't ask more, then everything was right with our world. Fear made me hold my tongue. That didn't stop anything, of course. No amount of pretending would change that.

Just before my fifteenth birthday, she called me to her. By this time, in midsummer, she was spending her days under an afghan on the divan in the parlor. She summoned strength only to climb to bed, and even those days faded. We took our meals with her in the parlor, though she insisted I continue to accompany Father. Both of us were sent out of the house each morning, never knowing if she would be there to greet us at the end of the day. Our days ended earlier and earlier, as she weakened more and more.

When she asked for me that evening, I came immediately. Father was already there, sitting within reach and holding her hand. "Come here, my darling girl," she whispered.

I went to her and curled up on the floor. I wanted to settle my head on her chest, hear her heart beat, pour my strength into her. But she was too fragile for that. I lay my head next to her, where she could stroke my hair. She sighed, more a breath seeping out than a sigh. "Louise, you and your father...cherish each other. Remember...I shall always be with you. Go on to do...wonderful things." Her voice weakened with pain, dropped below a whisper. "You have...mysteries within you. But I know...you can handle...anything. You and your father...together."

I strained to hear her, as even the whisper faded into "I love you both." She drifted into sleep, her chest rising and falling.

The morning light woke me, though I didn't remember falling asleep. Father was slumped, asleep, in his chair, fingers still entwined with my mother's. My hand brushed my mother's hand and I bolted upright. She was cold. No motion, no breath. My cry awoke Father.

***

We walked through the next few years one step at a time, holding onto each other every way we could. Neither one of us could handle the pain of taking out Bridie and Mother's trap, so we sold them to a worthy family that had admired both, and would cherish them when we couldn't.

Father's business stayed steady enough, though neither one of us put heart and soul into it. Everyone knew of Mother's death, and the devastation to my father and me. I acted the role of recovery, but it was hollow. I felt Father's emptiness too. We coped as best we could.

Then, one late summer day, Mr. Albert Wood showed up on the docks, looking harried and unkempt. One of the captains was pointing to Father. Mr. Wood trotted toward us, a sheaf of papers in his hand, looking as if they would escape to the winds at any moment. He slowed to a stop in front of us. "You Stephen Wright?" he asked, giving me a cursory glance. "Your daughter?"

Father frowned. "Yes, to both. What do you want of us?" Not his old genial self. Nor even his calm business style.

"I want you, my man." Mr. Wood clapped my father on the shoulder, then regrouped to juggle his papers back into some sort of order. "Albert Wood here. I'm looking for...Well, perhaps this is too abrupt. Let me buy you lunch." He indicated a dockside tavern, well known for its hearty stews and tasty cutlets.

"For what purpose?" Father asked. I slipped my hand into the crook of his arm. We were finished with our morning dealings, and were about to stop for lunch at that very establishment.

"I will explain everything. But let us retire to the pub there. I suspect you are both hungry..." *How nice of him to include me*, I thought, though not without a touch of sarcasm. He went on, "...and I *know* I'm starving. Come, humor me." He took my father by the elbow and steered us to the door.

Two hours later, my father's eyes shone in cautious interest, and, yes, perhaps even a bit of excitement. I couldn't help but being swept along with the tide.

Move from Green Bay to a small town, growing and vibrant, as Mr. Wood described it? I felt a kernel of hope. Would this lift the cloud from the both of us? The more Mr. Wood described his need to sell his mercantile, so as to spend the necessary time on his burgeoning ferry business, shuttling goods and people across the neck of the hourglass-shaped lake, the better it sounded. Father grew more animated as Wood described the town with its little church and village green, the surrounding farms with rich earth sprouting crops, the lake with logging rafts and thick with fish. Too good to be true? Perhaps. But it resurrected my father's faith in a future. And mine.

Within a few weeks, we sold what we needed to, including my little mare, bought what we needed to, and headed off with Father's draft team and wagon to a new beginning, in Woods Portage.

Chapter 7
Lou

Abe Johnson lived a "kissing corner" away from Lou, as he called it. Their backyards met only where the points of their lots touched. Abe, built like a fireplug, always joked he was catching up to Lou, age-wise. For a couple of months each year, they were the same age. Then Lou leap-frogged past him.

Today he even looked like a fireplug, with his red and black checked shirt and faded red fishing pants. Lou stopped herself from peering around to see if he left his waders on the back porch. She always thought of the two of them as a potential comedy team: stumpy jolly Abe and skinny string bean Lou. She'd play the sullen one while Abe delivered the zingers.

"She's reading *Little House on the Prairie?*" Abe said. "C'mon. Nobody reads Wilder anymore."

"Where have you been, old man?" Lou said. "Laura Ingalls Wilder is as popular as ever. Plus, she's a Wisconsin author. Teachers and parents love her. I don't really know why Kapi likes her. Plus, she's picked up every piece of historical fiction or history I've got."

They were closeted in Lou's kitchen peeling potatoes for dinner. Scalloped potatoes, ham slices, brussels sprouts with bacon. Heddy proclaimed a "get-together" and offered desserts. "Apple or mincemeat pie?" she asked. "Oh, never mind. I'll bring both."

She plunked them down on Lou's broad kitchen island. The island made the kitchen fairly narrow, but Lou liked to eat most of her meals there, standing and sipping tea. Until Kapi, that is. Then she insisted on them both eating at the maple slab in the living room or at the small table by the kitchen window, where the back door opened against it. Some semblance of family, maybe, she thought. Plus, we don't have to talk to each other if we're eating.

With only a window over the sink and the one by the table, Lou painted the kitchen lime green, installed a skylight and a new back door with a window to bring some light into what had been a dingy and inhospitable room. No window treatments needed here. The backyard was deep and backed up against an empty lot too wet to build on. When the leaves were down, she could see across Abe's street to the lake beyond. Even now, with the magnolia's flamboyant flowers already down, the lake showed a bit of shimmer in the twilight.

They munched on Heddy's imported goat cheese and whole wheat crackers. Abe's ham, when he opened the oven, was fragrant enough to fill the kitchen with threads of clove and pineapple. Heddy's three bottles of wine lay cooling side by side on the back porch.

Abe shoved the ham back in the oven and perched on a stool at the end of the island. He smoothed his plush white mustache. It was the only hair remaining anywhere on his head. "You want a hand with that?"

"Perfect timing, bozo. This is the last one." She brandished a naked potato, then sliced it with a deft hand.

Abe snared a piece of raw potato and popped it in his mouth. He got up and headed for the sink. "When's the

Terror coming home? I've only seen her on your back porch."

Lou poured milk over the casserole and slid the scalloped potatoes into the oven. "She is home..." A mere figure of speech, Lou thought. Kapi didn't seem to feel at home anywhere. Lou shrugged off the unease. "She's in the nook. Reading, as usual. At least she's subsided into grumbling *sotto voce*. A welcome change from the verbal 'love notes'." She made quotation marks in the air with her fingers. "I'll call her down in a bit. There might be strength in numbers if we're all here."

"Either that or she'll be scared out of her pants."

"You going anywhere this summer?" Heddy asked the others.

Abe chimed in first. "Heading up to Eagle River to fish. Got my cabin all rented. This year they've got canoes. I'd rather fish out of a canoe any day. It'll get me places a boat won't."

Lou laughed. "I'd love to see you get in and out of a canoe. Make sure you leave your gear on the dock, 'cause you're sure to put your foot on the gunwale and go right in the drink."

Abe bristled. "I'm no greenhorn, y'know. I canoed the Boundary Waters before." He opened the back door and snatched a bottle of wine.

"Before what?" Lou called after him. "The invention of the motorboat?"

Heddy snickered. This was an old and familiar skirmish.

Abe waved the wine bottle at Lou. "A lot you know. Before the invention of the wheel." He sent her a broad smile. He fished the corkscrew out of a nearby drawer and went to work.

"You two are the worst," Heddy said. "Who would believe you've been friends forever?"

"Since before the invention of the wheel," Lou said. *Since long before I met his late wife. Since high school,* she added to herself.

"Maybe earlier," Abe said. "I can't seem to recall." He poured a splash of wine in each glass. "Try this."

"Anyway. So, Lou. Have you decided yet what you're going to do about your trip?"

Lou shrugged. "Maybe." She opened the freezer and took out a bag of corn. "I *was* going to do a Meander again." The cold bag was getting to her hands and she turned to toss it in the microwave.

"The last time you did that, you came back feeling super relaxed," Heddy said. "Didn't you wander around Michigan? Where are you going this time?"

"This time?" Lou grabbed a cracker and slathered on goat cheese. "There may not be a this time. That girl..."

"*That girl* can go along, you know," Abe said. "No reason for you to deny yourself just because she's here." He held up his glass and they clinked rims. "To us."

"The Terror, you mean? You want me to take her along? I'd probably have to pry her out of the nook with a crowbar. She doesn't even want to eat with me." Lou gave them a wicked smile. "But I made it a house rule." She stuffed the whole cracker in her mouth.

"So make another house rule," Heddy said. "Like, 'Anybody living in this house comes along on any trips deemed necessary by the house mother. No complaining either.'"

Lou snorted. "As if."

"You never know unless you ask," Abe said. "Well, okay. Don't ask. Just tell. Need more?" He held up the bottle of wine.

"Heck yeah!" Heddy said, sliding her glass over to Abe. "This is good stuff."

"Sure, why not? Hit me," Lou agreed. She took a noisy sip. "I don't know. She's been with me weeks now and we still tiptoe around each other."

"Yeah, like you're so approachable," Abe said. When Lou opened her mouth, he added, "No, no. No protesting. We've been friends long enough, I can be honest."

"He's right," Heddy said. "You're going to have to make the first move. Ask her to go along. Besides, you need this for yourself, you know. I've seen you come home and work like a fury. Those Meanders energize you. And—" She held her glass up to the light. "You seem to see the stuff back here clearer when you get back."

Lou grunted and reached for another cracker.

Heddy swiveled to Lou, her glass still raised. "Here's to a summer Meander." She raised her eyebrows at Lou.

"Hear! Hear! I second that motion." Abe clinked his glass on Heddy's.

They both waited. "Come on, old lady. Commit," Abe said.

Lou grumbled something unintelligible, but she raised her glass and touched the other two.

"Announce it tonight," Heddy said.

"Good idea," Abe said. "With all of us here, she can't say no."

Lou laughed outright at that. "You two don't seem to get it. She hates me and she'll do anything to prove it. She can easily say no. And she will. You can bet on it."

***

By the time they opened the third bottle of wine, the scalloped potatoes were done, and the crackers and goat cheese were gone. The big maple table was set, including cloth napkins, a little touch that reminded Lou that civilization hadn't completely died out in her house.

The procession of food from kitchen to table began as Lou headed for the foot of the stairs. She stopped with her foot on the bottom step.

Best I don't go up. I'm all fuzzy warm from the wine and good company, and I don't want that disturbed by Kapi and her attitude. She took a deep breath. "Kapi. Kapi! Dinner's on."

"I'm on the way."

Lou raised an eyebrow and pulled her mouth down. Huh. Not even a snarky tone. Maybe... She turned back to supervise the table.

"Is she coming?" Abe asked. The thunder coming down the steps answered that question soon enough. Kapi appeared at the bottom of the stairs.

"Come on over and meet my friends," Lou said.

Kapi sidled to the table. "Yeah, I know—"

"Hi," Heddy stuck out her hand. "I keep seeing you flitting around, but we've never been formally introduced. I'm Heddy, Hedy Lamarr."

Abe guffawed. "Come on, Heddy. Stop pulling jokes."

With a sigh and a roll of her eyes, Lou chuckled. "Hedy Lamarr was a famous movie star way back when. This Heddy is just giving you a hard time." She took Abe's arm. "This is Abe, my—our backyard neighbor."

The look on Kapi's face shifted from frowning confusion to thunder. She swung on Abe. "And I suppose you're Abraham Lincoln, Abe?" Spinning to snag a chair at the table, she didn't count on Heddy planted in her way. It was like running into the Pillsbury Doughboy.

Heddy peeled Kapi off her ample bosom. "As I recall, house rule says we have to eat together. Wanna glass of wine?" She flashed Kapi a smile.

"Wait, what?" Lou froze in the midst of pouring herself a glass. "She's—"

Heddy flapped her hands at Lou. "Kidding. Just kidding." She rolled her hand. "Keep pouring." She turned to Kapi and winked. "Hope there's still some left for me. C'mon, sit down. Let's eat. I'm starving."

There ensued a very long period of time, broken only by murmurs of appreciation and the clink of silverware on plates. Conversation resumed when Heddy cut and served the pies.

"Yeah, Heddy." Abe waggled his finger at the pies. "A little slice of each. That's right."

"How about you, Kapi?" Heddy rotated her spatula over the pies.

Kapi shrugged. "Whatever." She picked up her dessert fork and examined the tines.

"Okay, mincemeat it is..." Heddy pulled over the appropriate pie plate.

Kapi sent Heddy a sharp look.

"...a-n-n-nd a piece of apple to go with," Heddy added.

"I'll go with the rest of you. One of each," Lou said.

Heddy dished up the same for herself. "So."

Oh, lord, here it comes, Lou thought. Heddy's "So" was a shot across the bow, a warning of something ... something ... to come. Lou speared a chunk of apple trying to escape the crust and shoved it in her mouth.

"So. Kapi, are you heading out with Lou on a Mea-"

"Just a little trip," Lou interrupted through the errant apple.

"What little trip?" Kapi sounded a bit alarmed. "What 'little trip'?" Air quotes with her fingers emphasized the words.

It was Lou's turn to shrug. "Just something I do every summer."

"Where?" Kapi asked, biting off the question. "Why?"

Heddy answered the second question before Lou could. "She goes out and—" She twirled her fork in the air, like a conductor. "—collects, you know, impressions of stuff. Colors, scenery, birds. You know, that kind of stuff. Then she comes home all relaxed and full of travel tales."

"So, where?" Kapi asked, a forkful of pie hovering above the plate.

"Don't know yet." Lou unloaded a hunk of pie into her mouth. "What does it matter?" came out garbled. She left the necessary part of the query unsaid.

But Heddy said it for her. "Wanna go along?"

If her mouth wasn't filled with pie, Lou would sigh. *Too late now, old lady. Damage is done.*

"You really should go, y'know," Abe chimed in. "There's lots to see out there. Lou always brings back plenty of stories."

"Abe is right," Heddy said. "You should go along. Better than sitting around here with the old folks." She pointed her fork at Abe. "'Cause that's where you'd end up, Kapi." She put her head down and concentrated on slicing off a piece of her pie.

"Speak for yourself, neighbor," Abe said. "I defer to the elders in the room."

Heddy snorted. "Have you looked in the mirror lately, grandpa? Anyway, whaddya say, Kapi? Us old folks—and I'm not really one of the old ones here—or the real dinosaur over there?" Heddy waved her fork at Lou.

"Go along?" Kapi's fork was still poised in midair. She swung her gaze to Lou. And waited.

Lou swallowed and washed it down with a long slug of water. *She's gonna wait, isn't she? I gotta say something.* She met Kapi's gaze. There was a moment from Kapi of...what? Fear of being left behind? Again? Lou lifted one shoulder, screwed up her courage and said, "Why not?" before returning her attention to her plate.

A mumble from Kapi resolved itself into, "Awright. I'll go." Then her fork clattered to her plate, and she pushed away from the table. Without another word, she picked up her own dish and one of the empty pie plates, and headed for the kitchen. Everyone else froze in place for a moment before resuming eating. It felt unnatural.

Kapi came back through the swinging door. "Going up to read." At the bottom of the stairs, she swiveled to add, "Nice meeting you all." She headed upstairs, taking the steps two at a time.

"What just happened?" Abe asked.

"Who'da thunk?" Heddy said.

"Well." Lou couldn't get out another word. *Guess I've got a traveling companion.*

Chapter 8
Lou

Mac would've loved this. And suddenly that tow-headed boy was there. Here he came, running down the driveway, his hair ruffled by the wind.

Lou never resented Mac's thick blond hair, inherited from Sam. It was the only thing he inherited from his father. His happy personality came from Lou. One would never know it now. But then...then, all was happy, serene, non-judgmental. No, that wasn't totally true. Enough followed down the line for that not to be true. She and Mac had the usual ups and downs as he grew, but never enough to cause a chasm between them. They were a tight society of two in their little boat, hauling out the oars when the waters got too rough for the sail. Battening down the hatches. Bailing out the bottom. She did all she could to make life realistic for Mac. The little boat holding two didn't last. Nothing does.

Lou was prepared for Mac to eventually fall in love, marry, have children. To let him go. Or at least to share him. But when Mac brought Becca home and announced their engagement, all in one fell swoop, Lou felt betrayed. She took a deep breath and prepared herself to like Becca, to accept her son's choice. But Becca never let that happen. On that first visit, she looked around Lou's comfortable front room, and with pursed lips and a curt nod to Lou, turned to Mac. "Come on, darling, it's getting late. Let's get going. Kapi's waiting in the car." Not a word to Lou.

The worst part? Mac went along with it. He shot his mother a look of apology. But he didn't contradict Becca. Becca never entered Lou's house again. Mac did, but mostly alone. He brought Kapi twice. All right, maybe three times. Hardly enough time to counteract Becca's poison.

Then Mac got cancer from that Agent Orange. Becca let no one near him until it was too late. For Lou, it became too late too quickly. Her own personality, crazed on the surface already, cracked into shards when Mac died.

Now, Lou, rattled to her soul, hardened herself as best she could. She took a deep breath and allowed the past to evaporate.

Yes, she remembered, Mac loved Meanders. She couldn't suppress a smile.

He always galloped around the car and the yard when they were getting ready to take off somewhere. Whooping and hollering and making up silly songs about where they were headed. "Goin' to the ocean! Drink a magic potion! Gonna do some fishin'! That'll be our mission!" Lou missed that happy-go-lucky attitude, and the boy that went with it. More the boy.

She outgrew the need to tent camp years ago. Even before Sam died, she graduated to cabins or bed and breakfasts. She never told Sam. But then, Sam was never with her anyway. Almost every summer, she tried for a week or so off on her own. Once, Sam threw a fit and Lou caved, just to keep the peace. But once Sam died, once

Mac was born, she had no one to answer to. Mac became her companion.

It worked out fine for everybody. In a way, that surprised her. Going off on a Meander, as she called them, was a chance to stuff her memory with images, people, places. A chance to unwind away from, first Sam, then just everyday life in Woods Portage.

Lou stuffed her duffel bag alongside the big cooler in the back of the SUV. She discovered the splendors of a plug-in cooler a couple of years earlier, and now it lived in the car. Farmers market purchases, grocery runs, anything that needed to be cold could be thrown in.

She rested her hands on the cooler and conjured up Mac chipping away at the bag of ice for his thermos of lemonade. "We *still* need ice!" he insisted. Half the fun was tic-tic-ticking away with the ice pick, so she always relented.

She smiled and could see Mac, well into his teens, still packing ice to chip for his drinks. That was before he left college to join the Army. The Green Berets. "If I'm going to join up, I'm going to join the best trained, the best equipped unit. Best insurance to get home in one piece."

They both knew those elite units were also the ones where life expectancy in the field hovered somewhere around five minutes. And they were always in the field.

Lou sighed. He had, after all, come home in one piece. At least on the outside. Inside, some insidious poison was working on breaking him down. Some best trained, best equipped, elite cancer.

She shook her head, dispelling the image of her lost son.

"Kapi? Come on! Shake a leg!"

"You don't have to holler." Kapi came up right behind her, Mac's old Army duffel sagging down from one shoulder. Mac's face seemed to hover just behind, a memory rather than a reality.

"God a'mighty, girl! You gave me a start," Lou said, turning to take the duffel from Kapi.

But Kapi held tight. "I can do it myself. Don't need your help." She slung the duffel bag into the back of the car, where it landed athwart two grocery bags.

Lou bit the side of her mouth to keep from saying anything. She'd check on the bags when Kapi wasn't around. If they had to eat squashed cupcakes, she'd make sure Kapi had the flattest ones.

"You're going like *that?*" Kapi flapped a hand in Lou's direction.

Lou looked down at her faded denim shirt, rolled up sleeves concealing a tear from some gardening tool years ago. And yes, her poop green pants were hanging loose on her skinny legs, but they were comfortable, dammit. "Yes. I am going like *this*. If you can wear that grungy t-shirt and—what are those? Combat boots? I can wear what I da..what I please."

Lou headed back into the house to grab the bag of ice from the freezer and the lunch bag from the refrigerator. When she returned and opened the back of the car, Kapi's duffel bag had been moved off the grocery bags and wedged in front of Lou's. Lou's eyebrows went up in surprise. She felt a moment of appreciation, but it didn't last long enough to emerge in words.

Kapi was already in the front seat, feet up on the dashboard.

"Get your feet off the dash," Lou ordered, leaning in the front window. "Seatbelts are *de rigueur* in my car."

"'Day rigger'? What the hell's that?"

"Language!" Lou was not above a few profanities herself, but wasn't going to take any from this little girl.

"It's *de rigueur*, not 'day rigger'. Means ya gotta do it. So buckle up. I'm going to check the house before we leave." She strode off and clumped up the front steps.

Heddy already had a key and the general list of where they might be driving. "Could change any day, though," Lou warned her. "But you know all that. I'll keep in touch, just in case."

"Don't you mean, *we*'ll keep in touch?" Heddy asked. She smiled, but her eyes questioned her own wisdom of pulling Lou's chain.

Lou pulled down her eyebrows, but didn't attack. "Two weeks, maybe three. But then again, I'm thinking maybe one will be more than enough." She sent Heddy a wry look.

"Time will tell," Heddy said. "And for Pete's sake, give it time! She's only been with you...How long now?"

"You know perfectly well how long," Lou shot back. "Over a month."

"Five and a half weeks to be exact," Heddy said.

"You weasel," was Lou's only answer to that one.

Now Lou cruised from room to room, checking the timer on one of the living room lights, making sure no water tap was dripping, rinsing the last coffee cups and turning them upside down in the sink. As her usual last move, she went to the basement and turned down the water heater.

She almost reached the front door before she remembered the earrings. She went back to the desk and whisked them out of the little porcelain dish where they lived. Her grandmother gave her the earrings, a cluster of long silver dangles and disks, "to help you fly." She always took them along on Meanders, and when she needed inspiration. She didn't even need to wear them, but they had to be within reach, so she could touch them, hear the silver pieces sing a bit, rubbing against each other.

She popped the earrings in her shirt pocket, then locked the front door and checked the mailbox, even though she knew it was empty. Old habits. When she got in the car and stuck the key in the ignition, she was greeted with two growls: one from the engine leaping to life and the other from Kapi.

"Are we actually getting out of here? Finally?"

"Well, what do you think, Miss High-and-Mighty? I just turned the car on. You figure we're vacationing in the driveway? Should I turn it off now and we can set up a tent in the front yard? Or do you prefer the back?"

"You didn't pack a tent." Kapi's voice rippled with arrogance. Then it dropped a tone or two. "Did you?"

Lou almost didn't answer. She took a deep breath to steady herself. "No. No tent. I'm too old for that now." She waited for a comeback. Nothing. That was a surprise.

Kapi snapped headphones over her head and retreated to the world of music.

Lou relaxed a bit. At least she wouldn't be expected to keep up a running conversation. Heddy would not be able to berate her on that account, anyway. Lou poked Kapi and waved her finger. "And get your feet off the dash." This time, her order was obeyed. And Kapi had her seatbelt on.

Lou shifted into reverse and eased out of the driveway.

"Finally. Let's escape this dungeon."

Lou restrained herself from stamping on the brake. She pulled over and turned to Kapi. "What?"

"What, what?" Kapi's headphones dangled around her neck. "Nothing."

"No. You said, 'Let's escape this dungeon.'"

"So?" Kapi began to slide her headphones back on.

"Your dad used to say that every time we left town."

Kapi shrugged. "Mom said it to me."

Lou pulled away from the curb. Maybe Becca and Mac built a family after all. "So all right. Let's escape this dungeon."

Kapi clapped on her headphones.

Lou headed north and stopped at Lake Street, the main road which ran up from the lake. Stop signs were hardly needed, though she heeded them nonetheless. The traffic in Woods Portage didn't amount to much, even when the fishing families came to town in the summer. Their cottages were lined up along the shore, north of the downtown, most of them hidden in the trees. The tourists appeared in the grocery store and the ice cream and candy shops, and once in awhile in the little church, but other than cruising the little gift shops in town, they pretty much kept to themselves.

Lou glanced east as she crossed Lake Street. The old stone ferry office squatted at the foot of the bridge across the neck of the hourglass that was the lake. The ferry itself was gone, having evolved from fur trappers to lumber wagons to cars, and finally, to obsolescence. The town council figured a bridge would have people flocking to the area. But the interstate highway just twenty miles east, built soon after the bridge, drew the flowing hordes of cars away. Everyone heading up north. Or back home again. Woods Portage became a charming backwater.

Lou was helping convert the ferry office into the town's historical society. The structure was still sturdy, in spite of looking like a miniature Chicago tenement. Her most spectacular find, intact upstairs, was an ancient rolltop desk. She'd pried open the lock and discovered dried out ink bottles and cracked pen nibs, receipts and orders, old account books, and even a pocket-sized address book—all belonging to Albert Wood, the original ferry builder himself and the man who convinced her great-great grandfather to open the mercantile store all those years ago.

She pulled across the intersection. As she came up on the old mercantile, she poked Kapi in the arm.

Kapi startled and popped her headphones off. "What the—?"

"This is my territory." Lou pointed at the mercantile. "My great-great-grandfather and his daughter started that store."

Chapter 9
Louise Wright

Because of changing weather, Father and I should have moved to Woods Portage a month or so before we did, but I didn't have much of a choice. The sudden opportunity to purchase the mercantile there was too good to pass up, but he had business matters to attend to before we left. He finally packed me up without a lot of warning and we were off. By the time we finished the train trip from Green Bay to Oshkosh, and then by wagon west to Woods Portage, my clothes were filthy, my boots were worn, my whole body was exhausted. I tried to persuade Father to allow me to drive the team once we were out of Oshkosh, but he'd hear none of it. "Louise Wright! No way for a daughter of mine—or any lady, for that matter—to travel out here," he said, "driving herself over these roads."

But I had nothing to keep my mind occupied, other than how I ached as we bumped along the primitive tracks. If I were driving, I could've focused on the horses, rather than the potholes. But no, Father wouldn't let me use the skills he himself taught me. At least, not until we were well away from civilization as we knew it. I finally wore him down. He knew I was a competent driver and his shoulders eased once he saw I could handle the reins.

Still, at times, to salve my weary backside, I walked, plodding along next to the wagon wheel. I plaited my hair into a long braid and tucked it up under my mother's old floppy canvas hat.

Though I inherited some of my mother's fine features and her raven hair, I had not inherited her shape. That was my father's. Not stocky, as he was, but not softly rounded either, as she had been. Sturdy would probably be the best description. A blessing, surely, as we covered mile after mile. Where she was tall, I stayed rather short. Where she charmed with her heart-shaped face, I approached everyone with a blunt square face. I inherited blue eyes from my father. But my smile came from Mother. On her, it fit like a well-made gown. On me, it sometimes startled.

But surprising smiles and blue eyes were not going to be much help to me, hampered with long skirts and long roads.

West of Pickett, I finally persuaded my father to lend me a pair of his old woolen trousers. If I was going to walk, or clamber up and down from ground to seat, I was not going to tangle myself up in skirts and petticoats, to say nothing of the dirt they'd accumulate. Father was reluctant, but I wheedled and cajoled. After extracting a promise—well, I implied—I'd revert to dresses once we got close to Woods Portage, he gave in. It was a small relief. But better a small relief than none at all.

I was used to more comfortable travel than this, and would've done much better riding my lovely little mare or settled into the padded seat of our carriage. After all, it was Father who insisted I learn how to ride in the first place. And how to drive. With gloves and a fine whip, I was as good as any of the young men of my age. Of course, not so good a driver as my father. Yet. Someday, I hoped to be.

But my mare and our carriage were back in Green Bay, sold to help finance our move. My dear sweet Mother was left behind too. Under the churchyard. Often enough, she'd whisk me away to the kitchen or the parlor and try to teach me everything she knew. By my soul, the woman could do anything! Her cooking was famous, her stitchery precise, her gardens replete with vegetables among the flowers. A bit eccentric? Of course. But no one who met her could resist her for long. Oh, to have her to cling to on that rocky road! She would've let me drive from the start.

Why did Father have to be so...so fatherly now? Soon after Mother died, when I was just shy of fifteen, he made me his business companion, I think to relieve his loneliness. He took me along on his buying excursions, oftentimes handing me the carriage reins. We'd go down to the docks to meet the Great Lakes schooners carrying goods up from Chicago or from the cities far to the east. I'd look at the bulge and flow of the full canvas sails and dream of the streets of New York or the bustle of Detroit. Never in my nineteen years did I dream I'd move west rather than east. West to Woods Portage to take advantage of the burgeoning town, a new place to make a new fortune.

Father wanted to escape the pain of losing my mother, wanted to begin again, to expand his business into the hinterlands. We still were to maintain a connection with the offices in Green Bay and Oshkosh, but Father's trusted managers would deal with that end, while we disappeared, for all intents and purposes, into the wilderness. Once or twice a year, Father said, would be enough to renew our acquaintance with civilization. I had a feeling even those visits would dwindle.

Once we reached Woods Portage three groaning days later, I was afraid I'd not have much time to set up the rooms behind the store before the cold weather threatened. It would make that first winter wicked, what with the lack of window hangings to keep out the cold, and the rush to preserve what additional vegetables and meats we could. Two more months would've saved me a lot of trouble.

"If it's this cold in October, what's going to happen in January?" I asked Father.

"Don't worry your head about that, Louise," he said. "We'll be packed in tight before then. I've hired a boy from one of the farms to split and stack enough wood for the winter."

I looked around the cramped store and shivered. "It's so damp in here."

"We're lucky," Father said. "This building is sturdy and we've a stove for the store and another for our living quarters. We get those fired up and the damp will disappear. Just you watch." He gave me a hug, which at least stopped my trembles. "Albert Wood built with plenty of room," Father said, "for his office and his living quarters."

"But it turned out to be too far from the ford," I added. "I heard the story." I thought of the new ferry office at the end of Lake Street, just before the wide dirt road ran out at the water's edge. The new Wood building was made of stone, and had a firm fieldstone foundation below its two stories. It was the only two-story place, not counting the house at the western end of town. That house was, as my father called it, a house of ill repute. I'd been around the docks in Green Bay enough to know that this house in Woods Portage was a place to "service" the men who worked the railroad to the west or the lumbercamps to the east and north, to say nothing of those who were probably some of the more upstanding citizens of Woods Portage, few as they might be.

Father did his best to protect me from the dark side of life, but I had ears and eyes. And our cook in Green Bay took it upon herself to teach me about all aspects of the world outside our doors. I knew a lot more than my father realized. I thought it best not to tell him everything.

But I was here now. In the middle of nowhere. I looked out the front window. At least our location on Main Street was well situated. The church was close, as were the taverns. Most of the other buildings and houses were strung along the true main street, the road coming up from the lake. Everyone else seemed to have battened down for the winter already. Our mercantile had a covered porch and a few chairs out front, but the weather was already autumn cool by the time we moved in, so we pulled the chairs in to our living quarters. Maybe in spring we'd be able to sit and socialize outside once in a while.

Father and I continued our practice of working together to do business. The store, while it needed work, could spare me a few minutes here and there in the mornings. As a result, I was able to commiserate a bit with the farmers' wives who came into town to supplement what they couldn't grow and barter off what they could. They were a hardy, pleasant bunch, rough around the edges, but glad enough to include me in their gossip, though they had little enough time for talk. I listened in on conversations with the trappers too, who came in from the north and west with pelts and furs to trade. They welcomed the chance to deal with Father, rather than having to go on to the river or, even farther, to Oshkosh, to sell their wares. With us as go-betweens, they could return to the woods and streams that much sooner. As for the loggers, they came mostly from the north, maneuvering small rafts of logs from the upper lake to the ford. Sometimes they unloaded a few logs at the ford, but more often they pushed on after a night in town, running their rafts down to the base of the lake, where an enterprising man had built a sawmill in the middle of nowhere. From there, it was easier to move the lumber than it was from Woods Portage. We didn't have enough room at the neck of the lake to accommodate such a large operation.

By the end of the first week, we'd unpacked the store supplies and arranged everything as best we could. Mr. Wood had a few supplies to sell and Father purchased most of his extra inventory. With our combined stuffs, our shelves looked fairly well-stocked. Customers appeared quickly, thanks to our daily forays into the community, such as it was. That, and my father's ability to make friends of anyone, assured we'd have plenty of business. I began to feel a bit better about our move. The weather remained cool but mild, the people I encountered were friendly, and the store was looking more like home. But Father was right about our customers not having a lot of time to chat. Most of the women I saw were farmers' wives, in town only for supplies. At this late date in the year, they were consumed with preparations for winter and didn't have much time for lengthy conversations with a young newcomer. Maybe in the spring. I'd have to bide my time.

Chapter 10
Lou

Lou slowed the car and pointed. "My great-great-grandfather's mercantile there? Stayed in the family forever."

Kapi snorted. "Clearly not forever, since you don't own it now."

Lou didn't really resent the implication. As she closed in on retirement age, she no longer had the drive to drag the business uphill. She sold the whole kit and kaboodle to a family determined to bring it back, who bought the lot next door and turned the empty lot into parking for their new-fangled grocery store, complete with gee-gaws for the tourists, and bait and lures for fishing. And wine, of course.

Lou ignored Kapi's sarcasm, and even softened a bit. "I didn't have the gumption to get the thing up to date and running like it should. I sold it and retired. The new owners turned it into a going enterprise. So, the mercantile is a place where natives and visitors mix, just like in the old days."

Kapi slipped her headphones back on.

Lou drove along the park across the street from the mercantile. Postage stamp park, outsiders might call it.

Large enough to play frisbee with a dog, but small enough to hail across to a friend. The little white church, still in use from the 1800s, stood across a street at the northern end. After Sam died, Lou donated some of his life insurance money to the church so they could renovate. She attended only off and on, but she had a soft spot for it anyway.

"Look," Lou said, poking Kapi again. "Where your dad was baptized." She pointed at the church.

Kapi released one ear from the headphones. "We didn't go to church much."

"Maybe we should start," Lou said, wondering how long they could sustain this conversation, one of the longest so far. "It's where I was baptized too."

"People here go back to the Pleistocene. Nobody moves." Kapi shifted in her seat to look at the church as they went by.

Lou had a snappy—and sarcastic—remark ready, but bit it back before it flourished. She remembered Kapi's raids on Lou's history books and historical novels. "Woods Portage might be a little corner of Paradise for most," she finally said.

"Or h— Dante's Inferno," Kapi said.

Lou couldn't help herself. She laughed. "Which circle?"

"I don't know the circles. We only talked about it being his idea of...you know."

"It's a literary reference. You can say hell like that." Lou risked a quick glance at Kapi. Her headphones lay against her neck, silent.

They cleared the last of the village shops and houses and the road swung toward the lake, visible now and then to their right. Cottages showed a bit through the trees too, but most were painted to blend into the landscape or were log homes, looking as if built for another era. Soon, even those petered out.

"How come there's no houses up here?" Kapi asked, gaze fixed out the window. "They just...stopped."

"This up here was Indian land. A bunch of ramshackle houses," Lou answered. "Now it belongs to the village. Nobody can do anything with it. It's too narrow, since they turned the old trail into a full-fledged road years and years ago. The Indians had a...I don't know what you'd call it. Extended families? Everybody crammed into one shack. Old cars and junk in the yards. From what I know, wasn't even big enough to be a town or a village on its own. Just a group of relatives living together. You can still find parts of some of the dwellings, they say, or the crap from the Indians. I've never looked for them myself." She took a quick look at Kapi and was surprised to see an angry face.

Kapi swiveled away from her to peer into the woods as they passed. "Native American."

"What?" Lou said.

"You're supposed to call them Native American, not Indian."

Lou knew that. But her era said Indian, and she didn't take the trouble to shake off the embedded term. Indian meant more to her than Native American. Native American was too...clean.

The road shouldered over closer to the lake, a lover headed for a tryst.

"This road used to be an old Indian and trapper trail, they say," Lou offered. Kapi frowned in her direction, but Lou ignored her and went on. "I'm still looking for maps. Maybe once we get the old ferry office building all cleared out, some of that stuff will turn up." The owner of the ferry office abandoned the building to the village—or to the bank, to be more precise—and it sat empty for many years.

Most people in town, other than a smattering of others, weren't really interested in retrieving the past. Was Kapi? She seemed to be, what with reading all those history books and such. Time would tell. If she—if they both—lasted long enough. At least Kapi wasn't harping on the Indian/Native American thing.

A project for another day. For now, she wanted nothing better than to concentrate on her—their—Meander.

Chapter 11
Lou

The first couple of days delivered on the weather predictions: sunny and warm. No storms on the horizon. Lou didn't discern many clouds in Kapi either. That could presage a decent trip and Lou could relax. Or it could mean crap was just over the horizon, waiting to barrel on in like the inevitable summer tornado. Just to be safe, Lou waited and watched.

The road was flat and the fields not much different. But soldier rows of pine trees alternated with soldier rows of early corn stalks. Knee high by the Fourth of July, Lou thought, though it wasn't quite close enough yet. Lou couldn't distinguish one grain field from another, though she knew wheat, oats, timothy were out there somewhere. Soy fields gave way to potato fields, acres and acres stretching away. She loved to watch the wind play tag with the fields as the summer wore on.

Lou sometimes wrote in a travel journal, just for fun. Gotta remember to write down "soldier rows" and "wind plays tag." She rehearsed the words over and over in her head. But by the time they stopped, her memory might fail. If she were alone... But she wasn't. But if she were, she would pull over and write it all down. The hell with it anyway. She slowed to pull onto the shoulder.

"Wait. Why are we stopping?" Kapi sat up.

"Give me a minute. Don't talk or I'll forget." Lou pulled out her notebook and scribbled down a few phrases. "Okay. Let's go." She stowed the notebook.

Kapi crinkled her forehead. "O—kay." She slid back into her music.

A moment later, they were back on the road.

"How come we have to take all these crummy roads through all these crummy little towns?" Kapi slouched down as far as her seatbelt would allow.

Sure enough. Here it comes. Lou tried not to succumb to pessimism. "All these crummy roads are scenic. Freeways get you from one place to another fast enough, sure. But these crummy little roads, as you call them, get you from one *person* to another. Big difference." Lou kept her eyes on the road. She could imagine the sour look on Kapi's face. She didn't need to see it.

"Yeah, sure." Kapi cracked her knuckles.

"You'll get arthritis from that."

"That's a bunch of bull— ... crap. I read that ... somewhere."

"Just don't do it around me," Lou said. "I've got enough arthritis as it is." She wasn't about to admit the pop-pop-pop drove her crazy.

"Fine." Kapi turned to stare out the window. "When are we gonna stop?"

To be fair, Lou knew they'd stopped for the day right after lunch before. But they hadn't even eaten lunch yet today. "What, you getting saddle sores?"

Kapi swung on Lou. "No, stu—. No. I just want to get out and walk around. Isn't there a waterfall or something around here? Something to look at?"

"You telling me that talking to the woman at the cheese factory yesterday wasn't enough? She pointed us to that great little nature preserve. Decent hiking along the ponds there."

There, the way the wind played with the reeds and the grasses could fill a whole page of notes in Lou's notebook. Some more on the different angles of light and shadow. And the birds! Rough sketches of shapes, wingspans, notations on colors, webbed feet, birdcalls. Anything and everything that struck her fancy. Kapi disappeared from her thoughts for a while.

Disappeared from her sight too. Lou found her crouched down in high grass, arms wrapped around her knees, watching a pair of mallards paddle along, followed by a slew of swimming fluff with orange beaks. Lou backed off without a sound. When she approached again, she shuffled her feet to announce her coming.

Now, Lou spotted a dense pattern of long rectangular fields separated by low dikes. "We'll stop here."

Kapi sat up and pulled off her sunglasses. "Here? There's nothing here."

"As good a place to stop as any. I'm sure there's a motel around here somewhere. Places like these aren't totally out in the middle of nowhere."

"This *is* the middle of nowhere," Kapi snapped.

"You don't know what that is?" Lou swept out her arm to encompass the fields. "Look carefully. You drink this stuff almost every morning."

Kapi sent her a look designed to wither, but Lou didn't even blink. "This is definitely *not* an orange grove."

"You don't drink orange juice." Lou refrained from adding, *stupid.* "And don't even think about mouthing off about tomato juice either."

Kapi clamped her mouth shut. "So, it's supposed to be cranberries. Right. Where are the trees?"

Lou couldn't believe it. How could anyone live in Wisconsin and not know that cranberries grew on vines in bogs? She bit her tongue and held her peace for a moment before setting Kapi straight.

"Vines? Then how come those dirt walls around them?"

At last, rational communication. "Those are dikes. The bushes are kept enclosed so the fields can be flooded."

By the look on Kapi's face, she was not about to reveal any more of her ignorance if she could help it. The look also said she wanted to know more. But wasn't about to lower herself to ask.

All right, smarty. Maybe I actually do know more than you do. "They flood the fields if the temperatures drop so the berries won't freeze." She'd better connect the dots. "If the berries are totally underwater, they won't freeze. They flood again to harvest. Cranberries float, so they can be gathered pretty easily."

"Who's going to swim out there, just to grab some crappy berries?"

Crappy berries. Cranberries. If it had been Mac, Lou would've pointed out the words and they both would've laughed. *No, Mac would've come up with the joke on his own. They still would've laughed together.* Lou snapped back to the present. Kapi wouldn't laugh. "Harvesting's done by machine. Used to be by hand, but not anymore." Lou parked the car and turned off the engine. She nodded at a figure walking along a nearby dike. "Looks like someone who knows all about this stuff. Are you coming?" She didn't wait for Kapi's answer, but stepped out of the car and closed the door. Lou waved at the worker and called out, "Bog looks great! Got a minute?"

She heard the car door open and, a moment later, clunk shut. She didn't turn around or even acknowledge she'd heard.

***

They dithered away a couple of hours at the marsh, picked the owner's brain about cranberries and then hiked the dikes. Lou did get some time by herself when Kapi, sighing and complaining, headed back to the car.

Lou was in no hurry to join her.

When they took to the road again, they didn't have to drive far to find a small motel perched on the edge of an even smaller town. What good luck that the town had a tavern that served superb hamburgers. That's about all it had, other than an attached gas station and a few scattered houses. But it had a lovely little lake that must have plenty of fish, considering the number of boats on it when they pulled up.

Lou unlocked the motel door and walked in. The room looked comfortable enough, with twin beds, and curtains with huge purple and blue flowers that matched the fluffy quilts. The one window looked out on a pine forest, but it was dark already.

Kapi disappeared into the bathroom with her bag. Dropping her own bag on the floor, Lou went to test the bed. She fished her grandmother's silver earrings out of her shirt pocket and set them on the nightstand between the two beds, then changed into her pajamas. She dug into her bag for her notebook, hunkered down in bed, propped up with pillows, and began to jot down more notes about the day.

Kapi emerged from the bathroom and plopped down on the bed. Kapi's long pink t-shirt was frayed at the neck and faded, but she wouldn't give it up. Considering she almost always wore black, it seemed an aberration. Back home, when Lou asked about it, Kapi growled, "Gift from my mom's friend." But Lou was the "friend" who sent it for a birthday. Apparently, Becca never told Kapi who it really came from. Lou wondered what else might surface. She went back to her notes.

"What're these?" Kapi said. She sat up and reached over to the nightstand to pick up an earring.

Lou almost missed it, so immersed was she in recording impressions of the day. She forced herself to put aside her notebook and focus.

Kapi held up the earring, the silver strands and disks glinting. "What're these?" she asked again.

"Don't—" Lou forced herself to a full stop. She took a deep breath. "Those are my grandmother's earrings."

Kapi jiggled the earring, making it chime. "Pretty."

Lou reminded herself to listen. This was an opening, of sorts. "My grandmother gave 'em to me. Told me to hang onto them 'cause they are family heirlooms."

"So, where did they come from then, if they were family heirlooms?"

"She said," Lou said, choosing words carefully, "they were her mother's. I think. Don't rightly remember."

"How could you forget something like that?" Kapi's tone made Lou's hackles rise.

"Easy," she said. "I'm old, remember?" She shrugged. "At any rate, she didn't know much herself." *There. That's enough to satisfy her.*

Kapi held the earring up to her ear. "How come you don't wear them?"

Lou sat up and swung her legs over the side of the bed. "Give it here." She put out her hand.

Kapi plunked the earring down on the nightstand, and sprang up from the bed.

"Where you going?" Lou's irritation showed.

"Duh...to brush my teeth?" The bathroom door clicked shut behind her.

Lou swore she heard a muffled "What's it to ya?" as Kapi slipped away. *Well, that was productive.* She picked up her notebook again, but everything disappeared at the shutting of the bathroom door. She slammed the notebook down on the bed. *Damn! I'm a hypocrite,* she thought. *To hell with fancy language.* This was so much easier when she got away by herself. Just too much distraction. Too much tension. Too much too much. *What right did that little...* She shook her head to clear it, and put her thoughts away.

Lou got up and slid open the window. A breath of a breeze cleaned the room before retreating into the night again. All seemed quiet on the western front. Or whatever direction she was facing. She was too weary to think about it. But not too weary to squint and check that the car was locked.

She closed the curtains and switched off the lamp on her bedside table. Her knees creaked as she maneuvered herself into bed. She tugged her old pajama top into submission. Her mouth curled into a crooked smile at the thought of her faded men's pajamas aligning themselves with Kapi's frayed t shirt. Funny how she herself avoided appearing in front of Kapi in her own house wearing her old pjs, yet here they were, sharing a room in old and tattered pajamas, both of them.

She sighed and pulled the blanket up around her shoulders. Taking inventory of any residual aches, she concluded that, all in all, she was holding up pretty well. In spite of—she really should stop calling Kapi The Terror, even if it was only to herself. She might very well slip, and out it would come. Not that Lou cared a fig for what Kapi thought about it. But she was Mac's daughter, after all. That should count for something. Her mind began the slow drift away.

Kapi emerged from the bathroom and crawled into bed. Lou almost missed the whispered "G'night" as Kapi turned off her light. Lou was too far into sleep to summon up an answer.

Chapter 12
Lou

The view from Pikes Peak State Park was just as stunning as Lou remembered. More, even. Maple trees, oak trees, even a hickory or two formed a rustling green canopy over a pair of rustic picnic tables. The fragrance was deep and musty from matted and decaying leaves, sharp too, from freshly cut grasses and clover. But it was a sweet harmony to Lou. Clouds heaved across the skies like galleons headed for battle. The sun danced in and out between them. The day was cool. Lou traded out her baggy green pants in favor of jeans. She was tired of her own silent defiance of Kapi's clothing biases. Besides the day being cool, the pants were starting to stink.

Lou stepped close to the edge of the cliff. The bluff dropped off so steeply that she felt like she could lean out and fly. It was impossible to see the bottom.

What she could see was the Mississippi River churning below, roiling, then calming, sweeping debris and boats along indiscriminately. The channels and fingers of the Wisconsin River, coming from the east, drifted into the Mississippi a shade bluer before Old Man River devoured her. Years ago someone told her about this park in Iowa, just across the Mississippi River. She took Mac and they stood stunned at the beauty of the place.

"Impressive, isn't it?" Lou noticed Kapi left her music in the car. That in itself was impressive.

Kapi nodded. Her braid came loose and she tucked stray strands behind her ears.

"Imagine Joliet and Marquette coming out into that big ol' river. They must've known they'd stumbled on something really stupendous," Lou said.

Kapi shaded her eyes to peer across the river. "1670-something. I think that's when they were here. How could they figure out where to go? They weren't standing up here where they could see everything." She drew figure eights in the air, trying to follow the multiple channels of water.

Lou stared at Kapi. *I didn't remember what year. Not even close.* She sniffed. The wind brought out a blush on Kapi's cheeks, but she seemed unaware. Lou took advantage of the moment. "I can't imagine setting off into such wildness with only faith in God and a canoe full of supplies."

Kapi shook her head, releasing more brunette strands. "Me either." She added, "Their canoes were twenty feet long or something. They could probably cram a lot of stuff in there."

A conversation, a real conversation. She remembered Kapi was interested in history. It was one of the most surprising things about the girl. Lou sank into nostalgia. "I brought Mac up here one summer. He loved it."

That broke the spell.

"Don't talk about my dad." Kapi didn't turn from the rivers, but her back and her voice hardened.

"He wasn't your dad. He was my son," Lou bristled. "No reason not to talk about him. I loved him." It was a low blow, but Lou couldn't stop herself. As soon as she said it, she twitched.

Kapi swung around, her eyes snapping. "You loved him? You *loved* him? *I* loved him. I don't remember much, but I remember how he hugged me. He was the only dad I ever knew." She wilted a bit before she stiffened up again. "If you loved him, why weren't you around when he needed you?"

"What are you talking about?"

"He was *sick* and you couldn't even spare an hour to come and sit with him."

Lou stumbled back against the nearest tree. "I couldn't?—What do you mean? I didn't even know he was sick until it was almost too late." She cut herself off. "You were what? Five? How the hell do you know what was going on?" Who cared about cuss words at this point?

"I knew. My mom told me. You wouldn't even drive down to see Dad. How could you do that to your own son? Your *only* son!" The words all came out in a rush.

"Your mom? Your mom wouldn't take my calls. Ever. Don't you think I would've driven to hell and back if it would've helped? I didn't give him that fucking cancer!"

They both froze.

Kapi's face crumpled. "Language," she whispered.

Lou spun away as fast as her arthritic knees would allow. When she got to the car, she dropped herself in and slammed the door. Between fumbling with the seatbelt and the ignition, she heard Kapi dive into the backseat. The rear door swung shut with a clunk as Lou spun out of the parking lot.

Not until she was at the bottom of the bluff did she slow and check the rearview mirror. She couldn't see anything of Kapi. But she could hear sobs. As for herself, she could barely see the road, her eyes were so wet.

We were doing so well. What a disaster. "Sit up and put your seatbelt on," she barked. She slid her hand under her nose and wiped it on her shirt. Who cares? We've really fucked up everything now, haven't we? She amended it. I. Haven't I.

But no. Kapi brought up Mac. Lou shook her head. Not true. I told her I took Mac up here. It set her off.

"We're going home. Right now." She saw Kapi sit up and squeeze herself against the door. She heard the seatbelt pulled out and clicked into place. But she couldn't see Kapi's face. Better that way. I don't know if I could keep my temper...at everything. We've both been duped. Lou couldn't wrap her mind around so many things roiling around in her head. Mac. Becca, the bitch. Kapi, caught. *Me*... I just can't deal with this right now. Later, when we get home.

Chapter 13
Louise Wright

Father stopped stock still when I came out of our living quarters into the store. "Louise Wright, you're not wearing that, are you?"

I couldn't help but laugh. "Yes, Father, trousers. I'm wearing trousers. You didn't stop me when we were coming out here from Green Bay."

"Well, yes, but..." He sounded flustered. "We're going out to deliver the goods ordered. I'd like to see you present yourself..."

I laughed again. "We're going out to the Burghardt farm. And you said yourself, the weather looks threatening, dress accordingly. So—" I spread my arms to display my weather-proof choices—heavy trousers, thick flannel shirt, wool socks and boots, for a start. "It's not practical to wear a skirt and petticoats. I guess you'll have to take me as I am." I went to him and kissed his cheek. "I don't want to get caught unprepared. I see you don't either."

His coat was long and heavy, collar turned up under a fur hat pulled low. We both looked like second cousins to bears. "You're right, Louise. We do need to be prepared. I've added blankets under the seat, along with a couple of bricks to heat, if Lorraine and Otto will take care of that before we head home again. The weather is sure turning bitter awfully early."

Weather was a whole different animal out here. Green Bay was on the water, which governed temperature, wind, humidity, all sorts of things. Here, in Woods Portage, we had a lake, to be sure, but it offered water challenges far more than weather challenges. The narrow neck of the hourglass lake might freeze in the winter. That shape, locals told us, made spring thaw an especially dangerous time, as ice breaking up and rains could cause a rush of fast water through the narrow channel. The town buildings were far enough back, and somewhat higher, so flooding didn't reach them. Any fool who built close to the neck of the lake would deserve anything they got in the spring.

"We'd better get going," Father said, "before anything hits. The sky doesn't look very cooperative, but we've got to get these supplies out to them before deep winter sets in."

"I'm just going to take a bolt of calico along, and a few other things, just in case Mrs. Burghardt could use them. We can always bring back what they don't want to buy."

"Always the business woman, Louise." He swept me into a hug. "All right, then. But hurry." He clumped out of the store, and went to the horses to check the harnesses once more, before we left.

I donned my heaviest coat and jammed my fur hat on my head. Before I added my mittens, I went to the shelf and pulled out a bolt of a calico I thought Mrs. Burghardt might like. I stuffed a packet of pins and a roll of ribbon in my deep coat pockets and joined my father outside.

He was already up on the seat, gathering reins in hand. I slid the fabric under the tarp covering everything in the back, checking that I didn't loosen any ropes that snugged everything down. I swung myself up to the bench next to Father and sidled under the blanket he spread over his legs. He clucked to the horses, and we were off.

I thought we had cold weather earlier, but once we broke free of the trees on the western edge of town, just past the big house, the winds took my breath away. The land rolled and bucked a bit, but it was mostly farmland, wide open to the elements. The weather all came from that direction, and it could be wicked. In the short time we were in town, we experienced a colder than average October. And now, we were deep into November. Even in Green Bay, there was no guarantee the weather would hold.

I examined the sky, looking for a slice of hope. The clouds over our village were heavy, but still rather high. However, out over the fields and lands to the west, the clouds were piling up and roiling, threatening. I couldn't judge how fast they were moving, nor whether they would deliver rain, hail, or snow. Based on the temperatures here on the ground, snow seemed likely. It made me shiver. Father shifted the reins to one hand and reached out with the other to pull me closer.

Before long, air began to sting, as a mist was driven into our faces. Even the horses lowered their heads. The clouds drew lower, thicker, menacing. It began to snow.

Between the wind and the snow—which grew heavier and thicker as we went on—I was afraid the landmarks, and perhaps even the road, would succumb to the snow. The horses plodded on. I hoped they could sense the roadway. This was not the time to be tipped into the verge. But we went on and on at a steady pace.

I leaned into my father, hoping he would hear me. "Maybe we should turn around." The wind made it impossible to say more.

He shook his head. "See that lightning-split tree just up ahead? That's getting close to the farm. We're better off pushing ahead. It won't be long now."

At that point, the horses slowed of their own volition, and it didn't make sense to urge them faster. They would know the safest speed better than we would. If only they didn't decide that the safest speed was full stop.

But they didn't stop, just kept pulling in tandem. The rhythm was rough, though we kept moving. By this time, the snow obliterated the road. If we didn't have fenceposts to guide us, who knew where our poor horses would deposit us? The snow was deepening as well, the wind creating drifts and waves.

I was losing hope when I spotted a large shadow looming ahead. I leaned into my father's shoulder, too cold to say anything. Our blanket was coated with snow and not providing much protection for our legs. We both hunched up inside our coats, hats pulled low over our ears. My father's beard was coated with ice, and I could hardly see past my eyelashes, they were so coated with snow.

Father lifted one arm free of the blanket and pointed ahead. I nodded in reply. Imagining a fireplace, I felt my chest grow warmer, though I'm sure it was merely illusion. We pulled up in front of the house across from the barn. The barn was our first glimpse through that maelstrom of snow. I could see a small square of pale yellow glowing, a window in the house.

A splotch appeared in the window, blocking out the light. A moment later, the door opened a bit, spilling a welcoming mat of light out onto a porch. Father got down from the wagon and pushed his way up onto the porch. He returned to the wagon, mounted, and turned the horses toward the barn. By the time he reached it, Mr. Burghardt,

I presumed, was sliding open the massive door and gesturing us in.

We drove in and the door closed behind us. I felt as if I'd gone from the middle of a howling hurricane into a muted gale. I unwrapped the scarf from around my head and face and took a deep breath of barn scent. Nothing smelled as sweet!

Mr. Burghardt strode to my father as I dismounted, wrung his hand and said, "We were sure you wouldn't be coming today, what with this weather."

"It wasn't snowing when we left Woods Portage," my father said. "But it's sure wicked out there now."

Mr. Burghardt chuckled. "We still gotta get back to the house. Let's get these horses taken care of. They've had a tough go of it. We can just leave the goods in the wagon. We'll get it all tomorrow, because you're sure not going anywhere tonight."

I felt nothing but relief. Other than getting to the porch, to venture out again in that storm, which raged and hollered beyond the barn door, was simply beyond my reckoning.

While the men unharnessed the horses, rubbed them down and fed them, I double-checked our load to make sure we hadn't lost anything, or things weren't shifted too badly. By the time we brushed off ourselves and the horses of the layers of snow, we were ready to brave the trek to the house. I turned up my coat collar and rewrapped my scarf.

"Whess go." I maneuvered wet wool threads out of my mouth. Pulling my scarf down enough to be understood, I said, "I'm ready. Let's go."

Mr. Burghardt opened the small door next to the large barn door. Snow swirled in before it was even fully open. He forced it shut again and turned to us. "There's a rope attached to the barn just outside this door. Before you step out, reach around and grab ahold. It'll get you back to the house. Whatever you do, don't let go. Old Man Wainwright froze to death a few winters ago when he lost the rope in a blizzard and got lost between the barn and the house." He shook his head. "Real tragedy, that was." He jammed on his mittens and pointed at Father. "You go first." He reached around and gestured to me. "You're next, Louise. Remember, don't let go. I'll bring up the rear, make sure everybody makes it." He opened the door again. "Go, Stephen! Go!"

My father was almost out of sight the minute he stepped out. I groped for the rope and thought for a moment it must have pulled loose. But then it slammed into my hand, pushed by the wind. My fist closed around it as if its life depended on it. Which it did, it dawned on me. I pivoted outside and fumbled for a grip with my other hand. When the wind whistled and gusted, I had no extra hand to secure my scarf once the end broke loose, determined to escape. I dug my chin into my coat and began the longest walk of my life.

The snow was up over my knees. Luckily, it wasn't a wet, soggy snow anymore, but the fact that it was powdery and light made for whiteout conditions. I could barely see the bulk of my father ahead of me. Couldn't see the house beyond. Couldn't see the barn behind, I was sure, though I didn't dare turn to check. It took all my strength to pull myself along that rope. It whipped around, up and down, full of snow and ice from the earlier, heavier snowfall. Several times, one hand or the other slid off the line, and I stumbled, convinced it would be my last step. I knew Mr. Burghardt was behind me, but I had no idea how far. Or even if he himself hadn't succumbed to the conditions.

Would I reach the porch, only to have to tell his wife that we lost him in the storm?

I slogged on, unable to hear anything but the wind screaming for a human sacrifice. I could hardly feel my feet anymore, and my hands were permanently formed into claws. I could no longer see from the snow stuck to my hair, my face, my eyelashes, my scarf. If I didn't freeze, I knew I'd die of suffocation.

My foot slid into something solid, and I lifted my chin enough to make out the form of the farmhouse porch in front of me. I had bumped into the bottom step. Thank God Almighty! I thought. I could no more have said it aloud than hopped in the air. My lips seemed frozen in place, puffing out great clouds of breath, worthy of St. George's dragon. I knew for certain my nostrils were stuck together.

I stumbled up the steps, with the help of someone's hand dragging me upward. I assumed my father's. But when I looked up, all I saw through the snow was a bear. I was too cold to care. I could imagine the obituary. Louise Wright, beloved daughter, eaten by a bear on the porch of a local farm.

The bear threw his paws around me and dragged me onto the porch. That's when I realized it wasn't a bear at all. I was crushed against the chest of a man wrapped in a bearskin with a deep fur hat on his head, and fur mitts on his paws—hands. I felt myself begin to fall, but his grip was so firm that I only dipped a little.

Mr. Burghardt pulled up on the porch at that moment, and from within the bear hug, I saw my father against the house door. Though I knew he was banging on the door, I heard nothing but the wind. We all stumbled closer, sheltering a bit next to the wood stacked on the porch. I could hardly breathe, but I had enough air to say, "Loose! Please, loose!" The man must have heard me, because the pressure against his chest lessened enough for me to steady myself.

At that moment, the house door swung halfway open, and Mrs. Burghardt reached out to pull my father inside. The "bear" pushed me ahead of him into the house, then stepped back to allow Mr. Burghardt to get in. Mrs. Burghardt was about to close the door, when she spotted the figure still on the porch. She grabbed a handful of fur blanket and pulled—him?—into the house too. She fought the wind, but the wind lost and the door thumped shut.

The sudden silence—or silence compared to what raged outside—disoriented me. I knew I was not outside for long, the distance from barn to house was not great, but I felt like I walked to the North Pole and back in that short span.

It took a fair amount of time to shed our winter outerwear, but the warmth of the fireplace encouraged me to hurry out of my greatcoat. It dropped a small blizzard of snow of its own on the floor before weakening enough in the warmth to allow itself to be hung on a peg. It took more than that to find the ends of my scarf and unwind everything, to say nothing of prying my hat off my head. It slid down so far, it felt glued to my eyebrows. By the time I sat on the floor to pull off my boots, the men shed their coats and all, and clumped to the fire to warm themselves.

Mrs. Burghardt bent to help me pull off my boots, and we got laughing so hard that I tipped right over. That's when she and I both realized the man wrapped in fur was still standing just inside the door, motionless. The men didn't even turn to see him.

"My soul!" Mrs. Burghardt's hand flew to her chest. "I didn't see you there! For heaven's sake, man, take off those wet clothes and come by the fire."

He reached up and pulled down the scarf muffling his face.

Mr. Burghardt jumped up so fast, he overturned the chair he'd settled in by the fire. "Indian."

My father rose and moved closer.

Mrs. Burghardt sent a glance of what looked like warning to her husband, then turned back to the man.

I could see then that, yes, he was an Indian. He had been coated with even more snow than we were, but much was melting away in the warmth of the room. Nothing showed but the top half of his face, blunt and square, with bright dark eyes.

He inclined his head. "Looking for shelter tonight," came through a bit garbled because of the scarf. But it was clear enough he needed a place to stay.

Mrs. Burghardt turned to her husband. "Can he stay in the barn? One night only." The last seemed a concession to Mr. Burghardt.

Mr. Burghardt jerked a single nod. "One night."

The Indian bowed a bit, quite hampered by his coat and fur blanket. "Many thanks." He turned to go.

"Follow the rope to the barn," Mrs. Burghardt said, "or you may not survive the night."

He nodded again and slipped out the door.

Father and Mr. Burghardt exchanged a glance full of meaning I didn't quite catch.

"Let's get those goods in the house," Mr. Burghardt said.

My father nodded acquiescence.

"Otto! You can't go back out there in this weather," Mrs. Burghardt protested. "Please. Just leave it until morning."

But by that time, the men were shaking out coats and sliding their feet back into their boots. "Get the boys, Lorraine. The two oldest can help from the porch." He reached for the door.

"I'm going too," I said. "I'm warmed up enough, and one more set of hands will make the work go more quickly." I pinched my lips together and silently dared my father to forbid me to come. He opened his mouth, then clamped it shut again. Though his face thundered disapproval, he didn't stop me.

***

As we began moving everything from the wagon to the house, the wind dropped, and the snow, though still falling, was diminishing. I could see the bulk of the barn, as well as the house. Strange how freakish blizzards could be, coming and going on a whim. But the cold was still brutal. Once again, I barely felt my fingers, though my feet seemed to acclimate, perhaps because I was walking back and forth. I met the oldest boy a short way from the porch and trekked things from there to the house, where the youngest handed off the load to his mother standing sentinel at the door.

The work took on a rhythm of its own, which was the only thing that kept me going. Take items from the older son transferring flour or grains or whatever to my arms, then inch my way to the porch. Luckily, the younger boy met me at the bottom of the steps. I didn't think I could make it up the steps, I was so weary.

When I felt I could not take one more step, my father appeared and turned me toward the house. I practically crawled up the steps and fell against the door. I lurched across the threshold into Mrs. Burghardt's arms. She helped me peel everything off once again, and led me to a chair near the fireplace. I was shivering so badly, I couldn't even thank her properly.

Once my body decided it was no longer so bitter cold and I retrieved my voice, I said, "Perhaps we should have left everything until morning."

The men looked at each other. "Lorraine, send the boys up to bed. I'll heat up some coffee." He winked at my father. "And get out the whiskey."

At their mother's direction, the boys scrambled up into the loft, and, after a bit of shuffling and prayers, silence descended.

In the meantime, Mrs. Burghardt motioned me over to the cook stove on the opposite wall and handed me a tin of coffee. I started to turn and go back to the fireplace, but she stopped me with a hand on my arm. She winked, a mirror of her husband, and tipped a drop or two of whiskey into my coffee, then did the same to hers. She whispered, "You've worked about as hard as they did, and are certainly just as cold. You deserve it." She touched her cup to mine and we each took a sip, hiding our smiles.

I couldn't help admiring her stove, crouched like a massive guardian dog. "Where on earth did you find such a beautiful stove?" I asked her. "Five cooking surfaces and two warming ovens? To say nothing of a main oven. It's amazing." I relished the coffee—and the whiskey.

She smiled. "I insisted we bring it from town when we moved out here. I hear that, when Mr. Lincoln was elected president, Mrs. Lincoln took her stove with her when she moved to the White House. I told Otto that if the First Lady could do it, so could I. He was so foolish in love with me that he barely blinked. He teases me about it endlessly, but he never complains about the meals I prepare on it." She cradled her coffee tin. "Let's rejoin the men."

Once we were resettled, Mr. Burghardt sighed. "If you are to live here, Louise and Stephen, you need to understand the Indian situation."

"Yes, please." My father turned to me. "Mr. Burghardt started to tell me about that."

I tilted my head, took another sip, and let my father lead the conversation.

Mr. Burghardt nodded as he packed his pipe. He picked a spill out of the kindling bucket and leaned over to light it at the fire. He drew on his pipe until it satisfied him, then tossed the spill into the fire. "They steal, pure and simple. Other than that, they're no trouble."

"They steal, pure and simple," Mrs. Burghardt echoed, but her tone was entirely different. She sighed, as if this were a conversation they had before. "They feel everyone should share."

"Yes," her husband said, "share as in 'What's ours is ours, and what's yours is ours.' They take your bread right off the porch railing when it's cooling, for heaven's sake."

"You know I always bake an extra loaf, because I understand what they want," she countered. "But, Louise, Otto's right, you do have to understand they're different than we are."

I knew that much from Green Bay. But maybe things were even more different out here. I'd just have to bide my time and keep my eyes open. I was pretty sure we would have Indians coming into the store eventually. I couldn't see turning them away, as long as they could pay. We needed everyone we could get on our side. I declined to join the conversation, but just nodded instead and sipped my coffee.

Mrs. Burghardt leaned over and patted my hand. "Well, Mr. Burghardt, we need to get these two to bed. They've had a very busy day."

"You two ladies take the bed. Stephen and I will bunk down out here and keep the home fires burning," Mr. Burghardt offered.

Mrs. Burghardt stood and pulled me up, for which I was very grateful. Exhaustion from the storm and the work set in quite suddenly. We linked arms and set off for bed. "Come on, Louise. I'll lend you a nightdress."

***

The next morning dawned sunny. Even though the wind abated some, it still flirted with any cracks it could find, and whistled me awake. Mrs. Burghardt was already gone, which was no surprise for a farm wife. When I rose and dressed, I could hear the rumble of conversation in the next room. I hurried out.

"Well, well, Louise," my father greeted me. "A very good morning. We thought you'd sleep the entire morning away."

"Considering my aches, I was hoping to," I teased. "I am sorry I wasn't up earlier to help with...whatever got the rest of you up."

Mrs. Burghardt handed me a cup of coffee and gestured to the table, where she deposited a bowl of hot oatmeal. "We sent the boys out to clear the porch and a path to the barn. We've just been enjoying breakfast and coffee while they do all the work."

The men laughed. "'Bout time. Gotta learn to pull their weight sometime. Might as well be now," Mr. Burghardt said. But I could tell he wasn't chiding his sons, just showing a bit of fatherly pride. My own father did much the same when I learned to drive properly.

I asked, "Is the Indian helping them?"

Mr. Burghardt shook his head. "They disappear pretty quick once they get what they want. Shelter the night, gone by the time we're out to milk." He shifted in his seat and reached to pour himself another cup of coffee.

"Sometimes they'll steal some milk before they leave. Never take it all though. Couldn't."

Father stood up and drained his coffee. "We should get going, Louise. We've taken a lot of their time already." He turned to Mr. Burghardt, as if he just remembered something. "What can we do to help before we leave? You've got plenty of chores, I'm sure. We should help."

"Naw," Mr. Burghardt said. "The boys and I can handle it."

We all turned as the door swept open. A blast of cold air shoved itself in before the boys could get the door shut again. "All set, Pa. No trouble to get to the barn now," the tallest one said.

"Did you get down the lane, like I asked? How's the road to town look?" Mr. Burghardt asked.

One boy dropped his coat on a low peg. "Our lane's pretty packed, but the wind's picked up a lot of the snow on the road, 'cause it's so open."

"Nothing a team of horses can't get through," the tall boy said.

"That's settled then," Mrs. Burghardt said. "It'll still take you longer to get back than usual. I've put up some coffee to take along. It should stay hot for a little while, anyway. And I'll get the bricks you brought in last night out of the stove. They'll keep your feet toasty warm for a bit."

Father was already putting his coat on, and I hurried over to retrieve all of my outer gear. My boots, left by the fireplace the night before, were dry and warm when I slipped them on. I stuck my hat on, wound my scarf around my neck and face, and maneuvered into my coat. Mrs. Burghardt came over and gave me a hug, as much as possible, being dressed as I was.

"You come back anytime," she said, and I know she meant it.

I sent her a smile before I realized she couldn't see it through my scarf. "Thank you for everything," I managed to get out.

Father and Mr. Burghardt were out the door and almost to the barn before I turned to go out the door.

"No, no," Mrs. Burghardt said, grasping my arm. "You just wait here until they get the horses harnessed and bring the wagon around. No need to get out in the cold before you have to."

I was relieved she held me back. I wasn't too enthusiastic to step into that cold again. The memory of the day before, and the struggle of it all sent a shiver up my spine.

At last, all was ready, and I swung up to sit next to my father. This day, I would be quite satisfied to let him drive.

The trip to town did, as predicted, take a lot longer than usual. At first, the snow was halfway up the horses' legs, though the roadway, once we were out of the farm lane, varied considerably in snow depth. For the most part, the wind had lifted a lot into drifts along the verge, or taken it completely over the fields. We stopped occasionally to get down and check the horses' hooves for ice balls.

Within a fairly short time, the weather warmed enough to clear all the snow off the trees, such trees as there were out here. Soon, the sun burned warm enough for me to unwind my scarf and stuff it under the seat. The snow too seemed to be melting down a bit. By the time we drove up to the stable in Woods Portage and unhitched the wagon, we could do it without mitts.

The stablehands settled the wagon in place, and even offered to rub down the horses. We set off on foot for the mercantile, and hoped the boy we hired kept the two woodstoves from going out.

I slipped my hand through my father's arm as the mercantile came into sight. "Look. There it is. Smoke coming from the chimneys too."

Father squeezed my hand against his side. "Home safe and sound."

Home. Yes, home. This is where we belong.

Chapter 14
Lou

Lou grabbed her tote bag and dragged herself out of the car. She plodded up to the front door, too tired to even put the car in the garage. With her luck, she'd bash in the frame, or even drive right through the back. When Heddy called out a "Hey! Thought you weren't coming home for another couple of days!" Lou flapped her hand and kept going. She'd know better than to bother Lou.

Kapi slid into the house behind her, backpack held like a breastplate, and headed upstairs without bothering to kick off her shoes. A moment later, Kapi's bedroom door slammed shut.

"Take..." The rest of it died before it was born. Lou turned to retrieve things from the car, but took one look outside, pushed the sight of the car away and closed the front door. *It's gotta be better in the morning. If Kapi wants something to eat, she's gonna have to get it herself. I'm going to bed.*

The sun would have to take care of setting all by itself too. No wine on the porch tonight. No rehashing the last few days with Heddy. No conversation—of any kind apparently—with Kapi.

Lou kicked off her shoes and shuffled off to the kitchen to get a drink of water. Her throat was raw from holding back tears and anger both. She set the empty glass on the counter. Lou started up the stairs in her stocking feet. Halfway up, Kapi was curled into the fireplace nook, her face hidden in arms clutched around her knees. Lou didn't even hear her come out of her room. She was tempted to stop, but she saw the girl tighten, and thought better of it. She stifled a sigh.

As she passed the bathroom, it called out to her. Lou backtracked a bit and went in. A hot bath would feel so good right now. A hot bath, then a good book and that glass of wine. Perfect. Except she wasn't in the habit of keeping wine in her bedroom. She sure wasn't about to go back downstairs to retrieve any.

She closed the tub drain and turned the spigot to as hot as it would go. She closed the bathroom door on the way out to send a clear message it was occupied. By the time she got back with a clean set of frayed and faded old pajamas, the bathroom was steamed up and the tub was issuing a clear invitation. She turned off the water and pulled off her clothes. Jeans, denim shirt, gray socks, purple bra and granny panties, all just dropped in a heap. Maybe she should just leave them piled on the floor, like Kapi used to.

Used to. That brought Lou up short. Kapi didn't leave junk dropped all over the house anymore. Lou had been too rattled with having her around to notice the change. She shrugged. Besides, she left plenty of her own stuff laying around. Standing naked in the bathroom, Lou tried to get her head around Kapi. But she was too tired to gather any loose ends together.

She avoided looking in the mirror as she lit the lavender candle on the counter and poured a blob of oil into the bath. Two of the few New Wave things she'd taken to. She took a deep breath and stepped in the tub. Enough water to sink down up to her chin, submerge herself even. And she did.

***

By the time she plumped up against a second pillow and pulled the blanket up around her shoulders—which were always cold, her mother's inheritance—she wondered if she'd have enough energy left to open the book, much less read anything.

Even though the sun edged toward the horizon, brightness still infused her bedroom, shafts coming through any gap in the curtains. It didn't make a stitch of difference. She was out like a light in less than two sentences.

At least until 2 a.m., when she snapped awake, convinced she was still somewhere along the Mississippi River. She lay in bed with her eyes closed, picking out familiar sounds outside her open window. Whispering maple leaves, the soft meow of a cat, then silence. She let her brain find its way home. Once re-occupying her body, she couldn't go back to sleep.

She sat up and swung her legs over the side of the bed. Don't just jump out of bed, her doc warned her. It's a great way to collapse when your knees haven't been informed they're expected to support you. Just sit and count to ten. Then get up.

Lou adhered to the routine, having learned the hard way that the doc was right. Only luck saved her from a broken something. The bruise on her hip disappeared before her next appointment, luckily.

She got up, pulled her twisted pajama bottoms back into place and padded out to the hall. Silence indoors too. She frowned and made her way past Kapi's door. Shut, which was a good sign. At least she hadn't sneaked out and run off somewhere. Lou checked the fireplace nook, but it was empty. Lou retraced her steps and stopped with her hand on Kapi's doorknob. Should she or shouldn't she?

Oh, hell. Stop second guessing yourself. She opened the door a crack, so it wouldn't squeak. The lump on the bed looked real enough, but it wasn't until Lou saw Kapi's foot, complete with black nail polish, sticking out from under that she knew Kapi was safely asleep.

"Afraid I'd run away?"

Lou drew in a breath so sharp, she was afraid she'd crack. She held it in her cheeks while her heart slowed, then eased it out through her nose. "Maybe."

Kapi pulled her foot under the covers. "Can't get rid of me that easy." She shuffled around, making the blankets ripple for a moment as she settled.

"Don't want to get rid of you," Lou whispered, surprising even herself. She pulled the door shut before either one of them could react, and trudged back to her room.

Her bed was cold, but Lou didn't care. She slid back in. As the sheets warmed, she tried to sort out what she said in the dark. Was that really true? She really didn't want Kapi gone? If that was so, then what the hell *did* she want? She fell asleep with a frown on her face.

***

At the light poking its nose through the striped curtains, Lou awoke with a start. She checked the clock. 7:30. Later than normal. At least this time she remembered she was home and not out on the road somewhere. Then she was slammed with the encounter—if you could even call it that—with Kapi in the middle of the night. She groaned.

Where do we go from here? Did she even hear me last night? Did I even hear what I said? Maybe it was all a bad dream. Although how really bad could it be to tell someone you could tolerate them? Or even wanted them around?

Maybe it was the lack of clothes drop-kicked into the bathroom corner. Maybe it was that outburst at Pikes Peak State Park. What did she say again? Kapi went on and on about the explorers and the history of the place. Like she really was interested.

But then the cloud descended. Mac. Lou sat up in bed to escape, but it didn't work.

If you'd really loved him... What did that little twirp know about love, especially family love? Kapi's mother poisoned her against her own grandmother. Becca gave Kapi the nightshirt Lou had sent for her birthday and told her it was from a "friend."

Wait. She called herself Kapi's *grandmother.* Was she? Well, wasn't she?

She shifted gears before she was overwhelmed. She backed herself up to Mac. When it came to Mac, Becca didn't want Lou driving to Milwaukee to see him. Lou squeezed her eyes shut. *To see my dying son. Hell, I was lucky he defied Becca and made the hospital call me.*

She barely made it. Mac hardly made a mound under the sheet, he was so wasted. Not that the vet hospital mistreated him. No, they did all they could. But by the time Lou got there—two weeks after he was admitted— nothing they could do would make it better. Pain medications made him recede from her, from all of them.

They took away almost everything else. But at least he wasn't hurting.

When Becca, with Kapi in tow, saw Lou sitting in the hospital, holding her son's hand, she was furious. She dragged Kapi back into the hall and turned back to snarl at Lou, "You have no business here, even if you are his mother. He's my husband." Her promise to have Lou removed trailed behind as she left the room and headed for the nurses' station.

Lou was flabbergasted. *She's caught Mac between us, the bitch. And Kapi's caught too, the way it looks.* She shook her head to clear the storm. Becca was not getting the satisfaction of seeing her thrown out. She stood up, leaned over to kiss Mac on the forehead and whisper, "I'll be back. I'll always be back, my beamish boy. Hang in there." She stopped at the door to look back at his emaciated body. She threw him another kiss, and left.

But by the next day, it was too late.

The marriage was a mistake in Lou's mind. She figured Becca was in it for Mac's money. Lou was never welcome. Visits trickled away to one day at Christmas, and then only in Woods Portage. And only Mac. Becca nixed taking a young girl on a road trip. It disturbed her routine.

Not that Lou hadn't tried. She'd call and say she was driving over. If Mac wasn't home, the phone just rang and rang. Sometimes, at first, she'd pack up and drive over anyway. She gave up after no one appeared to be home, even though a curtain would move, or a radio could be heard. On the rare occasion Becca was home, especially if Mac wasn't, the acid in the air on the front porch was simply too much to take.

Lou resorted to sending gifts on the appropriate occasions.

The marriage was a mistake, but was Kapi? Lou didn't know. She suspected Kapi was a surprise from Becca's youth. She didn't recall ever hearing about an earlier marriage. But Mac embraced both of them without a thought.

With such a mother, was it any surprise Kapi turned out to be such a...such a...

No, I'm not going to call her names anymore. She's my grandchild and I'd better get used to it. I wonder if she ever will.

But then Lou remembered their blowup at Pikes Peak. Lou lost her temper and let loose. What did Kapi say? Language. Lou couldn't help the miniscule smile that crept out.

I'm on Kapi for the crap she spouts. I guess it's only poetic justice that she calls me on it.

How could she be expected to keep herself calm, with the distraction of trying to keep Kapi in line? The bitterness could sometimes be distilled directly from the air when both of them were in the room.

The sound of rain seeped into her awareness. Oh no. We'll be stuck in the house all day. And the car is still packed. She groaned again.

Lou slid her feet into slippers and stood up. She squared her shoulders and figured she'd have to face the day—and Kapi—sooner or later, so she might as well get rolling now. When she shuffled over to the window and opened the curtains, her worst fears jelled. The rain was sheeting off the porch roof and the flower beds were drenched. A car went by and raised a rooster tail of water as it went through a low spot.

She closed her eyes, hoping beyond hope it was a bad dream. Stuck in the house was sometimes a boon, an enforced chunk of time to write. Today it was a bust, promising only a chunk of time, far too much time, to brood and frown and electrocute each other with charged glances.

No use standing here. Might as well enter the fray. She huffed. "Here goes nothing."

Chapter 15
Lou

By the time she reached the fireplace nook, Lou was surprised by the pungent fragrance of burning apple wood. Another one of those toss and turn nights for Kapi, Lou thought. She came around the bottom of the stairs to find Kapi curled up in one of the chairs, staring into a well-laid fire. Kapi didn't look up, but instead grabbed the book off her lap and pretended to read.

"Would work better if you turned it right side up," Lou said as she headed past on her way to the kitchen.

She missed any look Kapi might have sent her way, but she did hear the rustle of pages as Kapi must have rearranged the book.

"Thanks for the fire," Lou added as the kitchen door swung shut behind her. Let's see if that gets a rise out of her. But it didn't. At least, not that Lou could hear.

No coffee. Not that she really expected any. But with the fire, and the fact that Kapi wasn't hiding out somewhere made her hope that maybe... But no, nothing.

Lou went into automatic pilot in preparing tea and toast. What's this girl got up her sleeve now? No use trying to second guess. Bowl and spoon, both rinsed out, and a juice glass stood in the sink. Lou saw the residue of cranberry juice in the glass. She rubbed her wrist across her eyes, surprised by the rise of emotion.

Lou wondered how long Kapi had been up. Long enough to build a fire and make breakfast for herself. She couldn't remember if Kapi was still in pajamas—shorts and a t-shirt in her case. Lou looked down at her own pajamas, top button askew and bottoms held together with a giant snap she'd sewn on after the original snaps tore out. The blue pattern of the fabric was so faded, she couldn't even remember if it had been plaid or striped.

She shook her head. What difference did it make? No one else saw her pajamas anyway. Even Heddy. Lou's regular daytime wear of baggie pants and out-of-date shirts were nothing new to anyone who knew her. But her pajamas were the final gesture of defiance to the fashion world. They never mattered before. She wondered why they were bothering her now. Maybe they were only a statement to herself: *You don't care what you wear and you don't care what people say.* Except that didn't seem to make sense, now that she thought about it. If no one saw her most insolent clothing choice, she certainly wasn't saying anything to anyone, except herself.

And now she was getting confused over the message. If there's no recipient, what's the point of a message anyway? She wasn't prepared to say that Kapi might be the recipient. More to the point, she wasn't ready to say Kapi's response mattered.

The toast popped up and Lou hustled the pieces to a plate before they burned her fingers. The tea was ready. She felt the warm steam slide up her nose when she lifted the cup to savor the scent of apple and cinnamon. She slurped and swallowed. Toast with Door County Chunky Cherry Jam was the perfect accompaniment.

Slow down. Enjoy. Strange to have to talk herself into enjoying breakfast. Even with Kapi here, she was able to take her time and keep breakfast sacrosanct. She remembered C.S. Lewis's comment, "If you have lusted after bacon and eggs, you have already committed breakfast in your heart." She probably mangled the quote, but she didn't think ol' C.S. would mind. After all, he was dead. Anyway, the spirit of the thing was there. She smiled.

But something was a bit off this morning. Lou couldn't put her finger on it, exactly, but this wasn't a usual morning feeling. Kapi making her own breakfast; that was one thing, though not totally unusual. It happened before. The fire, that was another. Never done before.

But the quiet did it. Kapi never cared how much noise she made in the morning on the days she apparently didn't sleep well. She would appear downstairs with circles under her eyes and tousled hair. Sometimes on those days, Lou awoke to the shower running, or gargling in the bathroom. Even worse, Kapi seemed to make as much noise as she could, stomping around downstairs, as if she was determined to irritate Lou into early morning anger. Lou never gave her the satisfaction, though she wanted to.

Lou stuffed the last of the toast in her mouth and finished the tea. Enough was enough. Time to take back control of her own house.

She strode through the living room and upstairs. Might as well get dressed. This craziness was messing with her mind.

When she came back down in her usual baggy pants, Kapi was still curled in the chair. Dressed, Lou noticed. Jeans and a ratty plaid shirt. Maybe Lou should go back and change, considering she'd chosen a plaid shirt too. And a ratty one to boot. They were not exactly Siamese twins. What were their names again, those guys from the circus? Chang and something? She couldn't remember. With a start, Lou realized Kapi wouldn't even know who those Siamese twins were, much less know their names.

She grunted in Kapi's direction and went to stand at the front door. "Crappy day," she said, and got a grunt from Kapi in return. "I should've emptied the car last night."

"'t's in the laundry room," Kapi said.

"What? What's in the laundry room?" Lou said. "The car?"

"Crap from the car." Kapi didn't look up from her book.

Lou went to the stuffed chair across from her granddaughter and sat down. "You..." She wasn't about to jump to conclusions. Nor did she want to check the laundry room. The spell might be broken.

Kapi looked up. "I mean, I brought the stuff in from the car." Her voice felt noncommittal.

"All of it?" Lou matched her tone.

"All of it. I needed my music."

"But..." *But you brought my stuff in too.* Why? Lou thought better of saying it. It would sound snarky.

"Why did I bring your stuff in too?"

The girl can read minds? Lou simply nodded.

Kapi shrugged. "It was on top."

"You must've gotten soaked. It looks like it's been raining all night." It sounded inane, but was all Lou could come up with.

"I did. I toweled off in the laundry room. There's a load in the washer. I didn't turn it on."

Lou opened her mouth, then clamped it shut again. She had no idea what she wanted to say. Lacking words. That had to be a first. "Well, thanks. I'll go turn it on in a minute." She shifted in the chair. "I... That noise would wake me up for sure. I... Thanks for letting me sleep."

Kapi shrugged again. "I couldn't sleep anyway, so I figured I'd get all my...our junk in." She sneaked a look at Lou. "I was cold. So I built a fire."

"Great idea." Lou felt her way along. "Couldn't have built a better one myself."

Kapi graced her with a crooked smile. "Thanks."

"Can I ask you a stupid question?" Well, there's a great start, Lou thought.

Kapi looked up, but said nothing.

Lou forged ahead. "What's with the name? Kapi. Where did that come from?"

Kapi leaned forward. Her hair curtained her face. "My mom," she whispered, then looked up. "She saw a picture of a mountain somewhere called Capiton, I think it was."

"Yosemite," Lou said. "El..." She stopped herself from correcting Kapi.

"What? Yeah, Yosemite. I think that's right." She combed her hair with her fingers. "Anyway. She said she saw a photo of it when she was pregnant with me, and she figured it would be a cool name. But then she said I'd never weigh a ton, so she didn't add that part. She spelled it with a K so people wouldn't confuse me with the mountain."

Lou wanted to say, The woman really was stupid, wasn't she? But that might be going too far. "K is okay," she said instead. "Different, but okay, I guess." She cleared her throat. "I'm sorry I—" She was cut off by Heddy's announcement from the back door, the usual, "No need to get dirt on your floor," as she presumably slipped out of her footwear.

"The travellers have returned! Welcome home!" Heddy burst through the swinging door to the kitchen. She twitched a dishtowel at the two sitting by the fire. "Come on in. I brought you guys some breakfast. Egg casserole and…" Her litany of items was lost as she swept back into the kitchen.

Shards of words and thoughts rained down around Lou, slicing her as they fell. Damn! I love you, Heddy, but not right now.

Once again, Kapi curled up in the chair with the book clutched to her chest. While she didn't have storm clouds on her face, the smile was gone and her eyes showed blank. She unfolded and set the book on the floor. Not dropped it, not slammed it. Just set it down without a sound.

Lou cleared her throat. Kapi looked up. "You hungry?" Lou asked.

Kapi nodded and stood up. She waited a brief moment, then turned to the kitchen.

Lou followed. This better not have ruined everything. Or anything.

Chapter 16
Lou

Kapi withdrew to the fireplace nook with several books and didn't appear to be in any hurry to re-emerge and engage. Lou took up her usual post before the fireplace, in hopes of...well, perhaps in hopes of enticing her granddaughter to join her. But for two days, Kapi sailed from nook to kitchen to bed, and back around again, making sure never to occupy the same space as Lou.

What was the problem? Not the problem of what Kapi was eating, or where she would appear—or disappear—next. More the problem of how to come to terms with their relationship. At least Kapi didn't bolt from the house. That was something.

Time to take stock, Lou thought. I cannot figure her out. And I better start trying.

At five in the morning of the third day, Lou was already installed in her favorite overstuffed chair. She drummed her fingers on the chair's arms. She settled her head back on the chair's soft back. She closed her eyes. She tried to slow her breathing. She even put on her grandmother's earrings.

Oh, hell, she thought. I can't do this without writing stuff down. She levered herself up and retrieved a notebook and pen from one of the piles on the desk. After situating herself back in the chair, she slashed a vertical line down a fresh page in the notebook.

WRONGS, she wrote on the top of the left column. Then she added a question mark after the word. Maybe they weren't really wrongs. Maybe they were misunderstandings. But she wasn't about to cross out anything yet. She knew that much from years of writing in her travel journal. Never, but never, discard anything. You might regret it later.

She waffled over what to label the right column. RIGHTS just didn't work. Maybe HOPES. She scowled. Maybe FACTS? That felt closer to what she wanted. "Ah!" she puffed. Then wrote OBSERVATIONS on the top of the right column.

Where to start? Start with the dark stuff first. Then the other stuff, the stuff of contrast, might be easier to spot.

The first Wrong was easy: "Becca hated me." Even the second came quickly: "Kapi hates me." But she amended it with a caret and the added words "seems to." Fair was fair. If she was going to catalog what was going on with the two of them, right in her own house, she had to be as observant and objective as she could muster. Which didn't feel like much at the moment.

If she was being honest, then she had to also add: "Granddaughter forced upon me."

The list grew slowly. "K leaves stuff all over the place." That needed an immediate response, before she grew defensive. In the right column she scratched, "Not often anymore."

"K has lousy attitude." That too brought her up short, considering her own attitude wasn't the best. But she shook her head and moved on. If she was going to respond to every little thing, pretty soon she'd have a meaningless list, with everything balanced out. And Lou knew perfectly well that this life together was far from balanced.

"Didn't care if K got into the car on time at Pike's Peak." Fair was fair. Lou knew she had her own set of foibles. It's just that they had never really interfered with much of anything before. Her friends, she realized, gave her lot of latitude. Of course they do. They know I love them. "Don't know if I love Kapi" got added to the list. She went on, but the things she dug up became more and more trivial. Finally, in frustration, she scribbled "MAC DIED!" at the bottom of the page.

Then she threw the notebook toward the fireplace, where it landed with a slap on the stone hearth.

Lou set her elbow on her knee and tucked her fist under her chin. She squeezed her eyes shut to keep any tears from leaking out. Mac died. Was that the crux of the problem with Kapi? No, that didn't really make sense. Kapi was in as much pain as she was, maybe more. No, not more. Mac was the beloved child of her womb. That was closer than anything.

There. Maybe that was the kernel. Maybe Mac was too beloved for Becca. Did Becca think Lou was holding too tight to her boy? No way to know now, with Becca dead and buried.

Maybe there was a way to find out. Kapi. What did Becca tell Kapi about Lou, if anything? Lou knew Becca told Kapi a few things, but communication with Lou from that household was nil since Mac died.

Lou wondered if it was even worth asking. She didn't want to rake Kapi over the coals, considering she might not know anything. Lou did know that resentment and anger of one sort or another were eating at Kapi. There would be no peace unless she and Kapi could face things head on. Perhaps there were no answers. But "We'll never know" was a hell of a lot better than dead silence filled with darkness.

Lou heard footfalls coming down the stairs. She waited for Kapi to slide into the nook, but instead the sounds continued on down. Kapi must not know Lou was down here in the half-light of dawn. She dropped out of the chair and crawled over to retrieve the notebook. She retreated, tucked it under her chair in one quick motion, and resumed her seat.

"We need to talk," Lou said as Kapi cleared the steps and started for the kitchen.

To her credit, Kapi didn't bolt at the sound of Lou's voice. But she stiffened into immobility. She shoved her hands into her jeans shorts. Her shoulders lifted in a slow attempt to protect her neck.

Sit down, Lou wanted to bark. Instead, she said, "Come and sit down." She forced herself to lean back and fold her hands in her lap.

Kapi frowned. But she sidled over to the other chair and lowered herself. She stayed perched on the edge. Her eyes were fixed on the rug between her feet.

"We need to talk," Lou repeated. But she had no idea where to go from there.

A pause threatened to sprout mushrooms.

Kapi slid back into her chair and pulled her feet up. She set her chin on her knees and wrapped her arms around her legs. She still didn't look at Lou.

"Why did your mother hate me so much?" Might as well jump in with both feet. The splash might be overwhelming, but it wouldn't drown anybody.

Another silence.

"Look, I know she must've been jealous of me, because Mac and I were so close." She shifted in her chair. "But from the beginning, she never treated me like anything but an intruder. Even in my own house."

"She came here?" Kapi sounded surprised. "She never told me."

Lou sniffed. "Figures. She came in, said a few nasty things about my house, grabbed Mac and stomped out. Never saw her here again." She receded a bit into herself.

"But Dad came. Didn't he?"

Dad. Yes, Mac surely made her his daughter. She nodded to answer Kapi. "Yes, he came."

Kapi blew a sigh out through her nose. "He made me laugh. He took me places. We played a lot of games together, and he taught me a lot of stuff." She drew herself tighter together and set her forehead on her knees. "I miss him. I loved him." Her voice was muffled.

Lou opened her mouth to respond, but could only whisper, "I did too."

Kapi looked up. "She was a jealous bitch."

Lou shrugged. "Maybe of both of us."

Kapi sent her a crooked smile. "Aren't you going to tell me not to call my mother a bitch?"

"I didn't live with her."

Kapi echoed Lou's shrug. "She was, you know. A bitch."

The mushrooms grew. Lou waited.

"I think she resented any time you took from Dad. Especially when he got sick." She shivered. "She didn't want you around. That's about all I know."

"Well." Lou set her head back on her chair and tented her fingers. "That settles that, now doesn't it? Clear as a bell." Then she surprised even herself by starting to laugh. It started out as more of a snort, but soon escalated into a full-fledged guffaw. Lou's eyes were watering so much, Kapi became a wavering watercolor.

Kapi appeared immobilized.

Lou tried to suppress her laughter, but it sounded more like a dead-end sneeze.

Kapi put her hands over her face. But when she lowered her hands, her face had softened. Not quite a smile, but not a scowl either. She got up and headed for the kitchen. Just before the door swung shut behind her, she said, "I'll make breakfast."

Lou bent over and pulled out her notebook. Tearing out the pages she crafted, she crumpled them up and stuffed them in her pocket.

She hadn't expected even this much from Kapi. It'll do, she thought. It'll do. "I'll help," she called into the kitchen.

***

Breakfast was silent, but at least not of the poisonous variety. Kapi was putting away the milk while Lou filled the dishwasher when a rat-a-tat came from the front door.

"That'll be Abe," Lou said. "Must be guilt kicking in."

Kapi furrowed her brow. "Guilt?"

"Once a month or so, he gets feeling he ought to get to church. Then he pops over and wants me to go with. Never goes to the front door unless he's headed to church and wants company."

"And?"

"And what? Go let him in."

Kapi opened her mouth before reconsidering, then swung through the door to the living room. Lou heard Abe stomp his feet and say something that made Kapi chuckle. Lou wiped her hands and left the kitchen.

"You, um..." Abe always stumbled along on these particular Sunday mornings. "I'm heading off to church.

You want to come along? Nice weather out there for walking. And I hear the preacher's got a rip-roarin' good sermon prepared."

"You know no such thing, you old coot," Lou said. "How often do you commiserate with the reverend?" She snorted. "The older you get, the more you want to sidle up to Jesus. It won't make a difference, you know. He knows it all by now."

Abe drew himself up into a thundercloud. "Woman, I leave the judging up to Jesus. Don't you go telling me I can't grease the hinges on those pearly gates once in a while."

"Never hurts to try," Lou said. "And sure, to answer your first question, why not? I'll come along. Haven't heard a good hymn in a long time."

Abe smiled. "I'll even put in a good word for you, Lou." He turned to Kapi. "You too, little girl, if you want."

Kapi bristled.

"He doesn't mean anything, Kapi," Lou said. "You're welcome to come along, that's all."

Kapi stared at Lou a moment, then shrugged a one-shoulder okay.

Abe turned to Lou. "Get your Sunday-go-to-meetin' hat on, old woman. Time to enjoy the sunshine."

Lou shooed the others out the front door and locked up behind them. The day promised brightness and heat, and she was glad of it.

Abe swept his arm around for them to follow, and set off down the sidewalk.

"Say a prayer for your daddy," Lou said to Kapi, her voice low. "Your momma too. Sounds like she needs it just as much."

"And us," Kapi leaned in to whisper. "We need it too."

Lou and Kapi locked glances for an instant. The moment was gone like a blown dandelion, but it made its mark, brief as it was.

***

Abe pointed at the last pew, and Lou and Kapi went in before him. Lou moved far enough in so that more people could seat themselves on the aisle, if needed. In spite of the fleeting moment of presumed understanding between them, Lou was cautious. Were they really reaching an armistice? A resolution might be too much to expect, but a cease-fire at least would go quite a ways.

Lou felt a brush, a touch, a pressure along her arm. All thought ground to a halt. Kapi, it could only be Kapi. She didn't dare turn her head to look, but she reached underneath her seat with her left hand for the hymnal on the built-in shelf. In the process, she moved just enough forward to be able to see Abe out of the corner of her eye. He was leaning on the armrest at the end of the pew, chatting with someone across the aisle. A good distance away from Kapi. Plenty of room for Kapi to avoid Lou.

But Kapi's arm was still against her arm. Lou wondered how long she could hold her breath. All through the service, she stayed glued in one place. Her shoulder grew tired. Her neck stiffened. But she was not about to pull away. By the end, she had no memory of the sermon, no memory of the prayers, not even much of a memory of the songs, though she followed along well enough at the time, she thought.

In the rustle and chatter as people rose to leave, Lou almost missed Kapi's comment. "Not half bad," Kapi said, as she slid to the end of the pew to follow Abe out into the sunshine.

Maybe, just maybe, Lou thought, as she unlocked herself and headed out to join them.

Chapter 17
Louise Wright

"Louise, we need to call on the reverend," Father said. "He passed me on the street today and invited us to his service on Sunday, and to dinner after. Considering it's the only church in town, I accepted his offer. Seems like a nice enough man."

"Of course, Father. I think I can even find my good Sunday hat."

He laughed. "You'll be the hit of the town. I get the feeling there aren't too many cultured women around here, at least not yet."

I frowned at him, but I really wasn't serious about it. "I hope you don't expect me to start setting up afternoon teas and receiving visitors."

"You won't have time for any of that." He put his arms around me in a bear hug. "We've got to finish getting the store set up." He looked around us at the boxes and bales piled everywhere. "Besides, most of the women here are out on the farms. The town is mainly used by people passing through. But someday, you mark my word, this'll be a bustling center."

I doubted it. But I turned the conversation back. "Well, the wagon is unloaded and the horses are taken care of.

Everything we sent ahead from Oshkosh has arrived. Our beds are set up and the kitchen gear is at least in place," I said. "If nothing else, I can cook. I think the supplies we sent ahead will suffice."

He shook his head. "We'll have to rely on the farmers who are here too. Until we can get our own kitchen garden going next spring, I fear our meals will be sparse and simple. Winters can be brutal here on the lake, as you well know."

I wanted to ask him if this was the best decision, to move this far west, especially so late in the season. But I remained quiet. Such trepidation in my own heart would only add to his sorrows. Instead, I said, "We can ask advice from the reverend's family. I'm sure they'll be a wellspring of help."

"From what I can tell," Father said, "they've sunk good, strong roots deep into life here. I'm sure they'll be our best support." He released me from his embrace and began moving boxes, grouping similar materials together.

"How long have they been here?" I asked, bending to help him. I hoped the wife was young.

"I'm not rightly sure," Father said, "but I know they've been in and out of one post or another out here, or even farther west, for more than fifteen years."

There went my chance of a friend close to my age. Any woman following her minister husband for fifteen years was no longer young.

***

I never did find my Sunday hat. Father said I could go to church with my everyday one. We weren't, after all, in a city, where such niceties would be noted. I also, as promised, traded in Father's scratchy wool trousers for a dress.

Sunday service was small. Because I tried not to expect much, I wasn't greatly disappointed. I spent much of the service with my head bent to my prayerbook, but my eyes roved the congregation. Luckily, Father didn't insist on sitting in the front pew, as he had in Green Bay. We were no longer prominent citizens and didn't need to parade ourselves. Perhaps I should say we weren't yet prominent citizens, as I knew Father would rise quickly. His skills in procuring goods popular and stylish, as well as useful, coupled with his natural good humor made him a welcome part of everyone's life before. There was no reason to think it would be otherwise here. So far, it seemed to be going well.

Reverend Arne Iverson stood in the pulpit and expostulated on the gospel of the day, which I promptly forgot the moment he finished reading it. I tried concentrating on the words of his sermon, but other things got in the way. For one, the pastor's vestments were worn and faded, looking to be close to the end of their usefulness, but his voice filled the church. It was a fine, fulsome sound, resonating off the rafters and the plain windows. The Reverend set one hand on the Bible settled on the edge of the podium and never moved it for the whole of his sermon. The other hand waved and gesticulated so much, it made me think of a magician, a Merlin, casting a spell. His pale face, under a fluster of blond hair, flushed a bit as he talked and his blue eyes snapped. I slid my eyes away from him reluctantly. Although I wasn't processing the words, I was aware of his passion. His voice, his demeanor, his emotion, spread out to cover everyone like a Hudson Bay blanket.

I turned my attention to the congregation. In the first row sat a young man of about my age. From the rear, I recognized the same unruly blond hair as Reverend Iverson's. The morning sunlight caught in the strands, creating a kind of halo. The young man turned his head briefly and I saw the glint of blue eye. He had to be the reverend's son. I wondered where the pastor's wife was, as I didn't see anyone who seemed to fit with either the reverend or his son.

I wanted to look around more, but didn't trust myself to do much more than swing my glance from one side of the church to the other. Men seemed to fill the pews. I recognized Mr. Albert Wood, because he'd been in the store to see if we found things satisfactory, considering we purchased the place from him sight unseen. Mr. Wood, a burly man, well suited to these wilderness environs, sat alone. Father told me Mr. Wood was dedicated to making money, same as his father and his grandfather, the man who built the first ferry. But this Mr. Wood never married, instead choosing to stay on at Woods Portage after his parents and brothers all died. Mr. Wood sat quietly, listening to Pastor Iverson. I lost interest.

While Mr. Wood was dressed neatly, many of the men here were attired as if they came in from hunting. They reminded me of the deckhands and handlers back in Green Bay, skin tanned by the sun and wind, clothing heavy and mismatched. I saw trappers who'd already come in to trade beaver pelts for our provisions. I thought I could even smell them, even though they were across the aisle from me. But that might be mere imagination. I was still a bit unsettled and my mind played flights of fancy now and again. Scattered around were the loggers, padded in wool shirts and pants, big hands twisting caps in their hands as they listened to the sermon. I wondered where the farmers and their families were. None appeared to have made it into town this bright fall Sunday.

I put a gloved hand on the back of my neck and twisted to the side, as if relieving tension. It gave me a quick glimpse of the back left corner of the church. I was aware of a swath of empty seats around a cluster of women. My eye caught colors. Bright colors, reds, greens, golds. This in contrast to the earthy tones of the men's clothing. I didn't dare turn again, but I could still see, in my mind's eye, the women in the back pews, like colorful birds. I couldn't remember if they had hats or not, but in my imagination, I created hats for them. Large, they should be, but not too large. Just large enough to hold an ostrich feather or two, or perhaps a rosette of ribbon perched on the side. Who were these women? I couldn't put a finger on their ages with merely a glance, but I knew they weren't old. I had the impression of straight backs and buxom fronts. I closed my eyes. There, on the end, one of them impressed herself on the back of my eye. She did have a hat, one with a wide satin edge along the brim, I thought, that shimmered in the light.

My eyes snapped open and I must've given a little gasp, because Father turned to me and raised his eyebrows. I shook my head and gave him a tiny little frown, then settled my hands in my lap and feigned interest in the sermon, which appeared to be moving toward a close.

I was placid on the outside, but my insides were vibrating. Those were the women from the house at the edge of town, the two-story house. The house that came with a reputation. What on earth possessed them to come to church? Ladies of the evening in church? Well. This wasn't Green Bay, now, was it?

From the shuffle of feet and the general rustling from the congregation, I guessed the sermon came to a conclusion. Reverend Iverson stepped down from the pulpit.

The rest of the service went past me in a blur. I was too caught up in those women sitting in the back corner. I didn't even know how many there were, but I could still see the empty pews around them, a fence, separating them from the rest of us. Clearly, though they came to church, the rest of the residents here kept their distance. At least in public. I tried not to smile at that, and almost succeeded. What our cook in Green Bay didn't tell me, I imagined. Granted, my imagination only went so far, but I knew enough about how animals coupled and what drew men to women that I could imagine a few conclusions. I wondered how far afield my mind was from the reality of it all. Out here, beyond the edge of the cultured world, where all the fine veneer and polish of society were stripped away, I ought to be able to get to the heart of things so much easier. Father early on recognized my thirst for knowledge, my need for a sense of control. He taught me to listen with a businessman's ear, to drive with a firm hand, to bargain with the best of them, and to treat others with respect. I hoped it would be only the beginning.

***

Father held back, allowing others to walk out of church ahead of us. I myself turned in the pew, trying not to be obvious as I craned my neck and searched for the cluster of women. I was thoroughly disappointed to find their corner utterly empty. I don't know why I was surprised. Of course they would want to exit before anyone accosted them. Who knew what would be said? Granted, these men were the very ones who frequented their parlor, but perhaps they were also the ones who turned holy once a steeple was in sight.

I mentally shook myself. Surely not all of the loggers, trappers and sundry other men availed themselves of the services of these women. As Father took my arm to lead me out of church, I deliberately cleared my mind of such unholy thoughts.

"Well, Mr. Wright, I'm delighted to see you this fine morning." Outdoors, the pastor's voice lost some of its volume, but none of its energy.

"Stephen, please, Reverend."

"Call me Arne." He reached out to grasp my father's outstretched hand in both of his. "And this—" He turned to me without letting go of Father's grip. "—must be your daughter."

"Louise, yes." My father reclaimed his hand and took mine instead. "This is Reverend Iverson," he said to me, tucking my hand into the crook of his elbow.

"Pleased, indeed," Pastor said, sliding his hands into the full sleeves of his vestments and giving a little bow. He looked beyond us and called out to the young man I saw in church, the one with the blond halo. "Come over here, Gust, and meet our newest members."

The young man said a few final words, unintelligible at that distance, to Mr. Wood and another man and turned to stride toward us. Pastor pulled his hands out of his sleeves and reached out to slide an arm across the young man's shoulders. "My son, Gustav Iverson," he said. His face beamed with pride as he introduced us. "Gust, this is Mr. Wright and his lovely daughter, Louise. They've come in from Green Bay, via Oshkosh, and re-opened the mercantile store on Main Street, the one in the old ferry office."

Gust nodded in my direction, then greeted my father. "A pleasure to meet you both. I've noticed a great deal of activity around there the past few days. Are you getting on well with moving in?" He reached out a large hand, freckled with small spots, and engulfed my father's hand.

I had a moment or two to inspect him as he spoke with Father of the everyday annoyances of moving and unpacking and such. Gust Iverson was tall and lanky, fairly big-boned, but carried himself with dignity. Probably because he was the child of a clergyman. There was a certain demeanor required of the offspring of such an important person in any town, even out here. His hands and feet were almost too big for him and caused him to look a bit off balance, even when at rest. But his face made up for any deficiencies in his body. Under that thatch of blond hair was a face rivaling the cherubs painted on our church ceiling back home. Back in Green Bay, my mind amended. This was home now.

I shook my mind free. Before Gust turned to engage me in conversation, I took in his blue eyes and his porcelain face. Because of the freckles on his hands, I expected to find a spray of the same across his nose. But there were none. His skin was like the flesh of a peach, light and healthy looking, with a faint blush of rose underneath, ready to rise with heat or emotion. It seemed a silly comparison, but it fit. When he turned to speak to me, his blue eyes locked on mine. None of the hesitancy I almost always saw in the boys in Green Bay. Even Father's clients and customers didn't look at me with such openness. I saw it as deference back there, but now I realized it wasn't that at all. It was either pity or sympathy, probably for my mother's death. Or was it fear? What they were afraid of, I had no idea.

When Gust looked at me, it was as to a peer. No pity, no fear. He took me for what I was, a young woman close to his own age, apparently. Someone his equal, no better, no worse. I was never accepted so totally before. I felt cheered somehow. Perhaps Woods Portage would be a place where I could grow into who I really wanted to be. I smiled up at him as he took my hand in greeting. "I'm so glad to meet you," I said, keeping my eyes steadily on his. I meant it too.

We walked next door to the parson's house, speaking of how the men of the town, even the trappers who came and went with the seasons, came together to build the church and the parsonage, both in one summer season. Pastor and Gust were going into their fifth autumn here and were pretty much an institution by now.

It suddenly dawned on me that I'd not met Mrs. Iverson. I declined to inquire, as I thought she might be an invalid at home or perhaps off visiting relatives somewhere.

By this time, Pastor was up the front step and holding open the door. "Come in, by all means, come in. Hannah will have dinner on the table momentarily." He called down the hall as we entered, "Hannah! We're home." He led us into the parlor and asked Gust to entertain us while he informed Hannah of our readiness for a meal.

I was impressed. A real house with a real parlor. Granted, the house didn't look very large, and the front parlor clearly doubled as the Parson's office, but it wasn't at all what I expected. What did I expect? A log cabin? A one-room shack? This house had two rooms at the front, the dining room to the left of the front hall and the parlor to the right. The kitchen must be somewhere at the back, past a narrow staircase. I couldn't see behind the closed door at the end of the hall, but I could smell dinner.

Bedrooms must be upstairs. It was a small house, but perfectly adequate, from what I could see.

I turned to Gust. "Your mother must be very busy today," I said. It was an inane comment, made to mask my confusion over the fact she didn't participate in the church service. Apparently, she wasn't a total invalid, if she was in the kitchen. My voice must have belied my confusion, because Gust tilted his head and frowned. For some reason, his eyes seemed to go dark.

"Ah," he said, "you haven't heard. My mother is dead. She died six years ago this winter of a fever. She's buried in the cemetery behind our last church. We moved here the spring after she died."

"But Hannah..." I suddenly felt as if I were treading on shaky ground. "I'm sorry," I began, but Gust shook his head and smiled in a soft, sweet manner.

"No need to apologize," he said. "Hannah is our housekeeper. Without her, I think we would have gone under. Or had to move again. My father and I both depend on her to keep body and soul together. She cooks for us and cleans and generally shows us we're worthy to stay here."

At that moment, his father reentered the parlor, closing off the necessity of carrying on what could be a painful conversation.

"Come, all," Pastor said. "Dinner is served." He led us across the hall into the dining room, where the food sat steaming on the table.

We reached dessert without me putting my foot in my mouth and I relaxed. Mostly, I listened as the three men talked weather, gardens, water, travel, the store and myriad other topics. Finally, Gust turned to me and asked, "So, we've ignored you long enough. Tell me, what do you think of our little town?"

I threw my hands out in an expansive gesture, about to tell him I hardly knew the place yet. Unfortunately, that was the moment the housekeeper chose to appear behind me. My hand connected with a plate, upsetting what turned out to be a slice of apple pie, and dumping it directly onto the edge of the table. It tilted dangerously and slid right onto my lap. I froze in horror.

"Oh, miss! I'm sorry!"

The voice wasn't loud, but it startled me nonetheless. I looked up to see a dark, square face, framed in black hair, leaning over to try and reach the remnants of the pie in my lap. I shoved my chair back and grasped my skirt, like an apple-gatherer scooping up the harvest. I stood up and the woman backed off. "Let me take this into the kitchen. I can't eat it out of my dress." I tried a small laugh, but it sounded false.

"Hannah," Pastor Iverson said, "take Miss Wright into the kitchen and help her clean off. Thank you."

The woman, short and stout, gestured toward a door in the back wall and we set off together, me holding up my skirts. She held the door open and we left the men alone to eat their pie off of proper plates.

"Sorry," she repeated as she closed the door behind us. She didn't look up at me and it was hard to tell if she was truly sorry or just mouthing the expected words.

I stepped to the worktable and upended my skirts onto the smooth wood surface. The pie fragmented out, landing in juicy lumps. I didn't dare let go of my skirt. It was sticky with sugar, flour and apple juice. I looked from that mess to Hannah and back again. "I...I'm so sorry I ruined your pie. It smells wonderful, even if it is on my skirt and not in my mouth." My laugh this time was more sincere.

Hannah shook her head, then looked up at me. Her hair, coal black, rather than the raven's-wing black of my own hair, swung in a long braid down her back. Her dark eyes were deeply sunken in an apple of a face. Where my skin was dark with olive tones, hers was dark with reds and browns. Her hands, hardworking hands, matched her face. Without looking, I knew we didn't match there either. Me with pale hands. Yes, I drove horses, but not without gloves. Even stacking boxes and unloading supplies hadn't hardened my hands. I examined her hands again and wondered if mine would look like hers after a winter of hard inside work and a spring of outside planting. Her face was noncommittal. Though her eyes glinted, I couldn't tell if she found life humorous or if her eyes were only reflecting the sunlight pouring in the window over the pump. She seemed an enigma, examining me much as an unfamiliar dog takes the measure of an unproven companion.

I looked back at my skirt, wrinkling my forehead in consternation.

"Take off your skirt," she said, without ceremony.

"What?" I said. She caught me by surprise. Even out here, no one had been quite so blunt.

"Take off your skirt." Her voice grated with an edge of impatience. "I'll get you a fresh one. You can't go home with that one."

I watched without moving as she crossed into a back hallway and disappeared. I heard her in an adjoining room, opening a trunk or cabinet. Rustling noises followed and suddenly, she was back.

"Take off your skirt." This time, she spoke as to a child, slowly and deliberately, as if I weren't understanding her. She held out a simple calico skirt. "Put this on." She stepped in front of the closed door to the dining room to prevent any intrusion.

"I don't mean to take your clothes," I said. But after one look at her face, I unbuttoned my skirt. I worked with one hand, while crumpling the rest together in the other so I wouldn't drop any mess on her floor.

"They're not my clothes. The skirt was the parson's wife's."

"Oh, Hannah," I said. "Are you sure he'll be all right with this? I don't want to show up with her clothes if he's still...grieving."

She traded my soiled skirt for the clean one, dumped out the remains of the pie in the sink, rolled it in a tight ball and set it on the worktable. I stepped into the calico skirt and settled it around my waist. It was only a little large, but the length was perfect. "I'll wash mine and bring this one back as quickly as I can. Right now, maybe I should just go on home. Would that be better, do you think?" I picked up the bundle of my skirt.

She shrugged and pulled her mouth into a tight line. "What you wish," she said. "I can tell them you've gone."

I reached out and touched her arm. She had on a long, rather shapeless dress, protected by an oversized apron, but it suited her somehow. She looked more comfortable than I felt. "Thank you for your help, Hannah. I appreciate the gesture."

Her face softened, relaxed a bit, widening her eyes. I saw the deep brown and knew the glint therein reflected the humor she found in my predicament.

I smiled back, an honest smile this time. Though she hardly spoke a dozen words to me, I liked this woman.

"My name is not Hannah," she said, her voice so low, I wasn't sure I heard correctly.

I tipped myself closer. "Not Hannah? But the parson..."

"The parson can't pronounce my name, so he gave me the name Hannah. He said it's as close as he could get," she said.

"But you speak so..." I was about to say she spoke so clearly, so cultured. How could he not say her name? Confusion stopped my mouth. Perhaps I sounded pretentious, trying to put myself above her. If I had more schooling, it counted for nothing here. Latin and history wouldn't get us through the winter. I needed to learn from these people. I couldn't afford to offend them. I cleared my throat and tried again. "You're an Indian, aren't you? I remember seeing Indians in Green Bay occasionally. When we left Oshkosh, we saw some there too, at the wheelwright and..." I had a sudden vision of those we'd seen near the saloons or glaring at us from the blacksmith's back room. I seemed to be getting myself into more trouble.

"They...might be my people," she said, her voice quiet again.

"You have relatives in Green Bay?" I asked, surprised.

She smiled, but only her mouth, not her eyes. "My people, the Ho-Chunk—you call us Winnebago—are scattered. A few years ago..."

She stopped. I could tell there was more to tell, much more, but her face suddenly closed up. Her nose flared and the skin around her mouth tightened. Without another sign, I knew we were finished. "My name is Hiinuk Waka," she said, her voice deliberate. She turned and went to the outside door. "I will tell them you have gone home." She opened the door and made room to let me pass.

I knew the look I gave her was full of questions, but she never raised her eyes to mine. "Thank you, Hi..." I couldn't remember the rest of her real name and was ashamed to admit it. It was unsatisfactory, but I left with a simple,

"Good-bye," slipping out the door and down the back steps. I turned to wave or acknowledge her somehow, but the door was already closed between us, as if dividing us, one from the other, forever.

Chapter 18
Lou

Lou came into the kitchen fastening the last of her shirt buttons, which, truth be told, was held on by a mere thread or two. She shimmied her shoulders to settle the shirt and reached for the piece of toast sticking up from the toaster. A cup of tea, still hot, stood on the counter. "Thanks," she acknowledged Kapi's gift.

Kapi swung around in her chair and froze in place. "You're going to wear *that*?" Her eyebrows disappeared up under her hair. "That old shirt? Those old loose pants from last century?"

Again? Lou thought. "What's it to you?" she growled. She cringed at the sour tone. Any truce between them was still fragile. She cleared her throat. "What wrong with what I'm wearing?"

Kapi flapped her hand in Lou's direction at the same time she shoved a piece of bacon in her mouth.

Lou jumped into the gap. "Hell, I'm only going down to the ferry office to putz with dirt and dust." She slurped her tea. Deliberate. Defiant.

Kapi ignored any reference to language. She returned Lou's look in kind. "Fine. Wear what you want. Look like the old town tramp. Who cares?" She turned away and slapped jam on a piece of toast.

"Old town bum. I'm not the town tramp. Too old." She crunched down on her own toast, slathered with honey.

Kapi turned to her with her mouth open in retort, but apparently decided it wasn't worth it. She clamped her lips shut and took her plate to the small table. She mumbled as she finished breakfast.

Damn. Blew it again, Lou thought. She set her plate in the sink. She washed honey residue from her fingers, then scrubbed a wet hand across her mouth. "I'll be at the ferry office if you want me." She toweled her hands and mouth dry. "You...you can come down, if you want." She didn't wait to see disgust or maybe rebellion on Kapi's face. She swung through to the living room, and grabbed a tote bag already packed with notebooks and pens.

She scooped her key ring out of the dish and headed for the front door. In a moment of rebellious anticipation, she forced herself to stand still. So what am I hoping for? She'll come along? Fat chance. She stepped out onto the front porch and let the screen door slam behind her. She wanted to turn around, but was afraid Kapi might take it the wrong way. Perceived as too much control, maybe.

It was a short walk to Lake Street and a not much longer walk down to the old ferry office. Lou and a few others were resurrecting the building, or trying to. Though there was no official historical society, a number of residents wanted to preserve the place, in the hopes of bringing in a few more tourists. Or at least offering another attraction to those who rented cottages every summer. Plus, it was a matter of local pride. A few people turned up with items and stories about Woods Portage, all of which was stored in the mercantile's attic for the time being. Once the old ferry office was fitted out properly, with heat and appropriate furnishings, everything could be moved in and arranged properly.

***

The building itself might look decrepit from a distance, but that was only because it didn't fit in with its more contemporary neighbors up and down the lakeshore. However, its old foundation was fieldstone, still solid after generations. Except for the moss, the thick stone walls were in decent shape. A couple years back, a small grant, along with a passel of volunteers, paid for some much-needed work. Insulation, for one. Not terribly historic, but sorely needed if they were going to actually use the building. All arguments about authenticity went out the window, almost literally, when Abe insisted on meeting there in the dead of winter. That persuaded the last of the "authenticity" crowd. By the end of this summer, the leaky roof would be replaced. The ugly blue tarp was getting smaller and smaller, as more and more of the work was completed.

Even this early in the morning, two workers were busy on the roof. Lou gave them a wave and called up, "How goes it? It's looking pretty good from down here."

They both waved, but one kept his eye on the work. The other, a woman, put down her hammer and peeled off her jacket. "Finally warming up." Her voice carried like water down a pipe. "Roof'll be done soon."

Lou waved again. She pulled the key ring out of her tote, fought with the old lock, and won. She went in, propping the door open behind her. Abe, good at such things, updated the wiring in the old building. No heat though, other than an old cast iron stove, declared too dangerous to use until someone came to clean the chimney and the fire department cleared it for use. Or until they replaced it. Electric heat was too expensive for their small budget. Next year, a small furnace, maybe. Until then, any work in the cold months depended on a space heater. Lou never really trusted that contraption, having heard too many stories of fires, even though Abe assured her it was safe.

A couple more boxes and everything would be moved down from upstairs. The old rolltop desk, empty, would have to stay up there. Old Man Wood must've built the room around it, it was so big and heavy. No way could they fit it down the stairs, and she certainly wasn't going to heave it out the window.

She climbed the stairs. Apparently, Wood liked it up here enough to set up his living quarters. One big room, probably both living and kitchen area, was empty of anything but dust and dirt. An area off to the right once contained a broken down iron bedstead, removed last summer. At the far end, facing the lake, was the largest room, stretching the width of the building. Wood's office, with that big old desk standing kitty-corner so he could see the lake out of the only window set into the gable-end of the room. She had no idea if he was the kind of man to enjoy the view. More likely, he kept a close eye on the comings and goings of his ferry.

The desk chair was long gone, but in spite of her arthritic knees—or perhaps to spite them—Lou squatted down where it would have been. Her ritual when she came up here. She looked out the window and wondered what Wood saw in his time. Now, the bridge arched over the waist of the hourglass lake, taking up most of the view. If she ignored half of the window view, she could imagine the lake before the bridge, when the ferry was still there, moving on its cable across and back, across and back. The cable, pulled by any able-bodied hand on board, drew the ferry across, carrying skins, furs, trappers French and English, and a myriad of goods heading west for the farms or other small settlements. Going east, the ferry was essential for getting farm products to market, among other things. The road to Oshkosh, Fond du Lac, even Green Bay and Milwaukee was made a lot shorter by ferrying across the lake rather than trekking around.

Lou imagined rafts of logs coming down the lake from the incoming rivers, heading for the sawmill at the bottom of the lake. Maybe even long voyageur canoes with black-robed missionaries. Or Indians. She caught herself. Native Americans, Kapi says. Still Indians to me. Dirty Indians. Drunk and dirty. She shook herself out of the past.

She didn't know enough about the history of the lake. At least, she didn't know exactly who came through when. But the lake was clearly strategic, so any of her scenarios were plausible.

Someone stepped into the room downstairs. She grunted as she levered herself upright.

She hefted one box in her arms and shoved the other along the floor with her foot.

"Hey, up there! You working, Lou?" Abe's voice boomed off the walls and zoomed up the stairs.

Lou took a last look at what she could see of the lake out of the window and turned back to the stairs. "Yeah, you old coot. What did you think I'd be doing up here? Serving tea?" She was surprised at the hollow feeling in her chest. She'd thought it might be Kapi. Abe's haranguing took her mind away from that.

"Aren't you finished up there yet? How much crap can you stuff in one old desk? You got everything else out of that musty old upstairs months ago."

"Get up here and help an old lady, you bag of bones. Good for nothing." She nudged the box to the top of the stairs. "Here. Take this one down." She set the other box on the floor. "Then you can get your fat bottom up here and bring the last one down too."

Abe's head appeared, followed by the rest of him, accompanied by various mumblings and grumblings. He grabbed the box closest and maneuvered to head back downstairs. Lou was quick to move down behind him. She wasn't about to wrestle with the last box when Abe was around to take care of it.

Abe waited for her to get out of the way and clumped upstairs again. Within a moment or two, the last box was settled on the floor. "Okay, so everything's out of that bat-house up there. But now it looks like a hurricane hit here." He leaned back against the banister and folded his arms. "Where are you going to start anyway?"

"Right here," Lou said.

***

She plopped her hand on the nearest box. God only knows what's in here, and maybe even God doesn't know. She wasn't exactly excited about sifting through all this dusty junk, but when Abe and the minister approached her last fall, her mouth said yes before her brain fully engaged. Now she was stuck. There wasn't much, other than what had been locked away in the old rolltop. And that was stuffed.

Apparently, Wood's organizational skills were minimal when it came to the desk. Lou figured he, or maybe someone later, just shoved everything in somewhere, planning on putting it where it belonged later. After trying to figure out a system for herself, Lou gave up. She emptied each drawer and pigeonhole until a box was full, then folded it shut and moved on to another. Once everything was boxed, she stalled away the winter, which was understandable, considering the lack of heat in the place. But with summer well under way, the old excuses expired.

"What do you expect to find in those old boxes?" Abe asked.

Lou snorted. "If the boxes were old, I'd have no problem. Maybe they'd be labeled." She patted one box. "New boxes, old crap."

"There ought to be some really interesting stuff in there," Abe said.

"I don't know why I let you talk me into this," Lou growled.

"Aw, you know you're just as interested in it as I am." Abe chucked her on the arm.

"Only if I find some information on the old mercantile. You know my great-great-grandpa started that place."

Abe rolled his eyes. "Yeah, yeah. You've only reminded me a thousand times." His eyes twinkled.

"Stuff it, old man." Lou opened the flaps of the closest box. "I don't know much about them. Maybe Old Man Wood kept books on something that'll be useful."

"Don't count on it," Abe said. He peered into a box he opened. "Doesn't look very promising in here." He held up a sheaf of yellowed papers whose edges crumbled in his fingers.

"Damn, Abe. Be careful with that stuff. Old means fragile."

"You ought to know. You are."

Lou set her fists on her hips. "Old or fragile?"

"Take your pick." Abe grinned. But he set the papers down gently. "Where do you want me to start? What do you want me to do?"

Lou puffed out a breath. "Honestly? I don't know. Maybe if we take one box at a time and set things out chronologically..."

"I can help."

Lou and Abe both jumped, then turned, at Kapi's voice. "You almost gave me a heart attack!" Abe said, clutching his shirt.

Kapi stood in the doorway, hands jammed into her jeans pockets.

"You want to help?" Lou heard a weak wash of skepticism in her own voice. She cleared her throat and tried again. "You came down to help the elderly, eh?"

Abe stepped in. "We can use any and all help. Come on in, Kapi. We didn't see you there." He took Kapi's elbow and guided her in. "How about you clear off that table? We figured we'd try and make some sense out of this mess."

Kapi screwed up her nose. "It smells."

"The stuff is old," Lou said, then turned to Abe. "No smart remarks about old people." She shook her finger at him.

He put up his hands, palm out, in the age-old symbol of surrender.

"Let's get to work here," Lou said.

With a "Yoo-hoo! Who's working today?", Heddy swept in the door bearing a box from You Bet Your Buns Bakery and a cardboard holder full of coffees.

"Hey!" Abe beamed. "Second breakfast!" He helped Kapi clear one of the card tables. "Right here, lady. Right here." He took the coffee from her.

Heddy obliged. She pulled out the paper plates and napkins tucked in the box.

"You thought of everything," Abe said.

"Sarah thought of everything," Heddy said. "She even stuck in some wet wipes. Once she knew I was coming down here she said, 'That old hole? Dirty as a coal mine in there, I bet.'"

Lou snorted. "If she ever came down here and helped, she'd know." She wiped her hands on her pants and reached for a cruller.

"Uh-uh!" Abe handed her a wet wipe. "This first."

"What's it to you? It's my dirt," Lou said. But she took the wipe.

Abe settled on a step, balancing a coffee and a sweet roll.

"What was this place used for?" Kapi asked around a glazed donut.

"Ferry office," Heddy said.

"No, I mean after that."

"Well, the ferry closed down when the bridge went up. That was decades ago," Heddy said.

"So, it's been empty since then?" Kapi asked.

"I think so. Lou, you've been here longer than I have. What's the story?"

Lou shrugged. "All I know is old man Wood was long dead by the time the ferry closed down. Someone tried turning the place into a tea and coffee house, but it didn't last."

"Too small," Abe said. "No placc for a good in-house kitchen."

Lou reached for another donut. "Been empty twenty years at least."

"I remember when somebody opened a little gift shop here," Heddy said, "but that didn't last either. Too far off the beaten path for the summer people."

Kapi frowned. "It's not *that* far."

"Shows what you know," Lou said. "All the cottages were up beyond Lake Street. Most still are." She flapped her hand in that direction, letting loose a puff of powdered sugar. "All the other stores too, mercantile included."

"Oh! I almost forgot." Heddy reached in her pocket and pulled out a small plastic bag. "Julie up at the old mercantile gave me this to give to you. She found it in the back attic and thought it might be something from your family. It must've fallen...somewhere, and gotten stuck. Anyway, here it is."

Lou licked her fingers and reached for the bag.

Kapi snatched it instead. "Don't touch it! Look at your hands."

Lou harrumphed, but she picked up a wet wipe. By the time she finished, Kapi slid out a small packet wrapped in oilcloth. "Give that here!"

Kapi froze at the tone. She locked eyes with Lou, then shrugged. "Fine. It's nothing to me."

Lou took the packet. "Don't you idiots have something better to do than spy on an old lady?"

Abe and Heddy turned to the boxes. Lou knew their ears were on alert by the tilt of their shoulders.

Kapi didn't move. Nor did she flinch when Lou sent her a blistering look.

Lou lowered herself onto a folding chair and set the packet on her lap. She peeled back the oilcloth. Inside was a stack of papers, small and irregular in shape. Receipts and notes perhaps.

Even though they looked to be at least a hundred years old, they also appeared to be in pretty decent shape. As she lifted them out one by one, they crackled a bit, but they didn't fall apart.

She opened the first. A note, folded in half and written in ink. Faded, but not by much, protected from sun and handling, apparently.

It read: *Take a close look. You'll see what I mean. Heathen!*

Lou turned the paper this way and that. No date, no signature, nothing to indicate anything. When was it wrapped in the packet? And who wrapped it?

"What's it say?"

Kapi's voice brought her back to the ferry office. Lou's first reaction was to tuck it away, but the paper hovered only a second before Kapi snatched it.

"Be careful! It's fragile," Lou snapped. An unnecessary warning, it turned out.

Laying the note flat on her hand, Kapi read it. "What's it mean? Who wrote it? Who's a heathen?"

"How am I supposed to know?" Lou's voice grated. "It came from the mercantile attic, so what do you think?" She tried to tamp down her impatience. "Anyway, I've never seen this before." Maybe it was the vitriol of the note, but this felt like opening a Pandora's box. *Who wrote this crap?* she thought.

Kapi set the note on a nearby box. "What else?" She waggled a finger at the papers on Lou's lap.

Lou couldn't very well shove Kapi away. Maybe these papers would help their truce. She was getting tired of a snarky teen. Hard to admit, but she was getting rather tired of her own snark too. She took a deep breath and mentally bit her tongue.

The second paper fell into two pieces when she unfolded it. It was a receipt printed in pencil, and faded and damaged in spots. Some of the words were illegible.

Wright's Mercantile, Main Street, Woods Portage, Wisconsin

Order sent on... The date was illegible.

1 roc... cradle The price was too smudged to read.

Charge to ... Wood

To be...

Something was scratched out and the words at the bottom were a rough scrawl.

Rejected. No payment made.

Lou pored over the receipt. "To be...?" Delivered, maybe? To her great-grandmother Louise? Lou spotted a faint pencil mark, barely legible, along the side: File 1867. Was that a date? She squinted. No signature. Nothing on the back either. She ran her fingernail along the edge, pulled her lips into a tight line and set the receipt on the bottom of the pile. Who knows who it was for? Or why it wasn't paid for. Maybe the cradle was damaged.

She picked up the last two papers. A short note— handwritten in crabbed letters on a yellowed paper smaller than the palm of her hand, curled and water-stained—and an envelope.

The note was only a few words long: *The women get my silver earrings. Love, LWI.*

Lou squeezed her eyes shut. She was afraid to set the note down for fear it would disappear, gone like a dream. LWI. Louise Wright Iverson.

Her silver earrings. Had to be. When she was thirteen, her grandmother told her there were silver earrings put away for her. She'd not seen them until Grandma died and Lou's father gave them to her. "These're family heirlooms, Lou," her father said. "Take good care of 'em. Your grandma said they're the only things left, whatever that means."

Those lovely long spears of silver tinkling against a cluster of small silver disks. The earrings she took on every Meander. Her grandmother's silver earrings. No. Louise

Wright Iverson's earrings. Her great-grandmother's earrings.

The note. That was—had to be—Louise's own handwriting. Louise Wright Iverson's fingers reaching out of the paper to caress Lou's hand. The feeling was uncanny. But pleasant nonetheless.

Lou held the note to her face, as if some scent of Louise could remain. But there was nothing. She smoothed the edges and set it aside.

She took up the envelope. Freed of the oilcloth, it opened like a flower, glue having dried out long ago. But it was empty. Lou turned it over. The writing on the front was so pale, it seemed to dissolve into the paper.

She took it to the window and tilted it toward the light. Only a few legible words remained: *pins...flann...sugar...*

A grocery list, from the look of it, scrawled in a moment of haste on whatever was handy. An old envelope, who knew where from. Lou squinted and drew it closer.

Deliver...day late aftern...girls will be out.

The signature disappeared after the initial R.

"Why would someone order a cradle and then not pay for it?" Kapi's voice cut in.

"What?" Lou was jerked back to reality.

"A cradle," Kapi said. "Why order it and then send it back?"

"Why do you think?" Lou's irritation got the best of her.

"I think the baby died," Kapi said. Her voice was soft and sad.

"Let me see that receipt for the cradle," Lou said. "Please."

Kapi handed off the receipt on the flat of her palm. "A cradle for Louise Iverson, maybe."

Lou nodded in agreement. "My great-grandmother."

"The one who started that store on Main Street," Kapi said.

"Her father started the mercantile, not her," Lou said. She was getting distracted. Too much to sift through.

"She must've had kids. You're here," Abe said, coming up behind Lou.

"Of course they did," Lou said. She softened a bit. "My grandmother. They had my grandmother. There was another one, I think. A boy, maybe? But he died young. At least, that's what I was told."

"Aren't there church records?" Heddy asked.

"The books were all mildewed and stuck together. My mother mentioned once about the books being no good from a roof leak or something," Lou said. "But I don't know exactly what. Who knows what's up there?"

"Aren't you interested at all?" Kapi said. "I'd want to know everything."

Lou sent her a hooded look. Some things were better left alone.

"Anyway," Abe said, "what's this about delivering this cradle?"

"Maybe to Louise and Gust. You said her husband was Gust Iverson," Kapi said. She turned to Lou.

"Oh, thanks for that insight." Lou was suddenly not in a mood to tolerate Kapi's sarcasm. But when she turned to fire off another round, she saw Kapi's face. Smooth and interested. No sarcasm evident.

Lou satisfied herself with a simple, "I think Gust was a minister."

"You don't know?" Now Kapi was being contentious.

"No, I don't. He was dead long before I was around." Lou felt her hackles rise.

Abe stepped between the two. He took Kapi by the shoulders and turned her around. "That's enough for today."

Lou used great care in folding the papers and rewrapping them in the oilskin. She slid them back in the plastic bag. "I'm going home. Enough digging in the dirt." She tucked the packet in her pocket. *I'll get to the bottom of these yet.*

Chapter 19
Louise Wright

"Louise, I'm so glad you're here." Gust swung into the kitchen, letting in a burst of cold.

I saw Hannah tighten her lips, but she turned away without saying anything.

"Gust Iverson, you turn yourself right around and go back outside." I set my hands on my hips and he backed away, palms out. "Go brush those wood chips off outside. And stamp off the snow too."

"You'll be sorry when this winter gets really wicked and you're looking for firewood." Gust laughed as he went out the door and clattered down the steps.

"He knows better than that," I whispered. I shook my head and winked at Hannah.

Hannah paused a moment before turning back to her work.

I caught one of her brief smiles. Months into the winter, Hannah had finally showed signs of warming toward me. We didn't have many conversations, but at least the silences were more comfortable.

My curiosity rose. I wanted to know more about this taciturn Ho-Chunk woman. Perhaps now was the time to practice Hannah's real name. I tried in private to remember her real name, but I was reluctant to try anything out loud on her.

I took up the last of the apples. All were bruised and some were already softening, though they were just fine for the pies we were baking. I assured Reverend Iverson that it would be better to make the pies and sell them at the mercantile and use the money for the church, than let the apples rot in the root cellar. The winter trappers would be glad enough for a piece of homemade pie in the middle of a long cold winter.

I drew in a deep breath and, without looking up, said, "Thank you for helping, Hee-nuke Way-ka."

A moment of silence was followed by a cackle of laughter. "Hee-nuke..." Hannah stifled a giggle. "You try, but you fail." She lifted a ball of dough and loosened a finger enough to point at me. "Hiinuk Waka." She repeated it, lingering over the sounds. She raised her eyebrows.

"Hin-nook..." I crinkled my forehead and watched Hiinuk Waka's lips. "Hiinuk Waka," I repeated.

Hiinuk Waka bobbed her head. "Hiinuk Waka, yes. Snake Woman. I am of the Earth Clan." She dropped the ball of dough on the floured table and flattened it with her hand.

This was the opening I was waiting for. I decided to plunge in the deep before I lost my nerve. "Reverend Iverson said you lost your son just like he lost his wife." I went back to peeling apples. Better not to look at her.

Hiinuk Waka slapped the dough with the rolling pin. "I did not lose. He was taken." Her voice leaked vinegar.

I glanced up, apple and knife in hand. "Taken? By sickness, you mean?"

Hiinuk Waka raised her eyes. "No. Taken. Government men came and took him. Burned our homes. My husband died. All Ho-Chunk must go."

"What? I don't understand. Burned—? Go where?" I thought her son died.

"They said we had to go. To Iowa. To Minnesota. Then South Dakota. To Nebraska. Away from here. Away from home." She leaned into the rolling pin. Her hands turned white from the force of her grip. "I would not go. This is my home. My home."

"How could anyone throw you off your own land?"

Hiinuk Waka barked a short laugh. "They said go. We had to go. But many came back. My son did not." The rolling pin came to a stop.

I stood still as a statue, afraid to break the stream of words. But then my voice crept out without thought. "But why?"

"They wanted everything. Treaties broken. Families broken and removed." She shook her head. "I stayed. They wanted warriors gone so men would not fight. Ho-Chunk are not warriors like they said. We are People of the Big Voice. Farmers, hunters. Fighters when... But they wanted..." She picked up the pie crust and draped it into the pie pan. "I was only a woman. No danger. No fighter. But my son and grandson...."

"You have a grandson? Where is he?" I pressed the back of my hand against my mouth. Perhaps I was asking too much.

Hiinuk Waka took a deep breath and straightened to face me. She leaned to gather apple slices and filled the crust. "My grandson..." Her voice caught. "Ho-Chunk in Nebraska say he has left to come home."

"Nebraska? I thought you said..." I could only shake my head. How many times were they removed?

Hiinuk Waka bent over her work. "Many left Dakota. Many could not. My son died. Killed in Sioux wars. My grandson..." She picked up the pie, but hesitated before taking it to the oven. "My grandson went to Nebraska."

I had no idea what to say next. I whispered, "I'm so sorry, Hiinuk Waka. It's all so horrible."

"Huuwa Mani."

"What?"

"That is his name, my grandson. Huuwa Mani."

I tried it out, which drew a fleeting smile from Hiinuk Waka.

"Better you say Walking Elk."

I smiled back. "Walking Elk. Better than making a mistake and saying something vile in your language."

"Do you like Mister Gust?"

I felt my face flush at the unexpected question, but I refused to respond. "Here's enough for more than one more pie." I pushed more apple slices into a neat mound on the table.

Hiinuk Waka stood waiting.

I laughed. Apparently the diversion wasn't working. "All right, yes. I do like Mister Gust."

Hiinuk Waka went back to forming another crust. "He is a fine man for you. His face gets red for you too."

"And you approve?" I said. "I'd be happy if you did." It surprised me to say so, but it was true. I craved her approval.

Announced by another sweep of frigid air, Gust came through the back door. "I filled up the woodbox on the porch. That should keep you ladies going for a good long time." He pried off his boots and padded to the stove where he turned his back and sighed with pleasure at the heat.

Hiinuk Waka locked eyes with me. "Yes," she said. "I approve."

Chapter 20
Louise Wright

Walking Elk appeared at the parsonage's kitchen door the same day the trilliums blossomed in the woods behind the church.

I was helping Hiinuk Waka in the kitchen when he strode in the back door. He was taller than Hiinuk Waka, though he resembled her in almost every other way. The same snapping dark eyes to match black hair. The same warm ochre complexion. The same smooth nose, as if shaped in clay. The same look, wary, ready to pull shutters closed.

He levered off his boots, muddy from the early spring roads, and slung his heavy jacket over the nearest chair.

Then he smiled, and his face opened like embers fanned to fire. His grandmother, until then frozen in disbelief, exploded in a matching smile, the first time in a very long time she had a reason to do so.

Soon, everyone knew Walking Elk returned.

Before long, Hiinuk Waka's house door was tightened in its jamb, no longer needing fabric stuffed into the cracks along its edges. The sounds of chopping soon carried far and away; heavy, determined blows of a young axe wielder. As a result, Hiinuk Waka's woodpile grew high and wide.

The days grew longer bit by bit, and Walking Elk was often seen striding through town, his colorful shirt ruched up under his jacket. He looked a strutting bird next to the drab farmers coming to town to pick up provisions, nails, tools, baling wire. All those necessities for launching spring repairs and plantings.

Woods Portage grew lively. Farmers' wives rode in with their husbands, children along, bouncing with the excitement born of freedom from the confines of winter, women wanting a respite from the last of the canned goods they put up the fall before. Hungry for conversation as well.

I worked early and late trying to keep up with deliveries and demands as the ice broke up on the lake. Sven had constructed an icehouse the previous fall and now needed another padlock to secure the lower level. Ellie needed more flour, because her barrel had acquired a family of very large weevils over the winter. Albert needed more liniment for himself and his horse. And on and on.

"Papa?" I called into the mercantile. "I should go out to Juanita's to deliver that drapery fabric that came in." Juanita and her "girls" at the big house on the western edge of town needed our goods as much as anyone else. Father trusted me to drive out alone, or with Gust, and the townspeople learned to turn a blind eye to our doings. We reached a tacit understanding.

Father's voice came back to me. "Take that sack of sugar too, while you're at it." He stuck his head around the curtain across the doorway to the back rooms. "Walking Elk is here. He'll load it up for you. Gust is just coming back with the wagon." He popped back into the storefront.

Gust. I wet my fingers and smoothed back the stragglers in my hair. I slipped off my apron and checked myself in the long oval mirror that Father had delivered for Christmas before the weather went bad. A moment's turn, left to right and back again, a final pat of my hair. I pinched my cheeks to bring out a rosy glow and smiled at myself. I hoped Gust would notice. I went out to meet him.

"You look especially lovely today." Gust flashed me a returning smile.

Walking Elk stepped back just as I came down from the porch and fell into him. It was touch and go for a moment before Walking Elk could steady us with one hand on the wagon and the other grasping my arm.

"I am sorry," he said, turning me loose. "Did I step on you?"

"No, no." I shook down my skirt. I ducked my head so no one would see my embarrassment. "I should've been watching where I was going."

"She was so dazzled by my smile," Gust said from the wagon's seat, "she didn't see you." He chuckled.

I couldn't contradict him. I loved his smile. "I only wondered why you weren't helping load. It wouldn't hurt your smile one little bit." I set a foot on the wagon.

Walking Elk moved to help me up, but I swung myself up beside Gust before he could do more that brush my hand.

I felt Walking Elk's warmth, but by the time I settled on the seat and turned, he was gone. I shrugged and turned to Gust. "My rig, my reins," I said, grabbing the reins before Gust had a chance to react. I sent him a sweet smile and bumped his shoulder. "If I don't keep my eyes on my driving, I might be dazzled by your smile." At a look from him, I felt my throat constrict and my face go warm.

To hide my blush, I turned and saluted Father. I clucked to the horse and we were off.

Though Juanita's place was on the far west end of Lake Street, really where it turned into the road out of town, the house itself sat behind a fence and tucked in a grove of pines. Father and I made a number of deliveries there over the winter and now into spring.

"No reason to turn business away," Father said. "Everyone has to eat."

It didn't matter to him if the townspeople frowned at his serving the "ladies of the night," as he called them. He'd been the same in Green Bay, though the town there was considerably bigger, and most citizens were prone to ignoring what didn't directly concern them.

I drove the horse around the back of Juanita's establishment and, sticking my fingers between my teeth, gave a sharp whistle.

Gust startled, then laughed. "I didn't know you had such talents."

I grinned at him, then pulled the horse to a halt. "My father used to call me that way. I made him teach me. Now it's our signal to Juanita that we're here with a delivery." I crawled down from the seat and tied up the horse.

Juanita appeared on the back porch. "You alone today, Louise?" she called.

"Father is swamped at the store, so I offered to come. Your sugar order is here." I motioned at Gust, who was wrestling the sack off the wagon. He shouldered the sack and looked up at Juanita.

"Come on up here, honey. I don't bite." Juanita winked at me. "Don't worry, Louise, I won't corrupt your beau." She opened the back door to the kitchen. "Just put it in the pantry. You'll see the door to the right there."

"Your damask drapery fabric came in too. Gust can bring that in as well," I said.

"Let me get you two a drink of lemonade," she said. "It might be spring, but the day is warm enough." She led me up on the back porch.

Gust appeared at the door and I sent him to the wagon for the bolts of fabric.

"I'd send you into the parlor with that," she said with a wicked little gleam in her eye, "but I'm afraid of what the girls would think. There's room on the table right in the kitchen there." She followed him in and returned in a minute with a pitcher of lemonade and three stacked glasses. Setting them on a small table, she invited me to sit. She herself sat where she could hold the door open with her foot while Gust moved the bolts of fabric from the wagon into the kitchen.

When he carried the last of the load into the house, Juanita offered him a glass of lemonade, but he declined. Polite, but not warm.

"Anything else I can do for you, ma'am?" he asked. He sent me a look I was unable to decipher. Did he really want to simply ride away? I wanted to talk a bit, as we had over the winter when Father made deliveries. Juanita intrigued me. I liked her.

Juanita's look softened. "We got plenty of wood chopped, but it's still in the back forty. If you really want to be useful..."

"Got a barrow?" Gust asked. It sounded like he would rather work than join us, as if distance would keep him from catching anything.

Juanita pointed the way, and she and I were able to chat while Gust moved the wood to the woodpile. We never talked about anything too serious, but we laughed a lot. She wasn't evil, as the women in church seemed to think. From her viewpoint, she was providing a service to lonely men. I thought she was lonely herself.

Gust pushed the last barrowful into the yard and began stacking the wood.

Juanita reached out and set a hand on my arm. Hers was a hand that never touched a plow handle, or manhandled a foal out of a mare. But she didn't shirk hard work in her garden, or refuse to do her part in the kitchen. Her...clients were apparently quite willing to do the heavy work of splitting wood and such. But she and her girls worked their share, sewing, cooking, cleaning. Most of them sang or played piano. I sometimes heard them from the road or from the kitchen.

***

Father and I spent Sundays at the parsonage. Father and Reverend Iverson used the time to play chess or discuss the weather or argue theology, among other things. Gust and I whiled away the early spring afternoons, still cold, challenging each other in all the card games we knew, or could teach each other. Sometimes all we wanted to do was sit in front of the fire and talk.

Gust teased me about my lack of domestic virtues. I countered with, "Those 'finer skills' of city ladies have no use here. I can sew and cook. You've profited from my baking prowess too. And I can drive with the best of them. What more could one possibly want?"

"I know what else I would like," Gust retorted.

I lowered my eyes, imagining kisses and more. That made him laugh, though he didn't know what was in my mind. Or maybe he did.

When Walking Elk came in with the spring, he spent many Sunday afternoons in the parsonage kitchen with his grandmother, helping her where she allowed, or oiling harnesses, or some other such work.

One afternoon, I brought a paper of pins and a box of dress trims to the parsonage kitchen for Hiinuk Waka, far too small a thank you for her help over the fall and winter. Gust and his father were in the front parlor, rushing to finish Gust's studies for the ministry. By next spring, he could be ordained, if all went well.

Though I knew I could walk in at any time, still, I always announced myself. Today, I called Hiinuk Waka's name and pushed open the door. She was stirring something on the stove. I turned from her, and was startled by the bulk of Walking Elk who was lifting a deer hide from the table. "I didn't realize you were here. I didn't mean to disturb you and your grandmother." For once, his gaze held mine and I was aware of the depth of his eyes.

Though Walking Elk was there often, I only occasionally crossed paths with him, being in the front with Gust most times. I got the impression when he heard me coming toward the kitchen, Walking Elk left. I didn't know why.

I fiddled with the package in my hands, then thrust it out toward Hiinuk Waka. "A little gift. For you. From me. And my father." I clamped my mouth shut to stop my stammering.

"Why a gift?" Hiinuk Waka looked puzzled. "I have done nothing for a gift."

I chortled. "Oh yes, you have. You saved us from many problems with your advice." Hiinuk Waka opened her mouth to say something, but I held up my hand to stop her. "Father said you'd protest." I waggled my finger at her. "But I am not allowed to let you say no. We are very grateful to you."

Hiinuk Waka gathered the package to herself and said, "Thank you."

When I turned to go, Walking Elk was looking at me with such intensity that I felt caught. I forced myself away.

***

Early into June, Father and I ate as many strawberries as we could tolerate. After several mornings in the parsonage kitchen, Hiinuk Waka and I put up enough strawberry jam to see us well into winter.

I screwed down the last cover and said to her, "I'd love to find some blackberries. There's a scrawny bush or two out behind the mercantile, but they don't have enough berries for a pie, much less anything else."

Hiinuk Waka wiped her hands and said, "Tomorrow, you come with me and I will show you blackberries."

"Where?" I earlier ventured into the woods south of Lake Street. No blackberries in the clearings there, though I thought I recognized the low clusters of blueberry bushes. I explored north up the lakeshore, but found few berries of any kind. However, I found a wonderful cove for bathing and swimming, where the land sloped down to the water and the trees and undergrowth grew thick enough to hide anyone wanting privacy. I even went far enough north to find the worn path to Hiinuk Waka's home. But I didn't go down her pathway. She didn't need me bursting in on the one spot that truly belonged to her.

"Where?" I asked again. "I can't seem to find them anywhere."

She gave me a strange look. "There are berries and nuts all around us. I will help you open your eyes."

The next afternoon, after the rush at the mercantile slowed, I told Father of my plan and made good my escape. I met Hiinuk Waka just as she was coming out of the parsonage. "Come, we go," she said, and set off north along the narrow road skirting the top bulb of the hourglass lake. We walked in silence past the tree wrapped in bittersweet that marked the way to the secret cove. And then past the path leading to her house.

I could've walked on forever, the day was that beautiful. The blackberry patch was well worth the walk. We gathered two pails each, enough to satisfy us for a while. Besides, now that I knew where the berries were, I could come out and pick anytime.

Chapter 21
Lou

Kapi stretched over from the overstuffed chair by Lou's fireplace and nearly tipped herself out. "Wait. Let me see that again."

Lou found herself reaching, ready to catch, even though Kapi was too far away. But Kapi righted herself and tucked her feet under her again. "See what?" Lou said, settling back again.

"The receipt. You know, the one for the cradle."

The two of them were planted in front of the lifeless fireplace, papers strewn on the low chest that served as a table between them. One of the boxes from the ferry office sat on the floor, most of its papers piled higgledy-piggledy around it or added to the papers on the chest.

Lou waggled a finger. "It's right there. You can reach it better than I can."

Kapi leaned over and nabbed the receipt between two fingers. "I think I know who wrote this."

"It's from the mercantile. Who do you think wrote it? Pretty obvious, don't you think?" Lou said.

"Well, yeah. Mr. Wright, I suppose. Don't you think it could be Mr. Wright?"

"I have no idea." Lou sifted through another pile of receipts, but nothing seemed unusual. Orders from this farm or that. Big items that needed to come from Green Bay or Oshkosh, or Milwaukee. Things that the mercantile must not have stocked on a regular basis. Anything and everything that came in and went out the door. Bolts of fabric—not always the ordinary calicos, but satins sometimes, velvets—and ribbons. Fanciful, frilly laces. Buttons of mother-of-pearl. Who in God's name would need such stuff out here then?

"Look at this." She held up the order to Kapi. A peace offering of sorts. Though she hated to admit it, Lou found satisfaction in the small bits of sharing with this unruly granddaughter. "Who would order all this fancy-schmancy stuff for a town on the edge of nowhere?"

Kapi squinted. "Well, wasn't this town pretty busy then? What with the ferry and all?"

"Maybe. I guess so," Lou conceded. "But doesn't wool and flannel and practical stuff like that seem more reasonable?"

"I'm not finding much else from the mercantile. But Mr. Wood sure was busy enough with the ferry," Kapi said, holding up a record book of some sort. "He kept track of everything that went over and back."

"Before you look at that, here's a note signed by Stephen Wright. Just, 'Received from Albert Wood, full payment for use of horse and wagon.' Compare his writing with your receipt there." Lou handed it to Kapi.

Kapi set both pieces on her knees and bent low to examine them. Her hair swung back and forth as she compared the two. "Yup. The cradle receipt was written by Stephen Wright." She got up to set the two slips of paper on the television stand, where the other pieces from the oilskin packet sat. "So, Wood ordered a cradle and

Stephen Wright wrote up a receipt. Big deal." Kapi plopped back down in her chair.

Lou stopped shuffling papers. "It might be a big deal. The cradle was never paid for. Don't you think it might have been a cradle for Stephen's daughter Louise and her husband, Gust Iverson?"

Their gaze locked and Kapi raised her eyebrows. "They lost the baby somehow."

"That makes sense," Lou said. "Lots of babies died young in those years. If they didn't kill their mothers first."

"What?" Kapi said. "Kill their mothers?"

"Plenty of women died in childbirth. Having a baby was a perilous path for a woman." She pulled her mouth to one side. "What's the date on that thing?"

Kapi went to check. "Is no date. Why?"

"Must've been a baby who died, without taking Louise with it." Lou shrugged. "After all, she had my grandmother sometime in there."

"Did the family have a cradle?" Kapi asked.

"Lord, girl, I have no idea. That was forever ago. How would I know about that—" She refrained from her usual "crap".

"One way to find out." Kapi raised her eyebrows again.

"Okay, brilliant one. How?" She felt stubborn about making it easy.

"The church."

Lou exploded in a single guffaw. "The building was like a steambath. The records were gone. Mildewed beyond hope and stuck together, remember? They had to toss 'em all. Pfft!" The tone was there, but she bit her tongue before she was tempted to spit out something sarcastic. She went back to sorting papers.

"For an old fart, you don't have much—"

Lou held up a hand. She shot Kapi a look that exploded on impact. *This has got to stop. I really don't care what she thinks about me...* She caught herself again. Enough. Time to attempt disarmament.

They stared at each other, neither one seeing a way to exit.

"Whoo-hoo!" Heddy's voice preceded the back door thumping shut. Lou heard her shoes drop to the floor. "No need to dirty your floor." She came through into the living room. "What are you guys doing?"

Kapi leaped up. "Here. This is really your chair."

Heddy turned to Lou and pulled a long face that said What's with her? But she took the offer and dropped down. "So. What *are* you doing?"

"Trying to figure out—"

"—where to find out about somebody's baby," Kapi finished.

Lou and Kapi locked eyes again, but Kapi broke the spell. "It's that cradle thing." She settled herself on the floor between the two women.

"We wonder if the baby died." Lou hoped the *we* might smooth over everything.

"So, go to the old cemetery," Heddy said, picking up a pile of papers.

"There's a cemetery?" Kapi accused Lou. "Where is it?"

"Out behind the church," Heddy said. "Say, I brought some snacks. Mind if I go get them?"

Lou waved her to the kitchen. When she was gone, Lou turned to Kapi. "Don't get your hopes up. It's been overgrown for years and the old headstones are so worn you can't read them. No one's been buried there for a very long time."

Heddy came in from the kitchen. "New cemetery's outside of town. Lots more room." She set a plate of cheese and crackers on top of the papers on the chest.

"Hey, slob! You'll make a mess on those papers," Lou said.

Heddy swept the plate up and Kapi swooped in to rescue the papers. She stacked them back in the box. "So, we'll hit the cemetery tomorrow. Maybe we can do a rubbing or something."

"Have some cheese," Heddy offered. "Say, what about that crazy note about a heathen?"

Lou puffed out her cheeks. "I have no idea. Kapi, get that thing, will you?" But Kapi already picked up the note and was handing it to her.

"'Take a close look. You'll see what I mean. Heathen,'" Lou read. "I have no idea what that means."

Kapi bent over Lou's shoulder. "Well, Stephen Wright didn't write it. It doesn't match his handwriting from that other stuff."

"What about Wood?" Heddy asked. "Isn't there something there that he wrote? Maybe he wrote that." Heddy set to work looking through the papers in the box. "Here's an order from a Juanita."

"Wait!" Kapi said. "There's an easier way." She picked up the record book she'd set aside earlier, and opened the front cover. "See? 'Albert Wood, Ferry Proprietor.' This is his book."

"Let me see that." Lou waved her fingers.

Kapi frowned, but she handed over the book.

The signature was large, with flourishes on every capital letter. Under it all were the curlicues used in an earlier era.

"Prideful man," Lou said. "Look at that signature. A man full of himself."

"Typical of the times," Heddy said around a cracker.

Lou set the heathen note next to the page with the signature. "Doesn't this look like it matches?"

Heddy and Kapi leaned over, and all of them were silent as they examined the writing. As one, they looked up and nodded.

"Wood," Lou said. "It was Wood wrote this note."

Heddy picked up the note, adjusted her glasses and read, "'Take a close look. You'll see what I mean. Heathen.' Pretty nasty." She crinkled her forehead. "But what is he talking about?"

"It was in with the cradle receipt and that other stuff," Kapi said.

"May not mean a thing," Heddy said. "Any ideas?"

"Gotta mean something," Lou said. "Otherwise, why keep it?"

Heddy shrugged.

Kapi said, "Gotta be something a person could see. But..." She ran out of steam.

"Put the book in the box with the note. We'll take a closer look later," Lou said. "In the meantime—"

"In the meantime," Heddy broke in, "I'm hungry. Come on over. I've got a casserole in the oven. It's a new recipe and I need some guinea pigs." She got up and headed to the kitchen to put on her shoes.

Lou sighed. "Might as well go. She's not going to let up."

They left everything as it lay and followed Heddy out the back door.

Chapter 22
Louise Wright

At night, I often dreamed of a slender blond man with blue eyes and a smile like the sun. I was happy. Gust appeared, as if stepping out of my dream, whenever I visited the parsonage. Father released me, with gratitude, when times grew slack at the mercantile. Because then Hiinuk Waka took me in hand, and both Father and I benefited. I learned to cook what the farmers, the hunters, and the trappers brought in. Who knew that squirrel could make such a delicious stew? Butter and thyme, potatoes and tomatoes simmered with the meat, slow and bubbling. I never would have thought it so tasty. Green Bay seemed a long way away.

Gust would appear in the kitchen, lift the cast iron cover and take in the fragrance of whatever cooked there. One afternoon, he leaned over me as I stirred, and kissed my neck. Hiinuk Waka was not there or I might have reacted differently. As it was, I turned and, catching both of us by surprise, kissed him back. On the lips. Though it was merely a brush, the touch was like fire.

We stood frozen in place. "Do you mean that, Louise?" he asked. "I mean…"

"I know what you mean," I said. "Would I have done it had I not meant it?" I didn't blush this time, but met his gaze without wavering.

He set one hand on my shoulder and smoothed my hair with the other. He gathered me into his arms, and I stepped in willingly. We both began to laugh, a light understanding laugh.

I smelled something burning.

Gust turned with a whoop and, grabbing a nearby towel, he balled it up enough to push the stew pot off the hot burner. We moved, smooth as a matched team, he to sweep off the cover, I to scrape the ladle through the stew.

"We are meant to—" he began. But Hiinuk Waka walked in at just that moment. Though the spell was broken, I knew in my heart what Gust was about to say. My heart sang the answer, but I remained silent.

Not many days after, I set out for the blackberry patch Hiinuk Waka showed me, buckets slung over my arms. To satisfy Father, I wore skirts and such at the mercantile, but eschewed such finery—and such cumbersome clothing—in favor of trousers and flannel shirt when in the woods. Father pursed his lips at that, but learned quickly that I was not to be crossed in such matters. Coming home once from a serious entanglement with blackberry thorns was enough to convince him that trousers were a far more practical option. My grumblings as I attempted to mend the rips and tears of my skirt bordered on the language of some of the more colorful trappers that frequented our store, though I never crossed the border into such territory.

I hummed a favorite hymn as I picked berries and didn't notice Walking Elk approaching. When I stood and stretched, there he was, standing quiet at the edge of the clearing. The sun appeared to seek him out as it caressed his head, making his black hair gleam like the wings of a crow. His eyes, as usual, were hooded in shadow as he lowered his head. But I still felt the intensity of his gaze.

"I didn't see you there," I said, regaining my composure. "Have you come to pick for your grandmother?" I bit the inside of my cheek to keep from rattling on. He took me by surprise, but I didn't want him to know how I unnerved I was.

He shook his head and the sunlight sparked his eyes for a moment.

"There's plenty for both of us, you know." I held out a bucket. How stupid you sound, Louise, I thought. Stop being so nervous. Just settle yourself.

He lifted his eyes to mine and one corner of his lip sloped up a bit.

A smile. The barest trace of a smile. But a smile nonetheless. Why does he disturb me so?

Walking Elk swung away as if to walk into the woods on the trail to town. Or perhaps home to his grandmother's. He turned back to me. "I did not come to startle you." And then he was gone.

I wriggled my shoulders to relax, but was left with a residue of unease. Why did he come? He had startled me, unsettled me. Touched me somehow, I admitted. But why? And how?

Gust's blue eyes swam into my mind. I wanted them to be clear, defined and focused. But I felt a fuzziness. I closed my own eyes and took a deep breath. Louise Wright, concentrate. Gust loves you, you know, though he has not declared it so. Yet I knew it, could feel it every time we were together. And I was drawn to him, like a ship to harbor. He was safety and warmth. He was home.

That night, I dreamed of a slender blond man with a smile like the sun. And of a darker man with eyes that bored into me. I could neither discern nor remember much more. However, lurking in the background, felt, but not seen, stood an old woman rocking and keening without sound. I was unable to reach the old woman or even figure out why she was there. I recoiled from the identities of these nocturnal visitors. My mind refused to probe the depths of my dreams. So much so that I was left with only a vague form of the dreams when I awoke in the mornings.

But the dreams came often and unbidden.

***

July bloomed hot and I returned again and again to the little cove on the lake, not far from the blackberry patch. An old fallen tree balanced over the shallows, an invitation to slip off my boots and roll up my trouser legs. I could creep out to soak my feet in the cool water. The midmorning sun warmed the water and dared me to slide into the lake. I resisted. The cove was protected, yes, but I was never sure if someone would appear. Bare feet were one thing, but to go further might be inviting disaster.

I voiced my concern to Hiinuk Waka. "I would so much like to bathe in the lake. The water is wonderfully warm now, and my hair is so difficult to handle in the kitchen washtub."

"Many use the lake. I also, in your secret cove. After a long winter, it is good to enter the lake again."

"But I'm afraid someone will come upon me. That simply would not do," I said.

"Put a cloth just off the trail. It is a signal. The women of that house..."

Of course, I knew which house she meant. That house on the western edge of town. Juanita's house with the girls no one would sit near in church. The house reputed to have a large bathing chamber in the back. A room I'd never dream of using, of course.

"...the women of that house come here often."

"I never see them," I said. "How discreet."

"Often after church, when families go back to the farms or are visiting. Or very late in the afternoon. Then no one comes up the trail."

"I see," I said. "That makes sense." I was a bit uncomfortable, but the lake called to me. "So, if I place a cloth...?"

"Everyone will know to go on. No one will bother you. Tie it down the path a ways. Not right at the trail. No one needs the temptation."

I laughed. "I understand. I will have to see if I have the nerve to bathe in the lake. But it would be such a luxury from the kitchen."

"The lake will welcome you," she said.

So, this one July day, midweek, I slipped out under the pretense of looking for acorns and headed for the secret cove. Which I knew was not really all that secret. I did as Hiinuk Waka suggested and tied my red bandana on a sapling a little way in off the main trail, but a fair distance from the lakeshore. Far enough so that no one could see around the two or three bends in the path to the lake.

The cove's calm water reflected the shore and the trees. Though shallow near the shore, the water darkened out farther, a shade at a time, from blue to gray, the color of slate. It looked like I would not be surprised by a sudden dropoff.

I wanted to slip into the water fully clothed and then disrobe, but the idea of having to put on wet clothes stopped me. I left my boots and socks on the bank. After a thorough investigation of the area, I sat down and slid off my trousers. My shirt—almost long enough to be a nightshirt, came down over my thighs. I took a deep breath and slipped out of my underdrawers, folding them inside my trousers. After setting the rough bar of soap where I could reach it from the water, I hitched up my shirt enough so the hem would stay dry and stepped off the bank. The water lapped around my legs, warm as tepid tea.

Well, I couldn't very well bathe half-clothed as I still was. I turned my back to the bank and inched backwards until I was up against the fallen tree. I pulled my arms out of my shirt, lifted it over my head and balled it up. I set it on the tree. It would be the closest thing I could reach when I was ready to get out.

I grabbed the soap and walked out from shore until the water lapped my waist. Hiinuk Waka was right. The lake embraced me with its warmth. I submerged completely, keeping my eyes open in the clear water. My hair spread out around and above me like an ebony curtain as I sank. The sun streaked through the water, striping it with white and blue. When I couldn't hold my breath any longer, I lifted my face to the surface, letting my hair float. I checked the shoreline, but no one was around. I felt like I was scrubbing off the winter, the spring, and the sweat of the summer.

July permeated my skin. I finally felt I belonged. Woods Portage was truly home. Gust loved me, and I him. Father grew prosperous. Hiinuk Waka finally accepted me. Sometimes I felt almost a daughter to her, though we never spoke of such things.

I closed my eyes and turned to the sun. I wanted to stay in the lake all afternoon. But I would be missed. I didn't tell Father where I was going. Perhaps I needed one secret, one place to cherish for myself.

Whatever the reason, I knew I would be back to the cove. But for now, I had better get out and get back to reality.

Stretching out underwater, I stroked for the shore. I set my feet on the bottom and stood up. Closing my eyes, I bent backwards to let the water run through my hair. It felt so good.

I lifted my head and opened my eyes.

Gust emerged from the path.

We both froze for less than the blink of an eye.

I crossed my hands over my chest and sank into the lake. He turned his back so quickly, he almost lost his balance.

I wondered if I really even saw his face. And more importantly, if he saw...me. "What are you doing here?" I called. I would not lose my composure. "Didn't you see the bandana on the tree?"

"Yes," he answered, without looking back at me, "but I thought it was Walking Elk's." He cleared his throat. "I'd better go."

"Yes, you'd better," I said.

He walked away without another word, disappearing in a trice.

I waited a good long time before I summoned enough courage to get out of the water. Once dressed again, I realized I dropped the soap in the lake. I wasn't about to disrobe and go back to search for it. I wasn't even sure I'd ever come back to the cove. But yes, of course. I'd be back. The water would draw me back.

I tried to avoid Gust, but it was hard. After a few days, I gave up. Though we didn't talk about it, we seemed to come to an understanding about our...lake encounter. I, for one, knew I did nothing wrong. Truly, neither had he. We both turned away as quickly as we could have. I wasn't even sure Gust saw anything that would compromise me. And I knew he would never reveal stumbling upon me in the water. I certainly wasn't about to say anything either.

At first, we passed in the street, in the mercantile, in the parsonage without doing more than smile sideways. But the discomfort lessened. Gust even made a stuttering attempt to apologize, but I stopped him before he made fools of both of us. We nodded, smiled, and returned to...well, as normal as it could be. It fostered a new respect between us.

Gust stopped me in church that Sunday.

"Louise!" he called from the front. "Wait a moment, please."

I was hesitant to turn back. But the sun came through the windows, stretching out paths of light filled with shimmering motes, drawing me forward. Reverend Iverson's sermon was uplifting, fitting for the lovely day given to us. Gust's blond hair shone in the sun, glinting like a saint's halo. Just as in those stories, my heart gave a little jump.

Gust came down the aisle, striding in and out of shafts of sun. When he reached out to me, I went to meet him. I just couldn't help it. He was my comfort and my friend. His smile was like a bouquet of wildflowers.

"Come here, my sweet," he said, and I entered his embrace. I could feel in my soul what he wanted from me.

From the day he kissed me in the kitchen, I knew this was the man I wanted to spend my life with. He was so...solid. Soon, he would be ordained, and could assist his father here in Woods Portage. There was plenty of work for the both of them, what with the surrounding farms, the people coming and going with the seasons, and the growing town itself. It would be a comfort to his father to have Gust take some of the weight of the work off his shoulders.

I smelled the fragrance of soap on his shirt and looked up into his eyes. "I know what you want," I said. My discomfort melted away.

He threw back his head and laughed. "Do you now? And what would that be?"

"Oh, no, Gust Iverson. I will not take this from you." I smiled up at him.

He took my face in his hands. "I must say this quickly, before I lose my nerve." He cleared his throat. "Will you do the honor of being my wife? I love you, Louise Wright."

I couldn't contain myself. My laughter rose up through every pore in my body, I was so happy. "Yes! Yes, yes, Gust Iverson. I will marry you."

We collapsed to the floor in the aisle, kneeling before one another, arms still around each other.

"What is more appropriate than to promise this to each other here in this church," he said.

"Where we first met," I added.

He kissed me, deep and with such tenderness. "Come. We'll tell my father."

I held up my hand in protest. "My father first."

Gust laughed. "He already knows. I asked for your hand two weeks ago."

I batted his shoulder. "He never said a word!"

"I swore him to secrecy. But they're both in the parsonage, waiting for us." He released me and stood up, pulling me up with him. "Let's go."

We agreed to marry when he returned to Woods Portage after his ordination in the spring.

Chapter 23
Lou

Lou, Kapi, and Heddy stood in the overgrown cemetery behind the little church. The sunlight filtered through the trees, but it didn't make the place look any more inviting. Most of the headstones tilted at various angles, though some of them had tumbled flat to the ground, their remaining pedestals green with moss among the gray stone. The grass—weeds, really—was almost knee high, obscuring the smaller gravestones, turning the little cemetery into an obstacle course.

"Great setting for a murder mystery," Heddy said.

"In this small town?" Lou's voice scoffed. "Nothing so dramatic from what I've seen."

Kapi tsked. "All the horror books take place in small towns."

"Well, this isn't a novel," Lou said. She stooped to the nearest toppled headstone and peered at the engraving, made almost invisible by weather. "We really need to get the historical group in here to clean up this place. I never even thought about that before. It wouldn't take much with all of us working."

"It's a small bunch who care," Heddy said.

"I don't care how big we are. We can do this. We should do this," Lou said.

Kapi added, "Like eating an elephant." The others blinked. "You know, one forkful at a time."

A burst of laughter announced Abe's arrival. "She's right, ya know. Wouldn't take much, once we get started. Might take all summer, though, even with all this stuff." He was toting a gas-powered weed whacker and a pair of long-handled pruning shears. He balanced the shears on a nearby pedestal whose headstone lay on the ground.

"Who cares?" Kapi said. "Maybe we'll discover someone famous."

The other three looked skeptical. "Nobody famous ever came out of Woods Portage," Lou said.

"Well, you've been here longer than I have," Abe said. "But you never know. Who's to say who's important and who's not?"

"Fine, old man. I see you've got your tools and we've got our work boots. Let's see what we can dig up," Lou said.

"Dig up?" Heddy's laugh was deep and hearty. "Nobody's getting me to dig up anything!"

"For a smart woman, you sure are dumb," Lou said. She stuck her tongue out at Heddy.

Heddy was still laughing. "Takes one to know one."

"Okay, okay," Abe said. "Enough caterwauling. I've got a couple of wire brushes here, and some bleach. How's about we get to work?" He swung a backpack off his shoulders and set it on the ground. It almost disappeared in the weeds.

Lou held up two buckets and thrust them into Kapi's hands. "Here. Go get us some water. There's a spigot at the back of the church."

"I'll cut down some of these weeds. Where shall I start?" Without waiting for an answer, Abe dipped into his backpack for a pair of headphones, put them on, and started his weed whacker. He began clearing the area around him, then moving outward in circles. The greenery around him fell like snow melting on a hot stove.

Less than two hours later, Abe had swung into a rhythm that cleared a good portion of the little cemetery. Lou and Kapi scrubbed the headstones Abe cleared, while Heddy recorded the names and dates she could read. Some of the headstones had "Loving Wife" or "Beloved Child." A couple were more elaborate, and Heddy would assume a mournful voice as she read them out loud.

"Remember, visitor, this too is your destiny." "Angels carry her to the bosom of the Lord." "Typhus took this gentle soul."

Finally, Lou called, "Okay! Enough. It's a cemetery, not a t-shirt shop."

Heddy pretended to ignore her, but she ratcheted back on her volume.

Even after they were cleared, many of the gray stones were damaged or so weathered that only a portion of the engravings were readable, or even visible.

The sun moved overhead as they worked, supervising their efforts, dappling the ground. Slain weeds lay everywhere, flattened even more as they tramped around, cleaning and recording.

"Hey! I found something!" Kapi's voice boomed out from behind a tree. She stuck her head around and gestured them over.

Abe was still working away, oblivious to Kapi's call.

Heddy was kneeling in the deep grass, but levered herself upright and shuffled off to get Abe.

Abe shut off the weed whacker and followed Heddy to join the group. He slipped his headphones down on his neck and leaned the tool against a tree. "Got something, do ya?"

"So, we're here," Lou interrupted, flapping a hand at Abe. "What did you find?"

Kapi pointed to a small stone, almost flush with the ground. "Look at this. Katherine I-something. I can't read the last name. b—born, I guess—1870. d 1873."

Lou bent down. "I. Can't be Iverson. Can it? I wonder who?" She ran her fingers across the faint indentations. "Weather really did a number here. I can hardly read it."

Kapi poured a little water across the face of the stone and the carving emerged a bit clearer. Heddy captured everything that appeared. "'Beloved Daughter.' Wonder what she died of? Only three years old. What a pity."

Abe was rummaging around behind the little stone, sweeping his hands through the grass. He bumped up against a toppled headstone, broken into several pieces. "C'mere and help me push these together. It looks like a family headstone."

Lou crawled over to him. "Wait a minute. This doesn't make sense. This Katherine I. fits in the years my great-grandmother was alive. But I thought they lost a son. Maybe it's another family." She shook her head. "Huh. Far as I know, there weren't any other Iversons in town, though. Besides, my grandmother told me the whole Iverson family was buried in the new cemetery." She swept a hand across her cheek, leaving a streak of dirt behind.

"Now *that* doesn't make sense," Heddy said. "The new cemetery wasn't established until...what? Well, I'm not sure, but it sure wasn't in existence back then. This must be the original family plot. Did they move the bodies or something?"

Lou chewed on her lip. "I have no idea." She squinted down at the stone again. Bracing herself, she pressed her face closer. Squinting, she shook her head. She turned to Abe. "Abe, what's on those pieces you found?"

They gathered around and pushed and prodded the broken pieces of stone together. Most of the writing was so damaged, it was illegible. But bits and pieces of letters emerged as they scrubbed.

"Wait! Wait, wait!" Kapi held out her arms to stop them. "Look here across the top." She bent low over the largest chunk. "V-E-R-S. That might be part of Iverson, right?" She turned to Lou.

Lou swept her scrub brush across the face of the stone. ATHER appeared from the grime. "Father?" she said. "If that's right, then there must be a Mother there somewhere." Her hand started to tremble. "I don't think..."

"Here. Give me your brush," Abe said. His short strokes soon enough showed MOTHER emerging from the moss and lichen. "This must be the Iverson plot."

Kapi bent over the top, below what appeared to be the family name, and worked away until a weeping willow was visible.

"Stop a minute," Heddy ordered. When they sat back, she sketched what was on the broken headstone. The willow tree, bending over the two words, MOTHER, FATHER. "Okay. Go ahead. See if there are any dates down below there."

"Here," Abe said, motioning to Lou's brush. "You should do it."

But Lou didn't trust the steadiness of her hand. If this was indeed the old Iverson plot...well, it was too much of a surprise right now. "No, go ahead. Abe can do it. I'll watch for...whatever." She was a bit fearful that she'd be disappointed. She didn't want to ruin the whole thing by jumping to conclusions. Maybe there was another Iverson family, though she doubted it.

"Yeah," Kapi said. "You don't want to jinx it."

Lou was startled that their minds were apparently in synch. But she ducked her head and found a nearby fallen stone to perch on while she waited.

"Here," Abe said. "There's something else here, way at the bottom of this other piece that broke off. Lemme try..." Abe's brushing revealed what looked like a name and a date: TEVEN 1875. "Can't read the first letter, but looks like another Iverson, probably Steven. Only one year there, though," Abe said.

"One year," Heddy said. "That usually means a baby born who died a short time after birth." She added to her sketch.

Lou shook her head and tsked. "I've seen others like that. Sad story." She frowned. Something tickled at the back of her brain. Her thoughts were interrupted by Kapi.

"Something here too. Pretty faint, but there are some numbers here under that MOTHER." Kapi gave a final swipe at the stone.

Lou held her breath.

"LOUI—I can't read the rest, but the birth year looks like 1899."

"Too late," Lou said. "I know Louise was born earlier—"

"No, no, wait a minute." Kapi leaned in. "I don't think those are 9s." She rubbed across the numbers again. "1. 8. 9? No. That's a 4. There's another one. 1844."

Lou puffed out her cheeks and blew out a breath. "That sounds right. I think Louise Wright Iverson was born then."

"This must be her grave!" Heddy was sketching in the date.

They were silent as Heddy worked. A breeze came up, drying their sweat and sending the chaff of cut weeds spiraling up into miniscule tornadoes. The sun seemed planted in the sky, waiting for something to happen.

Lou shook her head. "No. This can't be Louise's grave. She's buried in the new cemetery. Well, at least I thought she was. Next to my grandmother, Marit Liebermann, her daughter."

The sun slanted down onto the stone, like a reading lamp on an old book.

"Died 1875," Kapi read from the stone. "Yeah, that's a seven. 1875."

"That's...that might be the right date, but I'd have to check." Lou pursed her lips and leaned forward, hands clasped on her knees. "Wait. What was that baby's year over there, Abe?"

"1875," he supplied. "Looks like Louise had a baby, then died the same year as the baby."

"Lots of women died in childbirth." Lou put her hand to her mouth. "The family story said she died of a miscarriage. But it looks like..."

"Look," Heddy said, her voice gentle. "This has to be your great-grandmother's grave. The Iverson grave. Somebody must've moved the bodies later. Or maybe they just put up a stone, like in memoriam, over at the new cemetery."

"That actually makes sense," Lou said, coming out of her slump. "I know that the new cemetery was established by the time my grandmother and grandfather died. Marit and Siegfried Liebermann were both buried there, and that was around—if I remember right—1930-something. No, wait. I was 15, so she died— that's Marit, my grandmother— in 1936. My grandmother died in 1936."

"So, the Iverson line could've been buried here. At least the start of the family. Like when Louise moved here from—where did she move from again?" Heddy asked.

"From Black River Falls, I think?" Lou answered. "I'm not sure of the exact year." She got up and walked closer to the old, broken headstone. "This has to be them. Doesn't it?"

Kapi was busy scrubbing below the FATHER on the headstone. "Gust," Kapi read. "Isn't that short for Gustav?"

"For some," Lou said. "But Louise's husband was just Gust, I think. That's what's on the stone in the new cemetery." She lowered herself to the ground, hearing her knees protest. "Any dates?"

"Just birth year. 1841." Kapi removed the moss she'd scrubbed loose. "That sound right?"

"I think so," Lou whispered. "This has to be them."

"You never knew their graves were here?" Kapi asked.

Lou shook her head. "I figured they were buried over there." She waved in the direction of the newer cemetery. "That's where my mother always took me to water the flowers. We went every week in the summer. I was the one who had to pump the water." She was lost in a memory for a moment.

She snapped back as Abe crab-crawled away from them, leaves and debris clinging to his pants. "I think there's something else here," he said.

"What do you mean, 'something else'? There was no 'something else' for Louise." Lou pulled on her nose. "According to my mother—at least, what *her* mother told her—Louise died when she had a miscarriage. But it looks more like a stillborn, or a baby who died quickly. You know, they didn't bury miscarried or stillborn babies in those years."

"Yes, they did," Heddy said. "Well, not miscarried babies. But stillborns were usually buried way back at the edge of the cemetery in unmarked graves, because they weren't really considered…well, babies."

"Either way," Lou said, "there shouldn't be anything else here in the old Iverson plot. Louise only had two children that died. Well, one child, one miscarriage." She frowned. "Or more likely, one toddler that died, one baby that died. And one baby that lived, of course. My grandmother, Marit."

"I don't know about that." Abe said, stood up and pointed down to a patch of thick grass. "Lookee here."

"Tell me," Lou said. "I don't want to get up." Things were appearing from nowhere, it seemed. She wasn't sure she trusted herself to stand steady.

"Get on over here," Abe said. "I think you need to see this." He pulled up some of the grass, exposing what looked like part of another stone.

"Oh, for Pete's sake, old man," Lou groused, partly to mask her confusion. But she sighed and stood up.

By the time Lou made her way to Abe, he had scraped away much of the dirt that covered the flat stone.

"This one was practically buried. If I hadn't seen a corner that looked a little too perfect, I would never have known it was another one," Abe said. He took one more swipe at the little headstone.

Lou set her hand on Abe's shoulder and leaned over. "The lettering looks pretty clear on this one," she said.

"Preserved under the dirt, the way it looks," Abe said.

"So, what does it say?"

Abe brushed off the last of the dirt. "Dorothea Winn."

Kapi giggled. "Who'd name a kid Dorothea Winn?"

"Was there a Winn family in town?" Abe asked.

Lou and Heddy looked at each other. Lou chewed on her lip and shrugged. "Not any that I know of. Pretty strange name."

"Who knows? But it's part of the Iverson plot, the way it looks, not a family named Winn. Maybe that was her middle name," Heddy said. "Anything else?" She sidled around the other side of the stone. "How about a date?"

Abe peered closer at the stone. "Maybe. Kapi, put some water on this, will you?"

Kapi dribbled water from her bucket over the stone. "See anything?"

"Maybe." Abe worked his fingers across the stone, searching for more indentations. "Yup. Look here. 1865."

"1865 what?" Lou asked. "Born, or what?"

"It says, 'Died an Infant'." Abe's voice was a whisper.

Lou and Kapi exchanged a glance. "We gotta go home and check some of those papers and receipts and stuff," Kapi said.

Cradle not paid for.

They were already out of the cemetery before Kapi's "home" struck Lou right in the heart.

Chapter 24
Louise Wright

I couldn't resist the cove. I knew, of course, that I'd go back. Gust bursting in on me so suddenly was an aberration. Now he knew to avoid the place when I was there. He knew my bandana. I took to tying it so it couldn't be missed. If I had my berry buckets with me, I left them there too, at the intersection of the trails. Right in the middle of the path, where they couldn't be missed either.

This day, the water was a brilliant blue. Out beyond, where it went deeper, even there the gray of slate had surrendered to the sun and the water was indigo. It didn't take long to disrobe and slip into the water. The water soaked clear down to my bones, washing away all the little aches and stresses.

I knew I wouldn't be disturbed again. But then came Juanita.

She came swinging down the path and planted herself on the fallen log next to my clothes. This time I had heard the whistle of a little tune coming down the path. I recognized Juanita's song.

Often when I made deliveries to her house—that house—she was playing her parlor piano. She knew I loved the tune, and loved to hear her play. I could hear her as I drove around the back to unload her order. My father or Walking Elk would deliver the heavier loads, but I always took the smaller ones.

She was older than I, and she treated me like a daughter. I suppose I needed that, my mother having died back in Green Bay. Whatever the reason, we had grown close over the months, even though she never acknowledged me in public, other than a slight inclination of her head, which set her hat feathers dancing. I did her the honor of doing the same. It was easier for both of us if we were seen to be only civil to one another. That, for some, was even too much. I paid them no mind.

"Louise, you are having far too much fun," she said as she settled her skirt around her.

I was up to my chin in the lake. "What brings you out here? Didn't you see my buckets or my bandana? You know the rules." Though to tell true, I wasn't disappointed to see her. It was the only time she ever sought me out. If indeed this was deliberate.

"I thought I would visit you on your territory instead," she said. She slipped her shoes and stockings off, tucked her skirt up under her, and dangled her feet in the water. "I hope you're not too shocked."

"Oh, Juanita, I'm delighted!"

She held up a hand. "Call me Rose. My name is really Juanita Rose, but my friends call me Rose." She sent me a dazzling smile. "My customers call me Juanita. And you, my dear, are not a customer." She gave out with a hearty laugh, far too deep for such a delicate woman. I loved it.

"All right...Rose," I said and smiled back. "But I'm curious. Why did you come out here alone?"

"I came to see you, of course. You, in your own environs. I've only seen you to talk to in my kitchen or on my back porch." She ducked her chin and gave me a sly look sideways. "This feels more...like friends." Her face took on a serious quality.

I couldn't help but giggle. She looked so vulnerable. It struck me that she couldn't have many friends. Perhaps none. Her "girls" were employees, or perhaps assistants. But I didn't think she would call them friends. "Well, we are friends, after all," I said. Her face lifted and her eyes twinkled in the sunlight. "And I am delighted to call you so."

"Even if we can't really—"

I interrupted her before she could say something painful, or shameful. "This shall be our secret. Rose. I like that name." Though she was considerably older than I, I felt a real bond with her. Both of us women alone, in one way or another.

"Well." She gathered up her stockings and shook her feet clear of water as best she could. "I must be getting back. My girls will be rising, and I need to get them cleaning and mending. No good fairies around to do our work for us, you know." She pulled on her stockings and slid her feet into her shoes.

"Rose?"

"Yes, dear. What is it?"

"I'll try and spend a bit more time when I make deliveries. And I can come by more often too. Father sometimes sends me out to the farms to collect produce and such. It's quite easy to stop on the way back into town."

Rose puckered her lips and frowned. "Won't your father mind?"

"He might huff a bit, but he won't mind. He has often enough said how he regrets how many of the people, women mostly, treat you. He knows how women need other women. He said it often enough to me after Mother died." I smiled at her. "He understands. I won't keep it a secret from him. But I won't broadcast it either."

Rose laughed. "Your father is a gem. Cherish him, Louise." She gathered her skirts and stood up. "I look forward to our next visit."

"As do I," I said, and gave her a little head bob.

"Finish rinsing your hair, Louise. You look like a ripe dandelion." She gave a merry wave and set off up the path. Within a heartbeat, she was out of sight.

What an odd visit! But I understood her need of a friend. Before we actually talked to one another, we had spent plenty of time sending the briefest of glances as we passed in church or in the store or on the road. Her entry into my world took courage for her. I could have easily denied her. That would have ruined any chance of harmony between us, and I probably would never have made another delivery to her "house."

But now she entered my world, willingly come to me. And given me the gift of her name. Rose.

I sank into the water and swirled my hair around. It made me feel like a mermaid.

I kept my eyes closed, blew out bubbles, and rose to the surface. I stretched my arms up into the sunshine and shook my wet hair down my back. When I opened my eyes, Walking Elk was standing on the bank, sunlight shining off his chest in sparks and glints.

I was too shocked to say anything. Or do anything. There I stood, water to my waist. But I didn't hide myself, as I had for Gust.

Walking Elk was looking at me, to be sure, but his eyes stayed fixed on mine. As strange as it sounds, I felt no shame, no guilt. Before he turned to go back along the path, he sent me a twitch of a smile. Which I returned.

And then he was gone.

Oh, Louise! What just happened? I spun around to face out into the lake, closed my eyes and sank below the surface. I should drown right here and now! But I didn't want to.

It took me a long time to gather the courage to go back to shore. It took even longer to stand up, gather my clothes, dry off and dress. Where was Walking Elk now? Watching me? No, that just didn't sound like him.

I started home, gathering my bandana and berry buckets where I left them. Wherever Walking Elk was now, his foray to the lake was a deliberate one. He saw the buckets and the bandana, I was sure.

My mind was awhirl with confusion. Why did I not hide myself when he appeared? Why was I so drawn to him? This, I knew, was forbidden. Only the early trappers took Indian wives. I knew of no Indian who had taken a white woman.

I caught myself up short. What was I thinking? Impossible. I would be shunned. Or worse. But I felt so...strongly toward him. This visit of his. All of his quiet ways and gentleness toward me, did he have feelings for me? Was this love of a sort? I could barely think the word, much less articulate it aloud.

Chapter 25
Lou

Papers and more were once again scattered on the chest between the chairs in Lou's living room. Kapi, sitting on the floor, and Lou, perched on the edge of her overstuffed chair, bent over the receipt for the cradle, reading, turning it over, peering at every letter, as if the paper itself would reach a point of irritation and explain itself. It didn't.

Abe gestured for Heddy to push a second box over to him. "Maybe there's something in here. We haven't checked out everything."

Lou lifted her head long enough to grunt at him. "Go at it, old man. But it didn't look like much of anything in there to me." She took the receipt from Kapi and held it up to the light, then shook her head. "Nothing."

"Can I help?" Heddy asked. She had pulled up Lou's desk chair and sat with elbows on knees, hands clasped in front of her.

Abe huffed and shrugged. "Looks like a bunch of junk in here." He slid his hand under a bunch of loose papers and peered underneath.

"Here. Let me take those," Heddy said. "I can sift through that and you can see what else is there."

Abe handed over the pile, and examined what was left in the box. "Whew! Smells like my grandmother's attic."

Lou looked up long enough to say, "Kind of like your shoes, wouldn't you say?" She missed the raised finger and the ready retort, cut off by Heddy before he could voice anything.

"We may be old, sweetie, but we still qualify as fragrance, not stink."

"Eau de skunkalicious," Lou said.

"Toilet water," Heddy added.

"What? Toilet water?" Kapi's hand poised in midair. "Who'd wear—"

"Merely another name for cologne," Heddy said. She laughed. "My mother kidded around all the time calling it 'collog-knee.' I was out of my teens before I realized that 'linger-ee' was really lingerie." The pile on her lap started a landslide and she whooped as she tried to grab the lot. Too late. Most of it slid to the floor. She got up and bent over to gather up what fell.

"Whoo-ee! What a view!" Abe whistled.

Heddy turned and batted him with a magazine.

"Watch it! That stuff'll fall apart," Abe cautioned.

Heddy ignored him. "I'm going home to pick up our supper. Everything's ready, I just have to run over and get it. I'll leave you all to the past." She set the last of the papers on her chair, straightening the edges so they wouldn't tumble again, and headed for the back door. "I'll be back. Hope you find something." And she was gone.

Abe shuffled through the papers stacked on Heddy's chair. "Doesn't look like there's anything here. Not even old newspapers. Just empty ledger papers and stuff." He set it aside and squinted into the box. "Humph. Couple of books in here." He pulled them out and riffled through the pages. "Numbers and dates. Costs and debts and payments."

Lou and Kapi set aside their work. "Anything interesting?" Lou asked.

"Maybe," Abe said, pulling out a thin sheaf of papers. "Here's a deed for land west of town." He separated the few sheets, setting them on the chest. "And a list of building materials—costs and such. And a final receipt for a house built on that land."

Heddy came banging in the back door. "Come and get it! Fixings for sandwiches and a pot of clam chowder." She came through into the front room. "Did you find anything?"

"Maybe," Abe repeated. "Stuff from a house built west of town somewhere."

"Where?" Lou and Heddy asked at the same time. Lou reached for the paper in Abe's hand.

Abe shrugged. "Not sure. You can probably figure it out."

Lou was nodding, followed by Heddy, who was looking over her shoulder.

"Yup," Heddy said. "I think I know which house."

"The Rose Arbor," Lou said.

"That big old Victorian that's a restaurant?" Abe asked.

Lou and Heddy nodded. "The year looks about right," Heddy said, "based on what the couple that owns it said."

"Who built it?" Kapi asked.

Abe laughed. "Here we sit, and no one thought to check that."

Lou smoothed out the receipt. "It says it was paid by Mr. Albert Wood."

Heddy was nodding. "Same here." She held up the land deed.

"So that old house was Wood's house," Lou said. "But I don't think he ever lived there. Everything I've heard is that he lived above the ferry office."

"All I know," said Heddy, "is that The Rose Arbor was once a cat house."

They all looked at Kapi. "What?" she said. "So, it was an animal shelter."

When they all laughed—all but Kapi, that is—Kapi's face took on the look of thunder. "What's so funny?" She started to stand up, but Lou put her hand on her shoulder.

"In those days, a cat house was a house for ladies of the evening," Heddy said.

"Oh, stop beating around the bush," Lou said. "It was a house of prostitution."

"What?" Kapi sank back down to the floor.

"Don't look so naïve," Lou said. "You know perfectly well what that means."

"Well, yeah, but..." Kapi ground to a halt.

"But what? You now having second thoughts about going out to eat in a restaurant that used to advertise a different kind of entertainment?" Lou chuckled.

Kapi sent her a crooked look, but didn't say anything.

Lou swallowed. "All right. It is kind of weird to think about it." Small concession.

"So, Wood built a house, never lived in it, then sold it to a madam and her girls?" Abe said.

"Looks like it," Heddy said. "But I'm starving, now that you mentioned the restaurant. Stuff's in the kitchen. Let's go eat."

"I have a better idea," Kapi said. "Let's go eat at The Rose Arbor." She sent the others a sideways smirk.

The others crowed. "Done and done!" Abe said.

Chapter 26
Louise Wright

For the next few days, I only saw Walking Elk at a distance, and could avoid meeting him. I was deliberate in that. But I couldn't really avoid his grandmother. What had been comfortable times in the rectory kitchen took on a whole new tenor. The air felt thicker to me, vibrating with secrets.

"My grandson is searching for a wife," Hiinuk Waka said one afternoon as we worked at mending.

I pricked my finger and thrust it into my mouth. The sudden taste of blood kept me grounded. "Ah, yes?" was all I could manage.

"Have you seen him in his bandolier?" she asked, never pausing in her stitches. For that, I was most grateful.

"Bandolier?" I asked. My voice shook so, I was afraid she'd look up and realize...well, everything. But she didn't.

"When young men are ready to marry, they wear those. A bandolier." She swept her hand from her left shoulder to her right side at her waist. "It is covered with fancy beading. I made the bandolier for Walking Elk. Only the finest beads and embroidery."

I flashed to Walking Elk at the lake, with the sun on his chest, on the beading, glinting.

"Like the birds." She knotted her thread and bit off the end. "Men birds have finery to attract the women. Human men do the same. Bandoliers are the Ho-Chunk way." She looked up and smiled. "I am glad to see him ready for a wife." She picked up a shirt and found the button which needed replacing.

I lowered my chin, hoping to hide the flush in my face. I could feel the heat. Before I could create something to say, she added, "He is a good age to take a wife and begin a family."

I nodded, but found I could not say one single word. Either I would burst into tears, or I would confess all. And then still weep. I felt such desire for him surge through my heart. And yet... And yet, there was Gust. I loved Gust. I knew that as well as I knew the sun would rise in the morning. My heart, my very soul, felt torn and ragged.

I set down my mending. "It's getting late. I must get back to the mercantile and help Father." I attempted a smile, hoping I would look relaxed. "I'm going out berry-picking tomorrow. Would you like some too? I'm sure I can pick enough for both of us."

She was busy settling the button in place, and didn't look up. But she said, "Yes. I will take berries for a pie."

I said goodbye and left before she had a chance to glance over at me. I stopped on the back porch and had to steady myself on the railing before I could make my way home. If Walking Elk was looking for a wife, why did he wear the bandolier to the cove at the lake?

I was frightened. But I was trembling inside. I was even more afraid to examine why.

The next day, once my duties for Father were fulfilled, I changed into trousers and boots, and gathered up my buckets.

"I'm off to pick berries, Father," I called into the store. "I shouldn't be long."

"Take your time," he answered. "We're not busy and I can spare you." He smiled at me in the doorway. "It's a fair trade-off for one of your pies."

I went to him and pressed a kiss to his cheek. "Flattery will get you everywhere." I turned to go out through our quarters.

"Take a hat!" he called after me.

I swept the old straw hat off the hook and sauntered out into the sun.

It didn't take me long to make my way up along the main street, and past the church and rectory. Within a few steps the cemetery disappeared behind me and I continued along the road taking me past the path to the cove, and up farther towards Hiinuk Waka's little log house. A mile or so beyond was that lovely berry patch. I never picked it clean. After all, the animals had to eat also, and there were plenty of berries for us all.

At that time of day, the sunlight dappled the ground without scorching it. The breeze was warm and comforting. I couldn't think of a better place to be. My troubled mind eased some, and I even began to sing a little. In church, I tried not to sing very loud, because I sounded like a frog in search of a mate. Not even like those sweet spring peepers that emerge as the weather warmed. I couldn't help but laugh out loud at the thought of my inept attempts at harmony.

I had begun on a third bucket when I heard a voice whispering my name. I stopped, fearful of what I would see if I turned to meet it. I closed my eyes. I took a deep breath. I turned around.

Yes, there he was, standing in the shade at the edge of the small clearing. In spite of that, I could see the beading on his bandolier rising and falling as he breathed. I myself couldn't breathe at all.

"I'll help." He came toward me and I had all I could do to stand still. Part of me wanted to run away. Part of me wanted to run to him.

I took in a great gulp of air. "That would be most appreciated," I said. I couldn't trust myself to say more. I handed him the last empty bucket.

We picked in silence for a while. My mind wanted me to say, "Look at me. I see your bandolier. I know what it means." But I quashed those thoughts. As for normal conversation, that well was quite dry.

Walking Elk picked rapidly, as if he must keep his hands busy. "I didn't mean to scare you," he said.

I knew what he meant. "You didn't scare me." It was the truth. But that, in itself, did scare me. Where were we to go from here? "Your grandmother tells me you...Tells me that the bandolier means you are..." My words stumbled to a halt.

"Yes, they mean I will look for a wife, a partner." He continued to pick, moving along in a smooth rhythm that was counterpoint to mine.

I nodded. I groped for what to say next. "I suppose you will travel to Black River Falls, to your people." I came to a dead end. What did I expect him to say? Yes? I'm looking for a Ho-Chunk girl to marry? If he left...then what? Foolish girl, I thought, of course he will marry one of his own kind. That must be the way it must be.

He stopped picking and looked over at me. "I will go, but not to Black River Falls, where my people summer." He frowned and resumed picking.

Well? I wanted to say, then where are you going? But I was afraid to ask it, to face his going away. Afraid I'd never see him again.

He got there ahead of me. "I am going to Nebraska." The words that followed were said so low and fast that I missed them.

"I'm sorry," I said. "What? But why Nebraska? Isn't that where you came from not so long ago?"

Rather than repeat what I missed, he answered, "Yes, Nebraska. I have friends there. Here there is Grandmother. I want her to come with me." His hands went still. "But she won't come."

I couldn't help myself. "Must you go? Really, must you?" I clamped my teeth together to keep myself from saying more, saying too much. My bucket hung from my hands. I simply couldn't make my fingers work when my mind was in such turmoil.

Walking Elk turned to me, and set his bucket down. "Yes, I must." His eyes said so much more. They spoke pain, loneliness. They seemed to reflect our future. My own eyes welled up with tears. His eyes shifted to hopefulness and to a control barely held in check.

"Will you come?"

By the way he looked at me, I knew he did not mean Nebraska. I nodded and he slipped the bandolier from his shoulder, letting it drop to the ground between us. We reached for each other.

***

Two days later, he was gone. But I knew he already found a bride in Woods Portage.

Chapter 27
Lou

"There's a box here," Kapi said. She pulled it out from under the yellow newspapers announcing various local events that no one remembered anymore. The papers disintegrated along the edges as she handled them. "It was at the very bottom."

"I don't know why I let you talk me into grubbing around in this stuff again tonight," Lou grumbled. "We had a nice dinner at The Rose Arbor. And wine always makes me tired. We should be going to bed." Abe and Heddy had already waved them goodnight and headed home.

Kapi glanced at her, but gone was the frown. Gone were the pinched lips. Gone was the vindictive look. Maybe things would work out after all. It was worth a shot. "All right, all right," Lou conceded. She plopped down in her chair and settled back. "You get to do all the work. I'll just sit here and you can tell me what you find."

Kapi sent Lou a smile. It was slow to develop, but it was a smile nonetheless. She cleared the top of the chest that sat between them, and set the small box on her lap. "Let's see what's in here." The corners of the top were crunched and torn, and the box itself sagged from the weight of the papers and such that had been stacked on top of it. Kapi took her time prying off the top. "Where did you find this anyway? Do you remember?"

"I think it was in one of the bottom drawers of Wood's desk. He had so much crap, I don't remember what was where." Lou leaned forward, setting her forearms on her thighs. "Whatcha got in there?"

Kapi used her fingertips to lift pieces up, one at a time. "Photos, it looks like. Not many." She pulled out sheets of onionskin paper as well. "This is between each one."

"Huh," Lou said. "Must've been stuff he really wanted to protect. Let's see."

Kapi began handing them off, one by one.

Lou lined up each photo side by side on the chest. "That's it? Only five?"

"I think so," Kapi said. She shoved the thin sheets of paper back in the box and set it aside. She scooted around the chest and hunkered down next to Lou. They both bent their heads lower over the images.

"Look at this one." Kapi picked up a photo of a man standing on the steps of a stone building. "Isn't that the ferry office?"

Lou took the picture from her and felt the edges bend and flake. "We'd better not handle these. They're apt to fall apart." She eased it back down on the chest. "But you're right. That is the ferry office building all right. Must be old man Wood there."

"Maybe there's a name on the back." Kapi picked it up again and turned it over.

Lou opened her mouth to scold, but shut it when Kapi showed off the back.

"Albert Wood. That's the guy, right?"

"Yeah, that's the guy. It's gotta be." Lou sighed, and waved her hand over the photos. "Well, you've picked one up, you might as well look at the rest." She wanted to add, *And don't ruin 'em,* but she refrained.

"Here's another one." Kapi waved a second photo in Lou's direction.

This time, Lou couldn't hold her tongue. "For Pete's sake, be careful! They're..." She knew she'd draw sarcasm if she added the automatic "old."

Kapi shrugged and prodded the photos around with her finger. "One of the ferry, by the looks of it."

Lou bent over to examine it. "Look at that old road. Slopes right down to the water." The ferry was already out on the lake, a stone's throw from the landing, ramp halfway up to vertical, obscuring much of what was being transported. "From what I can see, they really packed it full."

"Here's another one. A building."

"All right already. Anything on the back?" Lou's patience was wearing a bit thin.

Kapi turned it over and read, "The old ferry office." She flipped the photo and frowned. "But this isn't the old ferry office."

"Let me see that," Lou said. "That's not *our* old ferry office. But maybe it was Wood's old ferry office. Look at this." She bent down to Kapi. "Look familiar?"

Kapi squinted, then raised her eyebrows. "Is that...?" She steadied Lou's hand. "That looks kinda like the store. Doesn't it?" She looked up at Lou.

Lou nodded. "Yup. That's what I'm seeing too. That old porch is pretty much the same one that's there now. Huh. The mercantile that my great-great grandpa started must've been Wood's first ferry office." She peered at the photo again. "Funny. It looks pretty small. I can see why Wood built something bigger."

"I thought he built The Rose Arbor."

Lou set the photo down. "He did. The owners said they heard stories that house was too big for him, and too far from his beloved ferry. The stone ferry office we know had living quarters upstairs. He must've wanted to live above his business."

"Is that how your great-grandfather got the building for his mercantile?" Kapi asked.

"Great-great grandfather."

"Wait!" Kapi said. "There's another photo stuck to the back of this one." She slid a photo out from under one still on the chest. "This one looks like the same building." She handed it off to Lou.

The moment it was in her hand, Lou was transformed to her seven-year old self. Her father's voice came through loud and clear. He was brandishing the identical photo.

"Look at this! Dirty Indian! What the hell?" Her father's tone was angry, beyond angry.

Lou, the little child, cringed. He didn't see her or he wouldn't use that language in front of her. But she didn't run away. She hid where she could watch and listen.

"I always knew that someone back there..." He held the picture up and Lou could see the mercantile, with—were those people on the porch? Her father tilted the photo back and forth, then brought it close to his face. Shaking his head and frowning, he flipped it over. "Stephen Wright. Albert Wood. Pah! Louise Wright." That last name came out in a growl. "So, it's true. My mother-in-law always claimed there was Indian blood somewhere in my family. Shit!" He turned the photo over again. "And there she is. Louise Wright. There's the Indian, right there." He squatted down in front of the fireplace and grabbed the matches. "No one will ever see this. No one." But Lou already saw it. He set fire to the photo and watched it curl and crackle until nothing was left but ashes. "Don't need any dirty Indians in this family."

Lou swept back into her adult body. She couldn't have been gone long. Kapi still sat in the same position, waiting. Lou's first instinct was to burn the photo, just as her father had. But Kapi wouldn't understand, and Lou was not about to explain. She swallowed hard. "Yup, same building, but bigger. Wonder who the two guys are on the porch? They're too far away to see faces."

Kapi scrunched down to see the photo side. "There's three people there."

Lou frowned and handed off the photo to Kapi. Whatever was put in motion couldn't very well be stopped, now, could it?

"There're three names on the back too." Kapi held it so she could read the back, while Lou could see the picture side. "Pencil. Pretty faded. 'Stephen Wright and Albert Wood at the new Mercantile. Louise Wright,'" she read.

"Let me see that!" Lou took it from Kapi, heedless of its age. Was her father right? "It's the only photo I've seen of the woman, and she's too far away to see much." She shook the photo a bit. "Come on out of that shadow, Louise." She set it down with the others.

"She's really dark, isn't she?" Kapi said.

"She's on the porch, in the shade," Lou said. "Although people said she had the most beautiful black hair. At least, that's what I heard." Lou's stomach tightened. Could this be the answer?

"Well, she still looks dark to me. Are you sure she wasn't Native American?"

Lou snorted. "Indian? Not hardly. Look at her father." She stabbed her finger on Stephen Wright. "No Indian there." She glared at Kapi, daring her to say anything about her choice of words. She wanted to push it further.

Her father's words came unbidden to her lips, "No dirty Indians in our heritage," but she curbed the impulse and held her tongue. The knot in her stomach stayed tight. She batted an invisible ghost away, but Kapi was paying attention to something else.

Kapi held another picture, matted in cardboard with something written in ink on the back.

"That the last one? Let me see," Lou said.

Kapi nodded and held it to her chest. She looked down over the other photos. Her face was a mask.

"What's the matter with you? Hand it over."

Kapi shifted away from Lou. "I don't know if you want to see this one."

Lou flapped her hand at Kapi. She inched her way to the edge of her chair. "Don't you hold out on me, girl. What's in it?"

Kapi bit her lip, but handed the photo, face down, to Lou.

"Finally!" Lou said. "Someone who can write properly, in ink." She tilted it toward the light, the better to see. "For Louise Wright Iverson," she read. She turned it over.

She expected a wedding picture. Or maybe a photo of Gust, given as a keepsake. But it was neither of those. It was a studio portrait of a Native American woman, stout and a bit short, by the looks of it. She sat upright in a chair in front of a painted backdrop of clouds, and a potted fern on a stand of some sort. The woman was dressed in what must've been her finery, full skirt, print blouse, ropes of necklaces that reached clear to her lap.

She shifted to peer at Kapi, but Kapi was gazing into the fireplace. Lou checked the writing on the back again. "For Louise." Given to her great-grandmother.

"I don't get it," Lou growled. "My great-grandmother never had anything to do with...Indians." She pinched her lips tight and set the photo face down on her lap.

Kapi pulled her knees up and wrapped her arms around them. When she set her chin on her knees, her voice was so muffled, Lou almost missed what she said. "How do you know? You told me there were Native Americans"—she emphasized the words—"around here before."

"Yes," Lou said, "but not in town. They lived north along the lake. Where I showed you. But they weren't here when my folks lived here. My grandparents either, I don't think." She turned away from her thoughts.

Kapi spun around, still tucked into herself. "Then how do you know they were a problem anyway?" The words came out between clenched teeth.

"Because my mother told me how they used to live up top of the lake. Barefoot kids, stuff stacked all over the yard, old cars." She petered out. No way was she talking to a kid who had no understanding of...of what? How unwelcome the Indians were? What a nuisance they were? How different they were? Her mother always talked about Indians, years before, stealing vegetables right out of gardens, or bread set out to cool on the back porch railing.

"Maybe they were just poor," Kapi said. "Did she ever actually see any of them? Talk to them?"

"My mother—" Lou began.

"Your mother probably never even saw a Native American. I'll bet your grandmother didn't either. You said they were gone by that time. Probably so disgusted, they moved out." She stood up and went to the staircase. "I know I would." She disappeared up the stairs.

Lou hollered after Kapi, "Come..." She wanted to add something nasty, but couldn't bring herself to it. "Back here!" she added. But it was too late. Kapi was out of earshot.

She sighed and slid back into her chair. She picked up the photo and tapped it against her teeth. She rubbed her eyes. Don't be a fool, old woman. At least take a closer look at the thing. It had to be in the box for a reason. For Louise Wright Iverson. All right, so it was something given to her great-grandmother. Had Louise known this woman?

Lou turned the photo over and let her eyes wander. The woman was sporting so many necklaces that they looked like a horse collar. She looked placid enough. No smile, though. That made sense, considering how people had to sit so still for photographers in those years. This woman must've had plenty of patience. Every hair on her head was in focus, and her hands stayed still in her lap.

Lou looked at the woman's face, her eyes, her mouth. She picked up the photo of Louise standing in the shadow of the mercantile's porch. Her gaze went from one woman to the other. She shook her head more forcefully than she intended. "Nope. No resemblance." Even with that, she knew there was really no telling if there was any resemblance, Louise was too far away and too far into the shade to see details. "Of course she looks dark. She's standing in the shadows." It needed to be said aloud.

She set the mercantile photo down with the rest. Her eyes slid back to the Indian woman. Something caught her eye. But she had to narrow her vision and draw the photo close before she could be sure.

Her breath caught in her throat. "Can't be. Just can't be." She got up and retrieved her little porcelain box from her desk. She plopped down again, balanced the photo on the arm of her chair, and drew out the silver earrings her grandmother gave her. A beautiful drift of long silver slivers and clusters of silver disks.

She checked the photo again. The "can't be" turned into "it is." Lou's earrings were there, worn by that...Native American. And the photo itself had been given to Louise, her great-grandmother. Had anyone else known about this picture found in Albert Wood's hidden box? God forbid, she thought.

Chapter 28
Louise Wright

Within two days, Walking Elk was gone. Within three days, I knew. My body felt...softer, different somehow. I knew. Walking Elk left more than a bride behind. Within another week, my monthly courses, as regular as sunrise and sunset, refused to appear, and there was no denying it.

There was no denying, too, that Walking Elk wouldn't—couldn't—return for me. In spite of my dreams and hopes of that, it all evaporated the day Hiinuk Waka told me Walking Elk was staying in Nebraska. I was making bread, and the rhythm of kneading was the only thing to save me from collapsing to the kitchen floor. The room was hot and I hoped she saw me wipe only sweat from my face with my apron. I dared not cry, but my eyes leaked nonetheless. Hiinuk Waka was busy with her own rhythms of forming loaves and preparing the oven. With her back to me, I could see the flow of her work, relaxed, content, unaware of my anguish. I set myself to breathing in time to my hands, kneading, turning, forming. With focus, I could hold myself together, at least until night fell.

Then, alone, I purged my thoughts and dreams of Walking Elk in order to plan some kind of future. A future without him. I turned to face it, and was terrified.

My nights were spent in stretches of short restless sleep or wakefulness pacing the floor. Sometimes I sat at the window and watched the moon. I didn't cry. But I knew that what grew could not stay, could not live. But maybe, just maybe...no, I dared not consider it.

Back and forth, back and forth. Dreaming first of a child to cherish, all that was left of him. Shaking myself back to the reality of a ruined life if I followed that path. As strange as it seemed, I never asked why. Panic, yes. Fear. Abandonment, but not by Walking Elk. And never regret. Never.

How could half of me be so obstinate, so sure I could live, or rather, let live? With my feet planted firmly in Woods Portage, I knew it would never happen. I was stuck in my own world, unable to rise above, unable to uproot my feet. But unable to fall over also.

I walked, I cooked, I cleaned, I tended the mercantile. I ate dinner with Father, I flirted with Gust, I mourned the absence of her grandson with Hiinuk Waka. I talked at people, I listened. But all this was outside of myself. For two weeks, I moved through life and town without touching it. But then I woke up. I had to.

Father would need an order delivered to Juanita Rose in the big house, I was sure. If anyone could help me, Rose could. Her girls must need...help...every once in a while, surely. Wouldn't they?

I went to my desk and wrote. "Rose, A moment of your time, if you please. Perhaps when your order is delivered?" I sent it with one of the boys who was always hovering over the candy jars, hoping for a small handout. Father and I often accommodated. Enough notes flew back and forth among our customers, Rose included, that one more drew no special attention.

"Wait for an answer," I instructed the lad. He was back within the hour.

"She gave me this for you," he said, scuffing a toe as he waited in anticipation. I handed him a piece of his favorite horehound, and sent him off whistling.

I slipped into the back room—the mercantile was empty, for once—and opened the missive. "To: Wright's Mercantile. Order: 1 paper of pins, two lengths of blue plaid flannel, sugar (3 pounds, if it can be spared), the portion of rose damask ordered from Chicago (if it has arrived). Deliver Wednesday late afternoon, if possible. I will attend, as the girls will be out for the afternoon. J."

Wednesday late afternoon. The day after tomorrow. There was no standing mercantile order, so Rose clearly understood my haste in wishing to meet with her. I chewed on my lip, then chided myself for my impatience. Rose, no matter what the town saw as a woman of both low morals and plenty of leisure, labored mightily to keep her house in order, in every sense of the word. Because the women were the models of decorum while out in public, the women of both town and farms turned a blind eye to their...profession. It was a fine-tuned balance. I hoped not to upset it.

By Tuesday, I was almost frantic with nerves. Several times I plucked the wrong item from the shelf for a customer, and was finally reprimanded by Father.

"Louise, you are sorely distracted today. Whatever is the matter?" he asked. He stood with hands on hips, a sure sign of displeasure, though his voice remained even.

I had enough sense to blush, which I turned to a stroke of genius. "Oh, Father, I'm getting more and more distraught—" That was true enough. "Gust leaves shortly, and it seems we have so little time together before he's gone for the winter term." I congratulated myself on my shrewdness. I certainly wasn't lying. But then, I wasn't telling the entire truth either.

Father came to me and enveloped me in his customary bear hug. "My dear girl, you will soon enough have Gust all to yourself. I know waiting can be difficult, but it makes it all the sweeter."

"I shall content myself with dreams," I said, and gave him a kiss on the cheek. "If you can spare me, I'd like to take a little walk, just to clear my mind."

He released me and turned me toward the door. I untied my apron and laid it on the counter. "I won't be long."

"I can manage. Take your time." He waved me out as a customer came in the door.

By the time I reached the road leading to the ferry, I was almost in tears. With luck on my side, I met no one close enough to notice. I turned west, away from the lake, but did not go more than a dozen paces before halting to take a deep breath. Unsettled as I was, I could not go to Rose now, in the middle of the afternoon. Not today. If she were free today, she would have written to come today. I needed to control myself.

I turned around and headed for my sheltered cove. Soon, I set my feet along the path that took me to the shoreline. The water was slate-gray, as if in mourning with me. I couldn't bear to stay, it reminded me so of the morning Walking Elk appeared. I turned around and walked back under the trees, a welcome respite from the summer heat. The ferns were tall in spots along here, and the moist ground softened my steps. I stopped at the edge of a small clearing when I spotted a pair of red squirrels frolicking in the grass. They tumbled and chased, until finally they disappeared in the undergrowth.

I held everything tight to my heart, but the sight of those two lively animals so taken with each other broke the bonds. I sank to the grass and burst into tears. The larger part of me splintered into a million shards, while a tiny part reassured the rest of me that I was well out of the hearing of anyone. At that moment, that knowledge didn't take precedence.

Eventually, I made my way back to the mercantile, suitably armored in normality again. But inside, I vibrated and chafed. How could I possibly wait until the following afternoon?

As night fell, I didn't even bother to don my nightclothes, but instead exchanged skirt for trousers, and slid my feet out of my daytime shoes. I sat at my window, watching the sky darken from indigo to purest black, pierced by a few stars obscured now and again by scudding clouds. Rain on the morrow, I thought, which made my final decision easy. Leave now, before weather set in.

I picked up my boots and made my way down the stairs and out of the mercantile's back door. Thank heavens Mr. Wood built so sturdily that no creak of step or floor betrayed me. Though I'm sure Father would have understood my restlessness. However, he never would have condoned a walk after midnight.

I made my way without hindrance along the town green and turned west along the main road. The dogs all knew me, so those still abroad came with wagging tails, begging for a bit of attention. They retreated after a brief scratch behind the ears.

Before long, I was going up the walk between rows of roses, fragrant in the night. I made my way around the house to the familiar kitchen porch. I feared I would be too late, or perhaps even too early. Would the men who frequented such a place be gone? Or would the girls still be entertaining…visitors? Perhaps I would be too late and Rose would have retired for the night. It was far beyond midnight, and the night, though summer, held a certain chill.

As I came around the corner, I saw a glow in Rose's parlor window. I forced myself up the steps and drew up at the door to the kitchen. My hand froze in place, fist prepared to knock. I forced my arm to move, but the tap was so soft and tentative, I was sure Rose had not heard, even if she was indeed awake.

But the light from the parlor rose, as if floating, and before I had a chance to second guess myself, Rose opened the door a crack. Her face relaxed in recognition and she opened the door fully to admit me.

"Louise! What on earth are you doing here at this time of night?" Her brow furrowed.

"Oh, Rose…" My voice gave out. "I simply couldn't wait until tomorrow."

She took my elbow and pulled me into the kitchen. "The girls are asleep upstairs. I was just finishing up some bookkeeping."

A flood of tears threatened to burst, and I took in a deep breath to curb them. "I need your help." I could muster only a whisper.

She returned my whisper. "Come, come." She took me into her parlor, open only to the kitchen. I remembered the coral velvet chairs and lovely sheer curtains over the windows, now slightly open to the cool night air. Her desk was alive with paperwork, all of it aligned neatly in small piles awaiting her attention. A teapot near the fireplace puffed steam.

After settling me in a chair near the fire, she pulled a chair near to me and leaned forward to grasp my hands.

"You're white as a sheet, Louise. What's wrong? This isn't like you to be about so late." She rubbed my hands as if to warm them.

I looked down, letting my hair drop to shield my face. "I don't know what to do, Rose. You're the only one I could think to turn to." I raised my eyes to meet her gaze. I must be strong. I must. "You're the only one who can help me," I said, as my voice broke. The tears came, but I couldn't stop them. Nor could I cry out. Silent despair.

"Oh, my darling friend," she said. "I will do whatever I can to help you. Tell me what's wrong." She pulled a handkerchief from the sleeve of her dressing gown.

I stifled my tears and pressed the handkerchief to my mouth and nose. Perhaps I could suffocate and die right here, and all troubles would be over. But of course, that could not be. "I...don't know what to ask," I said. "I..." But I couldn't go on. I willed her to draw it out of me.

"Is this to do with the mercantile?" she asked, with a touch of what felt like sympathy.

A small laugh appeared unbidden. "No, thank God. All is well there." The mercantile felt trivial at the moment, though I knew our well-being depended on it. The catch in my throat betrayed my voice.

"Then what?" Rose asked. Her forehead cleared of furrows and she sat back in her chair. "Gust. It's Gust, isn't it."

I felt of sliver of opportunity open. My hands flew to my face, protecting what my eyes might betray. Walking Elk was gone. No one need know. I nodded, and felt my inappropriate laughter glide into frenzied tears.

"Oh, you poor dear. Did he retract—" She stopped herself. "No, of course not. You would have no reason to wait until the dead of night to tell me." I heard her slide forward in her chair. "He...ravished you."

I lowered my hands and met her gaze. I was afraid to say anything.

"Louise, did he force you? That is serious business."

I had the common sense to shake my head. "No," I whispered.

Rose relaxed. "My dear, from time immemorial men and women have coupled before marriage. It is not a crime, no matter what the locals might say." She floated her hand about in a dismissive gesture, then smiled. "You are engaged. There is no harm."

I sent her a skeptical look. Surely there was harm. I had to tell her. But she caught my meaning before I had a chance.

"Ah! And the result of that—"

I cut her off before she could voice what I couldn't bear to hear aloud. "Yes. The result."

She patted my hands, then grasped them tight in hers. "Your fingers are still ice!" She turned to the teapot and poured two cups, turning away, I was sure, to give me a moment to gather myself.

I must steel myself to bring up...what I needed to bring up. "I cannot do this, Rose. I'm hoping you can help me. Can you? Help me, I mean?"

Rose handed me a cup of tea. I wrapped my hands around the cup and lifted it, wishing I could hide my face behind it.

"My girls generally don't allow a pregnancy to develop," she said, lowering her eyes to her tea.

There was the word. The word I couldn't bring myself to think, much less say. I shivered so much, my cup rattled on the saucer. But here we were, at the point I hoped to reach when I sought her out. I waited.

Rose set her cup down and turned back to me. "We know many ways to prevent a...problem." She caught my reluctance.

"But?"

"But nothing," she said. "There are also ways to...expel."

My hopes rose. "So, you can help me?"

"I can't. But I know who can." She raised her forefinger and tapped alongside her nose. "You know her."

"Her?" I asked. If I knew her, wouldn't she also prove dangerous? Tell anyone she knew? Exposure would be devastating. Father would never recover.

"Don't worry, Louise. She is discretion itself. She would never betray anyone." She'd read my mind.

"Who? Can you be my advocate?" I didn't want to approach anyone until I absolutely had to.

"You won't need me to advocate for you. Hannah has helped whenever my girls needed her services." She shook her finger at me this time. "This doesn't happen often, I want you to know. I run a very careful establishment here. But on the rare occasion, I have used her services. Twice, as I recall." She rose and went behind my chair.

I felt her arms go around me in a warm embrace, and I leaned my head back against her chest and closed my eyes. If anyone could help me, I thought Rose would be the one. But I was frozen. Hiinuk Waka. How could I...? I shivered. It would mean... Her own great-grandchild. She would have to... I couldn't force my mind over that divide. I had to take action somehow. I had to do something.

Hiinuk Waka's grandson captured my heart, though I would never ever, in a thousand years, tell her what happened between Walking Elk and me. She would never know. She could help me, and she would never know. Could I do this? With Rose's arms around me, I simply couldn't even think about the next step. I certainly couldn't confide in Rose.

Tomorrow. I'll think about this tomorrow. I can't tonight. I can't.

Chapter 29
Louise Wright

We were sitting on Rose's kitchen porch, watching Gust unload firewood. He liked to take me along to keep tongues from wagging. Broad daylight and his fiancée along were enough to keep everyone happy.

"I couldn't do it," I whispered to Rose. "I got as far as Hannah's path, and turned around and went home." It shattered me to lie to her. I didn't even start for Hiinuk Waka's path. I sighed and added the one thing that would help me keep my secret. "I just couldn't do that to Gust."

"You haven't told him then," Rose said.

"No," I said, then turned to answer Gust's call. "Yes, I'm ready to go!" I grabbed my straw hat and went down to meet him at the wagon. I waved back at Rose, and called, "It's going to be beautiful!"

I scrambled up on the wagon and settled next to Gust.

"What's going to be beautiful?" he asked, as he drove out of the yard and headed back into town.

"Our wedding," I said. I hoped this would work.

He smiled and reached for my hand. "I know. I can't wait. It's going to be a long winter." He lifted my hand to his lips.

"I feel the same, Gust. I can hardly wait." That was true enough, but mainly because I loved this man to the depths of my heart and wanted a lifetime with him, not just because of the necessity for haste. "In fact," I began, "why do we have to wait?"

The horse slowed as Gust let the reins go slack. He sent me a sly smile. "I suppose we don't have to wait, do we? We can marry at Christmas, when I come home for the holidays." He shifted closer to me. "Can you plan everything without me?"

"To marry you sooner? Of course!" I patted his arm, then reached up to slide my hand along his cheek. "By why even wait that long? You leave in three weeks, so why not marry before you leave?" I held up my hand to stifle any objection, or even any conversation at this point. "I've thought long and hard about this, Gust," I said. "Who will be there to help your father when you are gone? Even you have commented on how his health is declining. If we marry before you go, I'll live in the parsonage and can do everything for him that you do now. And I can still help out Father in the mercantile. After all, Hannah is still there for all of us." I took both his hands in mine. "I love you, Gust, and I want us to be happy. If we marry now, we can have the best of both worlds. You need not worry about your father, and we can have some time…together before you have to leave."

"Louise, you are a marvel," Gust said. "I thought about this myself, but I don't want to put you in the position of having to get everything ready for a wedding so quickly."

Was this really going to be so easy? I laughed. "Oh, Gust, neither one of us has planned a wedding before, and our fathers certainly don't know how. I would want to keep it as simple as possible. I have a fine dress I've seldom worn. It will be perfect for a wedding. We can marry at a

Sunday church service, so all our friends will be there. And a picnic on the town square after would be just fine with me. How much more planning must we do?"

"Simple, yes. We don't really need a..." He flapped his hand.

"A city wedding," I finished. "A simple Woods Portage wedding is all I want. Most of all—" I leaned into his shoulder,"—I want you to be happy. I want us to be happy."

"If this will make you happy, then it will make me happy too," he said. "Are you sure? This is short notice."

I swiveled, and kissed him. "Yes. Yes, yes. I'm sure."

He clucked to the horse. "I hope our fathers don't give us grief." He shot me a smile. "But together, we can make it work."

***

It more than worked. Once our fathers knew what we intended, they surprised us with their enthusiasm. Soon, everyone in town knew. Mr. Wood offered to organize tables and such for a potluck on the square. Several of our best customers' wives arranged food and drink. Rose brought flowers from her garden, and even rode into town early to deliver armloads of roses for my bouquet and decorations for the church. No one seemed to mind that the madam from down the road was there, helping. She faded into the background with her girls, once people started to arrive. Hiinuk Waka made enough pies to feed an army, and even came into the church to witness our ceremony.

The day was beautiful, in every sense of the word.

We retreated shortly before midnight, though the party was still going strong. Father had discretely invited

Reverend Iverson to join him at the mercantile until Gust would leave for Iowa. We were touched by their thoughtfulness.

It wasn't long after midnight that it seemed the whole town converged on the parsonage, beating on pots and pans in a good old shiveree. We went to the door in our dressing gowns, but declined to rejoin the festivities. We were mightily teased for that. We returned to bed, and things quieted down before very long.

Gust left a week later to finish his studies in Iowa. I was sure by that time that my secret was safe.

Chapter 30
Lou

Lou couldn't sleep. She felt heavy. Not physically heavy, but heart-heavy. Kapi ran out on her. Well, not out, exactly. She just tore upstairs and slammed the door to her room. Over the earrings. No, Lou corrected herself, not over the earrings. Over... What was it over anyway? Yes, Lou was pretty obnoxious about family history. Oh, for God's sake, be honest, Lou. Not just Native Americans, but that managed to get all mixed up with where Kapi fit into things.

Kapi was caught between worlds. Lou surprised herself. She squirmed onto her side and punched the pillow. Kapi was forced out of Mac's world when he died. And now. Damn, I'm doing the same thing. I've kicked her out of my world too. And for almost the same reason. Mac. Mac leaving both of them in the lurch. Lou didn't want to share him. But Kapi opened up to her earlier, didn't she? Kapi admitted she missed her...dad. And Kapi loved him. Well, Lou loved him too. She chewed on her lip. *There's no reason we both can't love him. I should be happy to share. Isn't the old saying that love multiplies when it's shared?* "Well," she said out loud, "if it wasn't a saying before, it should be." She heard a soft tap at the door.

"You awake?" came a whisper. "I thought I heard you awake."

Lou propped herself up against the headboard, "Yeah, yeah, I'm awake."

Kapi's fingers curled around the door, followed by the edge of her face.

"Come on in. You might as well join the Insomniac Club." Lou pulled the quilt up under her arms and shifted her feet closer to the middle of the bed.

Kapi shuffled in and perched at the foot.

"Make yourself comfy. The club encourages bare feet tucked up." Lou cleared her throat. "Wrap up in that quilt down there. Too cold to sit there very long otherwise."

Kapi crawled up and wrapped the quilt around herself.

Lou began, "So. This is the best time of day to clear the air. Mac and I used to talk at night when he was worried about something. He'd come in and curl up, just like you're doing now."

"Didn't that wake up your husband?" Kapi asked.

"Naw. Sometimes I was off in a different bedroom. But if not, he always slept like a dead man." Lou regretted the phrase as soon as it was spoken. "Anyway, things get fixed in the dark better, I think. Don't have to worry about reading people's faces." She saw Kapi's head nod and felt the bed jostle a bit.

"Mac really loved you, y'know," Kapi said.

It was Lou's turn to nod. "I know he loved you too. He never said too much about love, but I can tell he loved you. And you already told me you loved him."

"I miss him a lot," Kapi said. "He listened. When my mom would go ballistic—which was a lot—he kept me safe. He got her to back off sometimes. When he died..."

"I know, Kapi. I know. It nearly killed me too." Lou's voice turned gravelly. "We both loved him. I know that now."

"Yeah. Love doubles when you give it away," Kapi said. "Dad used to say that. My mom laughed at him when he said that, but I think it's true."

When Lou got her breath back, she leaned forward and patted Kapi's foot. "Then we have come to an understanding. Considering we have a full quorum of the Insomniac Club, we can pass the resolution tonight." She waited.

"What resolution?" Kapi asked.

"We—you and I—resolve to accept the fact that Mac is gone. But the love he had for both of us will linger forever. Therefore, we resolve also to cherish Mac, because—"

"We both loved him, and that's okay," Kapi finished up.

"Meeting adjourned," Lou said, and slid back down under the covers. The weight that woke her up evaporated.

Kapi bounced off the bed, relinquished the quilt, and headed for the door. "I second that motion." She closed the door behind her and was gone.

No need for a second when the meeting's over, Lou thought, as she eased into sleep.

***

The next morning, the photos and their wooden box were still laid out where Lou left them the night before. So were the earrings. But they were draped over Kapi's hand where she sat curled up in the chair she vacated the night before.

Lou cleared her throat as she came around the fireplace into the room. "Couldn't sleep?" It was a conciliatory tone. She wasn't sure where the situation stood in broad daylight.

Kapi didn't look up, but she nodded. "Still kept waking up."

Lou lowered herself into the chair opposite. Better step lightly, she told herself. But Kapi beat her to it.

"I don't get it. Why would your grandmother have these earrings in the first place?" Kapi leaned over to set them next to the photo of the Native American woman wearing those very earrings. "Unless your grandmother was Native American."

Maybe we're good to go. "I know she wasn't," Lou answered. "But..." Her words wouldn't go where her mind was taking her.

"Then your great-grandmother must've been," Kapi finished the thought.

Lou sat with her chin in her hand, shaking her head back and forth in denial and disbelief. Years ago, when she was a child, there were rumors.

"Maybe she got them from somewhere. A gift from somebody. A craft show at a powwow or something."

Kapi snorted. "A craft show! Back then? I don't think so."

"You'd be surprised what went on in the past, young lady," Lou snapped. "They weren't barbarians, you know."

"I know that. But then where did they come from?" Kapi sat up so suddenly her foot hit the chest, making the photos jump. "Wait! Wasn't there something else about earrings? Wasn't there something in those other papers we were going through from the ferry office?" She jumped up and pulled a box out from under the old maple slab of a dining table along the wall.

Lou frowned. Yes, there had been something.

Kapi dug into the box. "Ta-da!" Kapi pulled out a packet of oilcloth.

Lou remembered in a flash. "Let me see that." She gestured for Kapi to hand it over. To her surprise, Kapi did, then curled up on the floor next to her.

Lou unwrapped the oilcloth and took a quick look at the papers inside. "Here it is." She set the rest down on the chest and read out loud the note they'd found before.

The women get my silver earrings. Love, LWI.

"See?" Kapi said. "Told ya those earrings were your great-grandma's."

Lou said, "Well, we knew that already, didn't we?"

"Well, yeah. I guess," Kapi said, the wind apparently taken out of her sails. "But then, does that mean that the Native American woman in the photo was her mother?"

Lou forced a shrug that she hoped looked unconcerned. "Doubt it."

"But look. There are the earrings. The photo says they belonged to that woman. The note says they belonged to Louise Wright Iverson, your great-grandmother. How'd they get from the old lady there to Louise? That's what I want to know." Kapi's brow looked like a newly plowed field.

"Maybe they just look alike. Two different pairs."

"Come on, Lou," Kapi's voice dripped skepticism. "The photo says it's to Louise, doesn't it?"

"I suppose," Lou conceded.

"It's clear they at least knew each other?" Kapi made it into a question. "You can at least say that much, right?"

Lou nodded, but her lips were pinched together. "Doesn't mean a thing." It was said more to convince herself. It certainly didn't seem to convince Kapi, who was shaking her head.

"There's a straight line from Louise to you, right? You know everyone in between?"

"Yeah. They're all up there in the cemetery."

"Wait. Wait, wait!" Kapi said. "The cemetery. This all explains that baby that died as an infant."

"You lost me," Lou said.

"Well, remember the cradle that wasn't paid for? And that crazy 'heathen' comment?" Kapi asked.

"Yeah? So?" Lou was connecting all the dots.

"Okay, so listen to this." Kapi scooted closer and set her hands on Lou's knees. "Albert Wood wouldn't pay for the cradle that he ordered for Louise and Gust's baby, right?" She scooted right on past Lou's nod. "Why wouldn't he pay? Because he realized that the baby was Native American, or at least half, 'cause Gust wasn't. But Louise was." She crowed the last line.

Lou shook her head. "But wouldn't he know if Louise was Native American? Why would he spot it just in the baby?"

"Here's what I think." Kapi settled herself down onto the floor. "I think Louise could pass. You know, as a white, not a Native American. Plus, if her father wasn't Native American—and it doesn't appear that he was—then Louise wouldn't necessarily look all that dark." She shrugged. "I learned in school that sometimes stuff shows up in later generations that wasn't there in the earlier ones."

"Maybe." Lou's voice came out flat. She could accede to the possibilities, even if she couldn't totally agree.

"So, okay. The buck stops with Louise, right?" Kapi pushed. "Where did Louise come from anyway?"

Lou shrugged. "Don't know for sure. If she was from Woods Portage, the church records were damaged beyond repair from that mildew. But there's nothing in the cemetery going back further. So, she probably came from somewhere else with her father when they bought the mercantile."

"Well, where did Louise's father come from then?"

"Good God, Kapi, I don't know. We never talked about that stuff. All I know is that he owned the mercantile in town here."

"I'll bet," Kapi said, "he came here to open that store, but then fell in love with a Native American woman—that woman in the photo—and had a daughter. Louise, your great-grandma."

It was becoming uncomfortable. Lou knew about the rumors, but she'd squelched those decades ago. If she shared that with Kapi, it might bind them closer. On the other hand, if she didn't, and Kapi found out later, a wall would go up that might be impenetrable for all time.

Lou took a deep breath.

Chapter 31
Louise Wright

When Gust returned for a Christmas visit, I met him at the ferry landing. The weather was already bone-chilling, and I wrapped myself in my warmest cloak. Father and Reverend Iverson both counseled me to stay home and wait, to preserve my health, to stay warm, to remember the state I was in. I laughed and assured them I'd be fine.

I swore both men to secrecy, once my breakfasts came back up my throat on a regular basis. I couldn't plead stomach flu for very long. No one in town knew, however, except Rose. I knew my secret would remain secret there. At this point, my waist was still shapely, though just beginning to expand. Easy enough to hide beneath aprons and dresses a bit fuller around the waist.

Hiinuk Waka had been the first to guess. "You shine from inside," she told me one morning. "As if you shelter a new life." She smiled and looked at me sideways.

I tried rippled laughter, but I could not contain myself. This was the great-grandmother, after all. "You see everything, Hiinuk Waka. Everything!" I took her hands. "Yes, I carry a child." I dared not say more, so afraid I would confide that the baby was Walking Elk's. He's your great-grandchild, I wanted to whisper. But I could not.

"A wedding child," Hiinuk Waka said. "A child of your first nights."

I nodded, overcome. But, no, I amended silently, a child of a warm afternoon, and a soft bed of ferns. Tears rose unbidden.

Hiinuk Waka squeezed my hands, then reached up to pat my cheek. "I am here to help you. I have birthed many babies. Even babies here in Woods Portage. When there is a first, or fear, I am called."

"I shall be most grateful to have you there." Hiinuk Waka would never know how grateful, or why.

***

"I have something to share," I said to Gust as we lay in bed. We had run the gauntlet of friends and the two fathers, spoken to everyone alive within twenty miles, I was convinced, and eaten a hearty meal at the mercantile before we were able to excuse ourselves to walk to the parsonage. Reverend Iverson once again repaired to the spare room at the mercantile so we could be alone for a night.

"Something to share?" Gust said. "But that should wait for Christmas. I have something for you also, but—" He leaned over and kissed my nose. "—you'll just have to wait."

I giggled. "My gift simply cannot wait. It is something to be shared between just the two of us. At least, for tonight."

Gust turned on his side and propped his head on his hand. "What could possibly be so important that it cannot wait a day or two?" He smiled and reached out to twirl a strand of my dark hair around his finger. "I have missed your raven locks, as the poets say."

I reached up and untwined his finger. "Give me your hand." I wanted to spoon my back against him, but I wanted more to see his face. I had to face him to make sure this would work. I kissed his fingers and set his hand on my belly. I flattened his hand against my nightshirt, wondering if he would be able to feel the faint flutterings I could. Doubtful, they were so like mere butterfly wings.

Gust, his face quizzical, switched his gaze from my face to my belly. Finally, his face cleared. "Are you...Is there...Will we...?" I nodded. Gust's face lit up like a summer sky. He burst into laughter and gathered me into his arms. "Are you sure?" he said into my hair. He pulled back just enough to see my smile and dancing eyes. This was going to be fine.

"I'm sure. I was sick every morning for a month," I told him. But when I saw the look of dismay on his face, I added, "But that's all over now. I'm fine."

Gust ran his fingers down my face, then bent to kiss me again. "How long? Will I be home before the baby is born?"

"May," I lied, knowing it was more likely to be April. "I hope you'll be back by then. And Hiinuk Waka will midwife for me. Between the two of you, all will be fine."

"I'll return as soon as they will let me leave, even if it means I must forego final ceremonies. I will be an ordained minister by then, at any rate." Gust caressed circles on my belly. "How can they deny a man whose lovely wife is carrying their first child?"

"I will not be so lovely the next time you see me," I said. "Probably fat and slow." Even as I said it, I knew he would not be home for the birth. It would be a baby born...early...for all anyone knew. Anyone but me. Rose and me.

"Fat and slow on you will still be beautiful." He drew me into his arms.

I sighed. All would be well with the world. I reached up and kissed him.

Chapter 32
Louise Wright

I was right. Gust didn't make it back in time for the birth.

The cramps began on an unusually warm late April afternoon.

"You're coming early!" the farmer's wife at the mercantile said when I gasped and doubled over in pain. "You'd better call Hannah. She's a wonder with early babes." She turned to her son. "Go up to the parsonage and fetch Hannah. Tell her Mrs. Iverson's time has come." She turned back to me. "How can I help you?"

Rose, waiting at the counter, gave a small nod to me.

There was a reprieve and I said, "If you can just go in back and get my father..." The farmer's wife went off.

"Come on, Louise," Rose said. "Let's get you home." She helped me out of my apron.

I grabbed Rose's hand as another cramp struck. "Will you stay with me? You know...everything."

Rose looped my arm through her own. "Of course I'll stay."

As dawn broke the next morning, I cried out with the last of my strength, and delivered a fine girl baby. Hiinuk Waka set her on my chest. I never saw such a beautiful baby. In spite of the blood and water, she glowed with health. Rose, crying as hard as I was, wiped my face, and Hiinuk Waka took baby Doe to clean her up. Rose helped me to change, and whisked off the birthing sheets. She propped me up in bed with pillows, and Hiinuk Waka gave me Doe, swaddled warmly. Hiinuk Waka went off with the bundle of soiled sheets and rags, while Rose made herself scarce when she heard my father open the front door.

Once Father cooed over his new granddaughter, I sent him down to the ferry office to send a telegram to Gust. But I made him promise he would include an injunction to Gust to finish his studies. Three weeks would give him full ordination. And me time to...return to normal. Father hurried off to send the telegram. And to announce, to anyone who would listen, the birth of the new babe.

"What a head of hair!" Rose said. "Black, just like yours." She smoothed the dark fuzz with one finger. She exchanged a glance with me. It was a cascade of words without sound.

"What will you name the little one?" Hiinuk Waka asked as she returned with a mug of hot tea. I could smell more than just tea. Hiinuk Waka would have infused it with healing herbs.

"Before Gust left, we decided on Dorothea if it was a girl," I said. "After his mother. But we'll call her Doe." That was fine with Gust. "Dorothea Winn," I added, before the lump in my throat dissolved into tears.

Hiinuk Wika stopped straightening the blankets around me. "Winn. Was that your mother?"

"My mother's name was Winifred, but everyone called her Winn." It was a fortuitous name, as it was also secretly short for Winnebago, what the whites called the Ho-Chunk people. That, and the nickname Doe, was as close as I could get to acknowledging Walking Elk.

I knew, as much as Gust wanted to leave the seminary and come home as soon as he received notice of Doe's birth, I wanted time to recover. That way, we could concentrate on each other, and on our beautiful new child. I knew he was reluctant, but he agreed, nonetheless.

In the time before Gust arrived, I tried, unsuccessfully at times, to keep Walking Elk at bay. Hiinuk Waka had little news from him, busy as he told her he would be, so I was spared that, at least. My mind slid to Doe and her dark hair. Would people in town see shades of Walking Elk in her? I worked myself into a passion of worry many nights. The closer Gust's arrival approached, the harder I worked to suppress my thoughts. Father forbade me from working at the store, so I kept myself busy with Doe, and helping Hiinuk Waka where I could.

Thus, Doe was a bit more than three weeks old when Gust came home. She had been fawned over by the women, doted on by both grandfathers, and settled into a decent routine by the time her father arrived. The comments about how robust Doe was for an "early" baby subsided, and I moved into the role of mother with great happiness. Her great dark blue eyes followed my voice, and I could see that, between Hiinuk Waka and me—and her father, surely—Doe was bound to be a spoiled little girl.

Doe, even so young, had my fine long fingers and toes. Her high forehead seemed to echo Gust's, in spite of... I still worried. But no one seemed to notice Doe's skin, suffused with a warm glow, and darker than my, and Gust's, tones. At least, I thought no one noticed. Until Albert Wood came into the store.

I was in the back room, settling Doe down in the box Father kept for her in the kitchen. I sang her a soft song and watched her eyelids flutter, then shut. I moved to the curtain that separated Father's living quarters from the store. He never put in a solid door, because he wanted to hear from the back if anyone came in.

I had one hand on the curtain when I heard Mr. Wood's voice. From his tone, he was there on some private business, so I remained out of sight, though I peeked through a gap in the curtain.

"Good day, Stephen," Wood greeted my father. "Fine day, fine day."

"Everything all right, Albert?" Father asked. "You look a bit flustered."

Wood puffed out his lips. He had a small scrap of paper in his hands, turning it this way and that, running his fingers along the edges. "I...well...I've decided not to take that cradle. The..uh...the babe it was meant for...well..." He planted his feet as if he needed the firmness of the floor to go on.

"Oh, no, Albert. The baby didn't make it?" Father shook his head and reached out to settle his hand on Mr. Wood's shoulder. "Of course, If you wish not to take the cradle, that is fine. Did the folks know you ordered it for them?"

Wood shook his head.

My father, his sympathy called upon, responded to Mr. Wood's distress. He took his hand from Mr. Wood's shoulder and smiled. "Not to worry, Albert. I'll give it to Louise for the little one."

I smiled at the exchange. But I was brought low with Mr. Wood's explosive, "No! I won't have it!"

My heart dropped. It burst upon me. That cradle was meant for me, for our baby, for Doe. I could feel it. But Mr. Wood didn't want Doe in this cradle. What did he see? What did he suspect? I shook that thought from my mind. Maybe I was seeing shadows where there were none.

Father's face was full of puzzlement. "As you wish." He cleared his throat, as if to give himself time to think of something to say. "It's a fine cradle. I'm sure one of the young farm husbands will purchase it when a new babe is due."

Wood looked relieved. But his hands remained busy with that piece of paper. I couldn't help wondering why he was worrying it so. "I, uh, I have something you should see. I have some...suspicions, you know." He drew his eyebrows in and looked down. He seemed surprised to see the paper clutched in his hands.

If I thought my heart dropped before, I was wrong. There were shadows. My legs gave out and I found myself crumpled on the floor.

"Suspicions? Of what, my friend?" Father leaned back against the counter. He was a master at making people comfortable—or uncomfortable, as the occasion demanded. This was somewhere in the middle. He seemed completely mystified.

I was not. A cradle refused. A man who did not acknowledge our daughter, except for peering into the folds of the christening blanket. After that, nothing. Suspicions, he said. I could barely breathe.

"Albert? You are most certainly distracted today. Does this have to do with that paper you keep twisting in your hands?" my father asked.

"What? No." Mr. Wood seemed to gather himself. He moved his feet, as if uprooting them. He stuffed the paper in his trouser pocket and reached out to shake Father's hand. "Nothing to worry yourself about, Stephen. My mind is just elsewhere today." He moved toward the door.

"Wait just a moment, Albert," Father said, grasping Mr. Wood's elbow. "Let me give you a receipt, showing you've cancelled the cradle delivery. It'll keep both of our books straight."

Wood took the receipt, stuffed it in his pocket with whatever was on the other note, and strode out the door.

The blood rushed back into my head and I could breathe again. Though for how long, I couldn't guess.

***

Not long, as it turned out. No one said anything, but sideways glances and what looked to me like simpering smiles eroded my sense of balance. I was sensitive to every look, every word. Most times, I could tell myself I was imagining things. But too many thoughts intruded.

At first, Doe was not the size of a baby born before time. After a month or six weeks, however, it hardly mattered— or hardly showed anymore. I could set that worry aside. Though there may have been talk before, and I was sure there was, all that blew away. Perhaps there would always be murmurs, but no one reacted overtly.

Doe's black hair caused no stir whatsoever, because my own hair was raven. Everyone knew that dark hair won over blond. Gust was white blond, but the two of us together could easily produce a child with dark hair. One more point I could dismiss.

But two things I could not dismiss. As she grew, she remained a golden brown, not a pale newborn, as most babies in Woods Portage and surrounding farms were. Granted, I was a dark-haired woman, but my complexion remained light. Not ivory, certainly, but that was mainly due to the weather and my tendency to often go out without a hat. Now, I cultivated a sun-kissed skin. Perhaps that would be enough to stop talk.

But I could not do one thing about Doe's eyes. I knew nothing about eye color, but some of the wives commented on Doe's eyes, how dark blue they were, whereas their own babies were born with pale blue eyes. Over several weeks, Doe's eyes had darkened even further, from sky blue to cove water blue to indigo with flecks of amber. Her eyes seemed to be turning brown as I watched. Of course, that was certainly not true. But was it possible? Over time, it was happening. Brown eyes from two blue-eyed parents. I could hear the talk in my head, and it was not pleasant.

With Walking Elk leaving when he did, would people put two and two together? Or would they continue to tease us with "Wedding Night Baby"? I dare not let my mind wander into such a trap.

My nights became restless again, for fear I would talk in my sleep. Even though Gust slept the sleep of the righteous, and never stirred, I slept the sleep of the damned. Sometimes I slept curled on the floor next to Doe in her basket. Sometimes I wandered the parsonage until I could only stumble to the settee for a couple hours rest. Reverend Iverson moved in with Father, in preparation for retirement. He and Gust shared church duties, but he insisted on bequeathing us the parsonage. I was grateful, for multiple reasons.

***

One afternoon, when Doe was two months old, I tucked her into my shawl, as Hiinuk Waka taught me, and set out for the cove. I had not been there since Walking Elk left. I turned off on the trail without leaving a sign behind.

The lake stretched calm before me. The sun was far behind me, and the shadows of the trees reached out into the water as if to scoop it closer. The water shone dark like slate. I took off my shoes and socks and hitched up my skirt around my hips. Doe was secure and sleeping against my chest in her shawl hammock. When I stepped off into the water, the cold almost sizzled around my ankles. I would have to go out a fair way before it dropped off.

The desire struck me like a knife. I wanted it to drop off. I wanted to walk along the bottom of the lake until there was nothing left of either of us.

What remained for us here, either of us? I had as good as committed adultery, condemning my beautiful child to a life of being shunned. Her dark skin, her dark eyes, her dark hair. All I could see in her was Walking Elk. I denied it long enough, but I knew now that she would suffer terrible indignities. She would be unwelcome in both worlds. White or Indian? Who would have her? What a barbaric life, to be haunted by such a legacy.

Because it was bound to come out. "Do you know about Louise Wright?" They would call me Wright, not Iverson, absolving Gust of any wrongdoing. "She lay with a man"—no, no—"She lay with an Indian." "Yes, and now there's an Indian child. A heathen child, for heaven's sake." Anathema. "And married to that wonderful Gust Iverson. I wonder if he's guessed?" I couldn't face that happening to any of us.

I began walking into the lake. The water was almost at my hips when Doe awoke and nuzzled at my breast. That stopped me, more than the cold water did. I unbuttoned my blouse and she nestled into me.

How could I not think of Walking Elk? This was his child. He would never know. That I vowed. But I could not...

I could not.

I turned and walked out of the lake.

Chapter 33
Lou

The Indian/Native American question was simply not going to go away. Kapi sat across from Lou in front of the fireplace, photos and earrings on the chest between them. Lou took a deep breath. "Kapi, I don't know any more than you do," Lou said. That wasn't the whole truth, was it? But then, what was?

Kapi sent Lou one of those raised eyebrow looks. "You must know something. Why can't Louise be a Native American your great-grandfather fell for and married?"

"Look, all I know is that Louise wasn't Ind...Native American."

"But look at her photo! She's standing there on the store's front porch, dark as all get-out. She had to've been Native American." Kapi put on her whiny voice.

"Impossible," Lou said. "All the In—those people were gone when my great-grandparents lived here."

"How do you know?"

"Because that's what everybody's told me." That snappish tone was out before she could stop it. "Sorry," Lou said under her breath, but Kapi wasn't backing off. "Abe is interested in all this, and he told me that those people that lived around here were all thrown out of the state. Even out of the territory before it was a state. So, there was nobody left."

"What do you mean, 'thrown out'?" Kapi said.

"Just what I said," Lou said. "The government removed them. More than once, the way Abe tells it." She hoped to divert Kapi from probing further.

"That's ridiculous!" Kapi frowned. "You just don't throw people out." She shoved invisible people away.

Lou shrugged. "Well, they did. That's why Louise wasn't Indian." She couldn't switch words quickly enough. "They were all gone."

"Then where did the earrings come from? And why's there a photo of that Native American woman written out to Louise? They must've known each other."

Kapi is right, Lou thought. It's what she herself feared. Fear, what an ugly reason to turn away. Then say it out loud, old lady. It won't kill you. "You're probably right. They maybe knew each other." Well, that didn't solve anything now, did it?

But before Lou could say more, Kapi grunted. "Probably? Come on, spit it out. What do you know that I don't?"

Lou screwed her mouth to one side. "All right, pushy. They knew each other. But that's all I know."

"How do you know? How?" Kapi was chewing on this like a wolf on a deer.

"Because she left a note with those earrings, that's how."

"So? Where's the note?" Kapi demanded.

Lou shrugged. "You're just gonna have to believe me when I tell you my mother burned it." After the rumors got too loud.

"Burned it? Then how do you know there was ever a note in the first place?" Kapi wouldn't let go.

Lou's temper got the better of her. "Because I saw it. Isn't that enough? Let it go, Kapi, let it go. My mother was ashamed. And so am I." She said too much. Kapi would demand to know everything now.

Sure enough. But Kapi's voice was almost a whisper. "What did it say, Lou? What did the note say?" And, unlike any other time, Kapi waited.

Lou levered herself up and moved to stand in front of the fireplace, her back to Kapi. If she had to say this—and she knew she did—she didn't want to see Kapi's face, no matter what the reaction.

"The note. I only saw it once, but I was about your age. My mother had the earrings out, lying on top of a piece of paper, a note. When she went into the kitchen, I read it." She scratched her nose, and took a deep breath. "It said 'Don't ever lose these earrings. They are your heritage. Pass them to the women of the family.' It was signed H.W., whatever that means." Lou waited.

After a moment, Kapi said, "That's it?"

"Isn't that enough?" Lou said. "The earrings are Indian, that's clear enough from that photo. Which means that you're right. Somewhere back there, maybe there's Native American in our family." She remembered this time.

"And that's so bad?" Kapi's voice fell soft on Lou's ears.

Lou turned around. "Up until now, it has been. Who wanted to be related to an Indian? Sorry, a Native American. No one, in my time."

"Yeah, but it's different now," Kapi said. "Isn't it?"

Lou shrugged again. "Depends, I guess." She slid her hands down her face. "I...I never wanted any connection." She sighed. "I guess now I don't care so much." I have you to thank for that, she thought. But she couldn't say that part. At least, not quite yet.

Chapter 34
Louise Wright

They increased. The rumors, I mean. Though my worst fears did not materialize—Albert Wood apparently did not say a word about his suspicions, as I knew they must be—fears still crowded about me.

The women. Always the women. Except Rose and Hiinuk Waka. The women looked, peered, stared. Held their tongues for the time being, but I could hear the words piling up behind their eyes.

"Oh Louise! What a lovely child."

"Thank you, Mrs. Sorensen."

Then a frown. "Her eyes are so...brown." A sideways look at my eyes.

"Yes, Mrs Sorensen, brown. My mother's eyes were brown." That only when my father wasn't around. My mother's eyes were green.

"Well." A subtle sniff, a shallow smile, and Mrs. Sorensen would be off, sometimes leaving her goods on the counter. "I'll pick those up later," she called over her shoulder. Sometimes she didn't.

More of them left the store with more than the usual comments about how busy they were. If I were in the back out of sight, they stayed longer, talking with Father, fingering new fabrics, debating whether to indulge their children with candies.

Sometimes, if I was helping Father, and Doe was in her basket, a mother might hover over her, curious to see if what the others said was true. I tried to silence the voices in my mind. Voices that said, "They know. They can tell she's not Gust's child." Or, when I was very tired and couldn't stifle anymore, "They know you lay with..." So far, I was able to repress the name of Walking Elk, but only just barely. If they could see Indian in Doe's lovely little face, they would see Walking Elk. Few young male Indians came through Woods Portage. Hiinuk Waka's grandson would be their first guess.

Even at church, Doe garnered sideways glances from the women. They noticed Doe was darker than either Gust or me. More, probably thanks to Mrs. Sorensen, noticed her deep blue eyes turning to soft brown. They whispered behind their hands.

"...she leave that baby out in the sun?"

Then a sudden silence as conversation ceased.

"Good morning, Louise. Reverend Gust had a lovely sermon this morning. Do pass along my compliments, as I see he's quite busy talking to Mr. Wood." Again, the smile without meaning and the swirl of fabric as she turned away to take up with some other woman.

"Your baby is certainly...growing." What would the word have been otherwise? I'd never know, because that was both the beginning and the end of the conversation. Duty done, the speaker became distracted by another friend across the grass. A touch on my elbow, perhaps, a quick word of "Enjoy your Sabbath," and off she would glide.

I felt like an island, with warm water swirling all around, but only storm clouds above.

Was I ostracized? Not exactly. Everyone was far too civilized for that. Perhaps I was turning too critical, too paranoid, seeing devils everywhere instead of simple people. Was anyone turning against me? I saw it everywhere.

Everywhere but in Rose, of course. Rose, who knew almost everything and yet treated me as a dear friend and not as a sinner. She had much practice in that, considering the business she chose. I never considered her a sinner either, so now we were a sisterhood of two, having a choice in common.

Day by day, I grew more and more fearful, though I tried to keep all that from public view, and especially from Gust. But what would Doe have to look forward to? More contempt and scorn than I was receiving. She would be a half-breed talked about behind closed doors and ostracized from...from everything, I realized. No friends in a schoolroom, if she was even allowed in a schoolroom. No one to share her secrets with. No one to call her out to play. No life as girl, woman, wife, mother.

My selfishness in loving Walking Elk condemned her to no life at all. I couldn't bear it.

I tried to cling to Gust, whom I loved with all my heart. He didn't see what others saw. Or if he did, I saw no sign of it. He loved Doe, that was clear. Of course, he left her care to me for the most part, but he leaned over her basket and gurgled at her, as one does with most babies. He was tender with me as well. I never saw a hint of reproach in him. He was a good man.

But I knew the time would come when he could no longer deny what seemed to be obvious to everyone but our fathers and him. Most of the men passing through our lives also didn't seem to notice, or perhaps just didn't care.

Some of them had probably taken squaws as wives. Or as...

But Mr. Wood saw. I knew in my heart that when he refused the cradle, he saw Doe for what she was. And I was filled with fear. He could destroy not only me—and after all, I brought all this upon myself—but also destroy every member of my family. My father and his business, my husband and his calling, Reverend Iverson. Undoubtedly Hiinuk Waka too, should he wish to.

But more than that, he would destroy Doe. My beautiful baby.

When Doe was almost three months old, I broke.

She was napping during a particularly warm afternoon, arms tucked tight against her chest, her little rump sticking up in the air. I reached down and rolled her over. She never stirred, but only stretched. I took the bed pillow and set it over her. It covered her body. I pressed. Tight. Closed my eyes. Held steady. I talked to myself. And to her. I told how her life would be if... And I apologized.

When all was still, I returned the pillow to our bed.

I was so very weary.

Chapter 35
Louise Wright

We buried Doe in the little cemetery behind the church. Everyone believed she died in her sleep. Babies died all the time, for all sorts of reasons. Sometimes the reasons were baffling, unknown, sudden. I wept constantly. When I wasn't weeping, I was sleeping. Nothing helped.

People came to the parsonage with food and condolences, but their own lives had to go on. Crops in the fields, animals in the barns, families to tend to. And on and on. I watched them dwindle away. Or rather, return to their full lives, even as I was the one who dwindled away. How ironic that these townspeople, so sympathetic now, were the same ones who whispered behind their hands when Doe was alive. I tamped down my thoughts, and welcomed as best I could their efforts at consolation.

Gust was helpless in the face of my despair. My father tried to keep me busy at the store. Reverend Iverson tried to keep me busy with church duties. None of them made a dent in my sorrow, though part of me could finally say the right things, do the necessary things. They saw it as an improvement. I saw it as a deception.

Hiinuk Waka drifted like a spirit between our kitchen and her lodge, saying little.

One day, after the height of summer, a few weeks after Doe was...gone, I heard Hiinuk Waka's light steps coming up the back porch. I sat with my back to the door and listened without turning. The coffee in my cup had long gone cold, almost as cold as I was.

Hiinuk Waka set a hand on my shoulder. Light as a feather, but it felt like lead. "Louise." She rarely called me by my name. It made me shiver. Not out of dislike or discomfort, but rather out of fear. Fear for what might pass between us. The thread that bound us was so very fragile already.

"Louise," she repeated as she came around the table to face me. "I have come to say goodbye."

It was enough to jolt me awake. "Goodbye?" I lifted my eyes to hers, but my hands still clutched the coffee cup, as if it could rescue me.

She nodded. "I'm leaving. My people are in Black River Falls for the summer. I go to join them there."

I pushed the cup away from me. Her people. Would that include...? I dared not ask, but it must have been there in my eyes.

Hiinuk Waka shook her head. "Walking Elk..."

My ears stopped hearing. "What?" Nothing but a whisper.

"He...Nebraska. He is with the ancestors now. Cholera. I will go to his resting place later." She lifted her chin and took a deep breath.

I froze in place. Gone? Gone from cholera, that deadly epidemic? I felt a piece of myself die on the spot. But I dared not show anything, say anything. Hiiunk Waka's voice broke through the fog.

"But now I go to Black River Falls," she said, "to be with my people..."

I imagined her adding, "to heal." But it went unsaid. Maybe we both thought it. For both of us.

"I have something before I go," Hiinuk Waka said.

I still sat, paralyzed.

"I have something for you. Something of the women of my family. To stay with the women of my family." She opened her hand and held it out to me.

I looked first at her, and then at her hand. There, cupped in her hand, were her silver earrings. Long tendrils of silver shafts, small shiny disks.

"For you," Hiinuk Waka said. "Yours, to pass on to your girl children."

I started to cry. "I have no girl children. I have no children."

She set the earrings before me, came around the table and put her arm across my shoulder. "You will," she whispered in my ear. "You will have more children. The earrings will go to a daughter, your daughter."

"Doe is dead. She will never wear them." I choked on my sobs.

"Yes, Doe would have."

I look up at her, and realized she knew. She knew who Doe was, who she really was. That was why she wanted to give me the earrings. I grasped her hands. But I could not speak. The words caught in my throat. I felt the force and honesty and, yes, acceptance, of her gaze. She scooped up the earrings and pressed them into my hands.

For the first time in many weeks, I felt a small kernel of balm. She was giving me an eternal connection to Walking Elk through her and her gift. She should have given them to whomever Walking Elk chose as a wife. Any daughters of mine would have no connection to her or Walking Elk. And yet, she chose me for the earrings, a gift that would seal the bond between...all of us. I closed my fingers around the earrings and felt the warmth of her hands lingering in the silver, and the warmth of my tears spilling over.

She left the next morning. I never saw her again.

Chapter 36
Lou

Lou turned to face Kapi. She wished there was a fire in the fireplace. She was cold, and it wasn't all the temperature. They were still talking about the earrings.

"So, the earrings were part of Louise's heritage," Kapi said. "You said the note said, 'Don't ever lose these earrings. They are your heritage.' That they're supposed to go to the women of the family. Right?"

"Yeah." Lou was still reluctant to admit to anything.

"So, what does this signature mean? 'H.W.'?"

"I have no idea," Lou said. Which was the truth.

As if reading her mind, Kapi said, "Abe said there were Ho-Chunk around here at one time. Maybe it stands for Ho-Chunk Woman."

"Believe it or not," Lou said, "I wondered. I have no idea whether that's true or not. By the way, there are still Ho-Chunk around. Just not in this town anymore."

Kapi frowned. "Maybe we can find some and ask."

"Ask what?" Lou said. "They're not going to know about some old photo."

"You never know," Kapi said. "Anyway, I think the H.W. stands for Ho-Chunk Woman." She shifted to an overstuffed chair and curled her legs under her. "I think that H.W. is that Ho-Chunk woman in the picture and that she passed those earrings down to her daughter, your great-grandmother, Louise. That's what *I* think." She grabbed a pillow and plumped it in her lap.

Lou knew that was as good a guess as any. She had always been ashamed of a possible link to Native Americans in her family line. Her own mother always wrinkled up her nose when Indians were mentioned. Her father spit, if they were outdoors. They both talked only about the old broken cars, the drunks, the peeling paint. Neither one mentioned the poverty, or any of the other reasons there must be for living that way. It came as a sudden shock that Lou herself never saw where these "Indians" lived. Where had her parents gotten such views?

Kapi didn't seem to have that hangup. She was walking into things with curiosity and an open mind. In a way, Lou was reluctant to let go of her old feelings. They were a bit of a buffer, a protection against the hostilities of the world. They gave her an excuse for being irascible.

She frowned. What was the need now? Her grandmother's and mother's old prejudices were just that. Prejudice. Intolerance. Their hostilities weren't Lou's anymore. Besides, her mother and grandmother couldn't have known about where the earrings came from. They wouldn't have found or seen that old photo with Wood's stuff. And the only note left was the one leaving silver earrings to the next woman in the family. Nothing about where they came from.

The only thing hinting at anything was the note that was burned. Hardly a hint there. But her mother *had* burned it. Why? Maybe they'd never know. Whatever, now Lou needed to refocus. Kapi was her center now, not some old stories and rumors. Could she make that shift?

It wouldn't be easy. Maybe now that Kapi was with her and actually talking, she could. If not change totally, at least make some adjustments.

Hell, I've made plenty of changes already, she thought. What's one more?

Nothing was a sure thing. The whole truth lay in the past, out of reach. That fog didn't really bother Lou, but she knew Kapi sought more solid ground. If this gave it to her, after all the crap she'd put up with in her life, more power to her.

Chapter 37
Louise Wright

Hiinuk Waka's silver earrings proved a talisman for me. I only wore them when I was alone in the parsonage. They gave me courage to keep moving. Doe would always be with me. Hiinuk Waka, with Walking Elk standing behind in the shadows, would always be with me.

I never went back to the berry patch. But I could still picture every patch of sunlight, every path and branch. The vision gave me a tiny piece of comfort when I felt alone.

But I continued to visit the cove. The lake, in its various colors, gradually washed me clean. Finally, I no longer saw Walking Elk on the bank, but only the embarrassed Gust the day he caught me bathing. I smiled rarely, but I found solace in Gust's arms.

Enough solace that three years after...after...I was pregnant again. This time, there was no Hiinuk Waka as midwife for me. There was a doctor in town finally, which was a blessing. But he also banished Rose from my room. I labored with no comfort around me. Doe's birth lingered in my memory as a slide into life. A wet bloody emergence, a birth full of joy.

With Marit, I screamed and screamed until I could hear Gust outside the door, his voice gruff with terror. Terrible pain. A fitting punishment for...what I did. As I worked to birth the child, I was so wet with sweat that my hands could find no firm purchase on the bedposts. Hours and hours. Finally, the doctor could see her head. That was enough for a valiant effort, and Marit was born. We named her after Gust's grandmother.

After the birth, I was shaking so from the exertion that the doctor wouldn't give Marit to me, but instead handed her off to his helper to clean and swaddle. I barely remember the afterbirth emerging.

I spent the next two weeks in bed, rousing myself only to nurse. Gust had a fulltime attendant for me so I could recover.

I feared a distance would grow between this baby and myself. After Doe, I wasn't sure I could love another as I loved her. So, I took special care while nursing to gaze into Marit's eyes, stroke her cheek, play with her downy hair.

I wept over her. Everyone thought it was from joy and happiness. Which it was, of course. But it was also from the loss of Doe, the loss of her father whose name I forbade myself to utter or think. That Louise was no more. With the birth of Marit, I discarded that Louise and molded myself into a different woman. Neither better nor worse, but only different.

**

Gust lowered his newspaper. "Perhaps we should have a brother or sister for Marit. It's been...Marit is almost three years old."

We were in the parlor, toasting before a cozy fire. Marit was on the floor playing with her doll. I set my sewing in my lap. "Perhaps," I answered. "To have no sisters or brothers can be very lonely." I caught Gust's look. He knew

I had no siblings, and thus spoke out of my own experience.

He looked down at our daughter, his forehead wrinkled in thought. "But I don't want to put you through the pain you had with Marit. I can't bear to have you suffer like that again."

"Put your mind at ease, Gust," I said. "I have no trouble carrying a child. And delivering is over in...well, in due course. It doesn't go on forever." I clasped my hands until my fingers were white. "After all, I've done it safely twice before." I smiled at him.

His eyes sparkled and I loved him all the more.

***

Though Katherine was an easy baby to carry, she was not an easy baby to birth. This time I furnished myself with a roll of thick rag long before I entered labor. I could at least keep Gust from anguish if I could stifle my screams. I endured the pain as a punishment.

After more than two days, the doctor said enough. He administered chloroform and I retreated from the world. From what he told me later, he pulled Katherine out of me. Her shoulder caught, and he reached in to turn her. That wrenching, and the amount of blood I lost, meant I was too weak to nurse, but I had no milk anyway. Gust brought in a wet nurse, one of the local women who birthed a babe not three weeks before.

Katherine was a small baby who grew into a small child. She seemed to catch every cold that appeared. Marit adored her and they played for hours before the parlor fire or near me in the kitchen.

I can barely speak of her life, short as it was. With two children, I could muffle the loss of Doe a bit. But Katherine was not meant to be with us long.

***

Children were dying. Young children. The disease crept from farm to farm, and then found its way into town. And into our home, I feared. "Gust! Get the doctor! Bring him now!" I heard the hysteria in my voice. I was so afraid.

When Katherine's glands began to swell, we moved Marit into our bedroom, hoping to contain whatever it was that was afflicting Katherine. She had swollen glands before, but never like this.

Gust was out the door before I said another word. I sent Marit to stand by the front window and watch for her father to return. I wanted her as far as possible from the sickroom.

"Wait in the parlor, please," the doctor said, "while I examine her. I'll be quick."

Gust took my elbow and steered me away, though I protested I wanted to stay with Katherine. "She needs me. I want to stay."

But by that time, we were at the parlor door. Neither one of us could sit still, so we paced while Marit plied us with questions we couldn't answer.

"Is Katherine going to die?" A question only a six-year old could ask so forthrightly.

We had no answer. If it was what we feared... With that, we could not face the answer.

But we had to, of course. Diphtheria, the doctor said. The thick gray mucus draped across her throat.

We sent Marit to live with another family in town until the crisis was past. If it would pass.

We watched Katherine slowly suffocate. We held her day and night, but nothing helped. She died in Gust's arms one mild night just as the full moon rose over the trees.

We hung a funeral wreath on the front door of the parsonage and praised God that neither of our fathers was alive to see the pain of losing yet another child.

***

On my thirty-first birthday I found I was expecting again.

"This one is a boy." I finally screwed up enough courage after two months to tell Gust. "I can just feel it." But that wasn't the only feeling. The further along I could get, the more confident I could become. Maybe.

He laughed and laid his hand on my belly, not showing even the tiniest bulge yet. "I can't feel a thing. How can you tell?"

"Women's intuition," I said. "I'm going out to tell Rose."

"It's a good thing you are above reproach in this town, Louise. I must admit, Rose has done a lot of good things, but the women still shun her." He kissed my forehead. "I'm glad you're a good enough Christian to minister to her, as a friend."

Above reproach. Oh Gust, I'm glad you never guessed what kind of woman that other Louise was. For just a moment, Walking Elk slid through my mind. I could see his face and his walk, and almost feel his hand caressing my cheek. I closed my eyes and forced a smile. "Rose is a dear friend who has helped me in more ways that you can imagine. I'm glad you don't forbid me seeing her."

"How can I forbid you anything?" Gust crushed me in a hug. "Don't be too late now."

"I'm afraid, Rose," I said. We were bent over a pot of tea and a plate of shortbread cookies.

"What in heaven's name are you afraid of? You've had babies before." She lifted her cup and the steam tendrils curled up her cheeks.

"I don't know, Rose. I don't know why, but this baby— this birth—terrifies me. The others..." Rose knew how easy only the first had been.

Rose leaned over to pat my hand. "It'll be fine."

I shook my head. "I don't think so. I'm older now. And I've been having terrible nightmares. Lots of water and blood, and that's all I can remember. I wake up when everything seems to go dark." I couldn't put into words the terrors of the nights.

Rose smiled over her teacup. "Bad dreams, Louise, that's all they are. Just bad dreams. You've not had any problems so far, have you? No, I didn't think so. It'll be over before you know it and you'll have a lovely baby again." She held her palm up toward me. "But don't worry. If something happens, I know your favorite songs to sing at your funeral."

I dropped my napkin and bent to pick it up, hiding my face from her. When I sat up again, I fronted her with a silly smile. "Just don't sing Nearer My God to Thee. I'll be near enough then, if it follows that path."

We both laughed, but I knew. I just knew...

Chapter 38
Lou

The rain lessened to a drizzle, leaving the afternoon gray and cold. The fire Kapi finally built snapped and crackled, while she sat curled up in one of the big chairs. Lou set another log on the fire and stood gazing down as the flames took hold. They were in the middle of a discussion about Louise.

Lou sighed. Unanswered questions sometimes bothered her, but not as much as she knew they bothered Kapi. "Look, Kapi, whatever happened back then, with the Native Americans and the earrings and such, we may never find out anything. Some things just disappear into the past. We looked at everything from Wood's stuff, and I think we've done pretty well figuring out what we could. The rest we're just going to have to let go."

"So, what did we figure out, anyway?" Kapi said, tousling her hair. "It's so frustrating."

"What? That we don't know everything?" Lou said. She set her mug of coffee on the mantel and bent to poke at the fire. "Nobody ever knows everything about the past."

"But I mean, what did we figure out? My brain is all fuzzed up and I want to straighten it out." Kapi wiggled her fingers in her hair, giving herself a head massage.

"Okay, okay. Let's just take a look." Lou grabbed her mug and shuffled to the chair opposite Kapi. She plopped down. We know the lineage from me back, don't we?"

Kapi closed her eyes and tilted her head back to lean on the chair. "So. You, then your father—" She held up one finger.

"Nels Liebermann," Lou added.

"—who did not give you the earrings." Kapi said. "Then his mom, Marit Liebermann, your grandmother." A second finger went up.

"Who did give me the earrings," Lou said. She slurped her coffee.

Kapi clasped her hands behind her head. "Marit's mom was Louise Wright Iverson, right?" Kapi said, then answered herself without waiting for Lou. "Right. And that's where we run into problems." She opened her eyes and rolled her eyes to Lou. "By the way, what's with all the headstones in the old graveyard, anyway? That's what's confusing me."

Lou sat up straight. "Okay. So. There's the old Iverson stone, with Mother and Father. That's Gust and Louise Iverson, my great-grandparents. Then there were three other stones, right?"

Kapi nodded. "Yup. All of them kids really young."

Lou ticked them off on her fingers. "Katherine, died at three years old. That baby, probably named Steven, who apparently didn't live very long, because there was only one year on the stone. And then Dorothea Winn, died as an infant."

Kapi giggled. "I remember. That weird name, Dorothea Winn."

What about Kapi? Lou thought, and smiled. "Those three babies. We knew there was Marit, my grandmother, too, but she's buried in the new cemetery many years later. She survived. But those three babies..."

"Yeah." Kapi ground to a halt. "I don't even know what to ask." Her face brightened. "But what about the earrings? Louise had a Native American connection somewhere in there," Kapi insisted.

Lou leaned forward. "All I know is that Louise left those earrings for her descendants. My grandmother got 'em, and she gave 'em to me."

"Don't you have photos of your grandmother with those earrings?" Kapi asked.

"Nope." Lou puffed out her lips. "You know, I don't ever remember her wearing them. But then, I didn't pay too much attention."

"But she kept them, didn't she?"

"Yeah, she kept 'em. Must have. We've got 'em, don't we?" Lou sighed. "I wonder..."

"What?" Kapi said. "Why she didn't wear them, you mean?" She leaned forward and tapped the photo. "So, why did she keep them then? I'll bet she was so afraid someone would notice they were Native American and wonder where she got them."

"Interesting point." Lou settled back in her chair and tented her fingers in front of her face.

"So, what do you know about these women? I mean, what happened to Louise? At least we know what happened to her earrings."

Lou tilted her head back and closed her eyes. "Well, let's see. Louise died young. In her 30s, I think. Her dates are on the tombstone, remember." She shifted in the chair. "I was fifteen when my grandmother died. At that time, I wasn't really interested in her life, or what came before." She sneaked a look at Kapi.

Kapi shot Lou a quick grin before lowering her head so her hair shadowed her face. "Kind of like me." A mere whisper, but Lou felt the power behind it. The slight shock that produced caught Lou by surprise. But it was a pleasant realization.

"Yup, me too." They were silent for a moment. "Anyway, my mother married into the family, so it was really my father, Nels, who knew about the earrings from his mother, my grandmother." She shook her finger and nodded. "That's why my mother never wore them. They really weren't hers to wear. Grandma never gave them to her. Or to my dad either."

"So, then you got them."

"Well, yeah, eventually."

Kapi chewed on her lip. "So, Louise—your great-grandmother—gave them to her daughter. What was her name again?"

"Marit. Nels was her son. There were no other children. Nels was the only one."

"Okay, so Louise to Marit. Marit to Nels. Nels to you. Right?"

Lou nodded. "Well, pretty much. I actually got them from my grandmother, Marit."

"Then my dad," Kapi said.

Mac. A pang straight out of nowhere. Lou folded forward, holding in the pain.

"You didn't give them to him, or to my mom, did you." It wasn't really a question.

Of course not. They were to go to the women of the family. Becca wasn't family. Besides, they probably wouldn't be sitting right here in front of us if I bucked the heritage part, and gave them to her. Becca would've thrown them away. Lou drew herself together and rejected the vitriole of what she would've said earlier. She came so far. There was no reason to clothe herself in that again. Kapi deserved more. "No, I didn't. I didn't give them to Mac or..."

"I know why." Kapi reached out as if to pat Lou on the knee. But she couldn't reach that far.

"I'm sure you do." Lou looked up, her eyes swimming with wet. She spoke before Kapi could voice it. "Becca and I never...hit it off. It didn't seem the appropriate thing to do, to give her the earrings."

"Mom didn't...like you much," Kapi said behind her hand. "I understand."

Lou smiled. "It's okay. So do I."

"Look," Kapi said, "we'll never know for sure about Louise, I guess. But that's okay. It's okay if Louise was Native American, Ho-Chunk maybe." She cleared her throat. "It is okay, isn't it?"

"It will be," Lou said. "It was so long ago. It shouldn't matter anymore, should it?" She's pulling me forward. I can't go through life walking backward. My grandmother is dead, so are my parents. Mac, and Becca too, God save her black heart. Both gone. Kapi's lost so much. With a start, Lou realized she herself lost just as much, probably more. She must let go of all that. Kapi was excited about her newly acquired family. How could Lou quash that? She couldn't.

"No, it shouldn't matter anymore. It doesn't." Kapi's hair swirled as she shook her head. "We should be proud of that heritage. There's so much there."

"And we still have the earrings." Lou heard the naturalness of that *we*.

"We do," Kapi agreed.

It sounded so good coming from both of them. "And now they're yours, Kapi. It's time to pass them on."

Kapi's smile lit up the room. But her head was shaking no. "Not yet. You still need them for your Meanders."

"Our Meanders, don't you mean?" Lou said. She had a sudden inspiration. "Next summer, we should go up to Black River Falls. That's where those Ho-Chunk people have a center, I think." She took a deep breath. "We need to go see Mac's grave too. Together."

"Really?" Kapi sat up straight. "I'd like that." She bounced a bit. And then she started to giggle, but put her hands over her mouth to suppress it. "We can't go to Dad's grave."

"Why ever not?" Lou asked.

"Because I stole his ashes."

"You—wait. What?" It was not often that Lou was dumbfounded.

"Mom promised Dad she'd scatter his ashes in the woods, but she never did. She stuffed the box in the back of her closet." Kapi scratched her nose. "So, I stole 'em."

Lou opened her mouth, but not a trickle of sound emerged. She cleared her throat, then asked, "Where are they now?"

"Here," Kapi said.

"Here?" Lou felt like a parrot. "Where here?"

"In my backpack under my bed." She chewed her lip. "Can we maybe scatter them in the old cemetery behind the church?" Her words came out in a rush.

Lou blew out a great breath. "Ya know, legally, we're not supposed...Oh, hell. Why not?"

"We don't have to tell anybody," Kapi offered, leaning forward as if in supplication.

Lou sent out a "Huh," followed by, "Sometimes, it is best that secrets remain secrets." She flapped her hand in Kapi's direction. "Of course we can do that. Whenever you want."

"A sunny day. On a sunny day," Kapi said. "Dad would like that."

Lou nodded her agreement.

"Can we really do that? Scatter my dad, and go up to see the Ho-Chunk center?" Kapi asked. "Really?"

I've got a chance to give Mac—and me—closure. Kapi's given me my son back. Lou sent her a smile. *Girl, you enrich my life.* Someday soon, she'd tell Kapi just that too. "Yes, really. Really to both." It startled her to realize that the Ho-Chunk connections would also enrich her life. She skooched to the front of the chair and held out her arms to Kapi. "C'mere."

Kapi put her hands to her face. When she took them away, they were wet. "I...I don't think—"

"Hugs don't require thinking. C'mere." She waggled her fingers.

Kapi moved across, knelt down, and leaned into Lou, who enveloped her in a hug. She settled with her ear on Lou's chest. "I can feel your heart."

"So can I," Lou said. "So can I."

Author's Note

What happened to the Ho-Chunk in Wisconsin was indicative of what happened to tribes all over. Beginning in 1829, the government offered the Ho-Chunk money for their land. The offer was made again in 1832, but coupled with an attempt to remove the Ho-Chunk west of the Mississippi River, but the tribes there were fighting, and the removal attempt failed. However, over the next 30-plus years, the government removed Ho-Chunk from their ancestral lands. In 1837, they were removed to Iowa. The 1846 removal to far western Minnesota was designed to provide a human barrier between the warring and raiding Sioux in the west and the white settlers in Minnesota. Between 1853 and 1855, the Ho-Chunk were removed to Neutral Ground in Iowa and southern Minnesota. In 1862, they were removed to South Dakota, but most escaped to Nebraska, where a Ho-Chunk community remains to this day, called the Winnebago Tribe of Nebraska, Winnebago being the whites' original term for the tribe. Finally, in 1874, the government gave up after the attempted removal of that year failed. During all of these expulsions, many Ho-Chunk refused to go, and many others returned from exile as soon as they could.

About the Author

After earning Bachelor and Master degrees, Mary Ann Noe spent 29 years in Waukesha classrooms, first teaching 7th grade Language Arts & Social Studies, followed by 22 years of high school English and Psychology. Upon retirement, she joined a writing workshop, where a good instructor taught her that the slash and burn of editing doesn't leave scars. Mary Ann publishes poetry, nonfiction, and the novels *To Know Her* (2021), *A Handful of Pearls* (2022), and *Hannah's Eyes* (2023). Her poetry is in many print and online publications. She spends time reading, writing, baking, and happily communing with nature in Wisconsin. Visit www.maryannnoe.com for her blog, a collection of photos, a contact link, and more.

Other Titles by Mary Ann Noe

Note from Mary Ann Noe

Word-of-mouth is crucial for any author to succeed. If you enjoyed *Water the Color of Slate*, please leave a review online—anywhere you are able. Even if it's just a sentence or two. It would make all the difference and would be very much appreciated.

Thanks!
Mary Ann Noe

We hope you enjoyed reading this title from:

BLACK ROSE
writing™

www.blackrosewriting.com

Subscribe to our mailing list – *The Rosevine* – and receive **FREE** books, daily deals, and stay current with news about upcoming releases and our hottest authors.
Scan the QR code below to sign up.

Already a subscriber? Please accept a sincere thank you for being a fan of Black Rose Writing authors.

View other Black Rose Writing titles at www.blackrosewriting.com/books and use promo code **PRINT** to receive a **20% discount** when purchasing.

www.ingramcontent.com/pod-product-compliance
Lightning Source LLC
Chambersburg PA
CBHW050150120726
47903CB00002B/570